"You cannot allow yourself to live your whole existence through without ever knowing the pleasure of two people enjoined. Two hearts so close they seem, indeed, to beat as one," he finished softly, and moved her clasped hand against his own beating heart to illustrate his point.

But Emmalie, albeit in a whirl of emotions, resented his resorting to his obvious courtier's ways and retorted, "Is that the way you act with all your ladybirds? For shame! I am quite content with my heart beating its own quiet, steady beat on its own."

"Are you certain of that?" he whispered. "Enough to put both our hearts to the test? You, who so love testing others, are you willing to test yourself?" And he pulled her back into his arms and kissed her thoroughly.

THE AGE
OF
ELEGANCE

Helen Archery

FAWCETT CREST • NEW YORK

A Fawcett Crest Book
Published by Ballantine Books
Copyright © 1992 by Helen Argyris

Library of Congress Catalog Card Number: 91-93148

ISBN 0-449-22055-9

Manufactured in the United States of America

First Edition: April 1992

To the most elegant of all ladies, Astera,
and our mother, Calliope-Carol, and our
father, Thomas.
For their example of grace and courage
and the delight of humor.

With love, I take off my Plumed Hat to you all and N.N.

CHAPTER ONE

"NOTHING SHALL INDUCE ME TO AGREE TO THAT CON-
nection," was all Miss Emmalie Marlowe would say,
no matter how many arguments and how many times
her mother put forth Viscount Wynnclife's name.

"But he is the beau-ideal of the Haute Ton—second
only to our dear Prince Regent himself."

Miss Marlowe did not reply to that, but her eyebrows
rose and arched so noticeably at the mention of the
Prince Regent that her mother quickly added, "No, he
is considerably junior to our dear Prince Regent. And
his highness has a grown daughter, while Reggie has
never before permitted himself to even consider marriage. Heavens, if you knew how many mothers have
all but burst holding their breaths in the hope of his
coming up to snuff! Society is strewn with these expired
expectations. And still he is pursued. Yet he skillfully,
nimbly evades every web. Actually, I almost lost my breath
myself—expending so much of it begging him to consider
you. And to be so rewarded for all my breathlessness by
your cold face and that . . . insipid sentence."

"Nothing shall induce me to agree to that connection," Emmalie said again, without any consideration
for her mother's sensitivity to redundancy.

"Enough! Have I brought up a daughter with such a
paltry vocabulary? Can your mental facilities be so limited and your filial devotion so skimpy that you cannot
offer me more than that response? No, preamble of,
'Much as I am obliged to you, Mother, for the extraor-

dinary efforts on the part of my unworthy self . . .' No, not even that courtesy! Forgetting the respect due your parent, could you not for variety sake have found a dozen different ways to express your rejection? Certainly in my lifetime I have rejected hundreds of men, and I pride myself on never *once* having used the same sentence. Not that I would have been so dull as to have used your choice of words even once! But forgetting the style of your remarks, let us come to their purport. Can you explain *why* you do not wish to accept that connection? About Reggie himself, you cannot possibly have an objection. Not only is there nothing about him to give one a disgust, but even you must agree on the excellence of his person. In all respects, he is precisely what every woman would dream might come her way: tall, with the tongue of a Greek scholar and the face of a Greek statue. But you have seen him. You must recollect his devastating smile. That alone has entrapped the hearts of the most devious ladies of experience, not to mention their equally devious, though inexperienced, sisters. You have had a Season! You have seen the selection of gentlemen on the Marriage Mart! Is there one who can be mentioned in the same breath of eligibility as Reginald Lancaster—the fifth Viscount of Wynncliffe? No! I cannot allow that it would be his person!''

No response from Miss Marlowe. Her face was set, staring resolutely ahead. Lady Leonie could only hope she was making some inner impression on her daughter, for certainly there was no sign of outward response. Yet, she continued with her panegyric of the offered lordship—having by now reached his manners. ''They have a degree of elegance that must be a model for every young gentleman. Need I even put into words the quality of his conversation, which is renowned for wit and perspicacity! Actually, I am acknowledged no mean wit myself, yet I have been occasionally brought to a stand by his brilliance! I allow that *you* cannot judge in that area—but you must take my word. And lastly, his

2

fortune. Comparing him to nabobs would not be over-stating. Where then, in heaven's name, can you find an objection? In what area are you so nice that he would not be suitable? I cannot fathom! Why I have been told, *entre nous*, that no less than the queen herself, in regard to a certain princess, has let it be hinted that she should not be adverse to *that connection* herself! Yet apparently what is desirable for royalty is not suitable for a mere mousy Miss Marlowe!''

''Nothing shall induce me to agree to that connection.''

''*Emmalie!* You are trying my patience too far! You have gone your length and then some! Have I raised such a ninny as you now seem? Such a totty-headed, bird-witted widgeon! You are foolish beyond permission! I despair of you and your future. But mostly I regret that such a goosecap should possess my genes! What a waste of inheritance! Even your father, though given to fits of deplorable cockle-brained humors and notions, was generally a man of some sense—as evidenced by his seeking out my hand. But you, you have never given me an instance of the slightest sign of intelligence. If I did not have the greatest confidence in Nurse Mary, I should seriously suspect that you were switched in your cradle and are the daughter of a country bumpkin. I must repair to my apartments to recover from this your latest, but certainly your most wounding . . . *disappointment*.''

And Lady Leonie Marlowe walked nimbly away from her daughter's apartments, having immediate recourse to her fan to cool her agitated countenance. When the footman closed the door behind her, Emmalie finally allowed herself to come out of her rigid stance and sink down on her settee—in pure relief.

She had not relented! Thank heavens, she had not given in, as she usually did, to her mother's forceful-ness. No, she had remained firm, under the protection of her one unequivocal, irrevocable sentence. And once again repeating her infamous statement, she added the period of a small satisfied smile.

As for Lady Leonie, now in her own apartments, her only regret was that she had not physically shaken her daughter out of her rigidity! So overcome was her ladyship, she was nigh to asking for a vinaigrette. But having always made such a point of despising all those ladies who had continual recourse to vinaigrettes or vinegar-soaked cloths (not to mention sips of hartshorn and water) to restore their senses, she could not now allow herself to sink so low in her own opinion. But she did, however, sink onto her own sofa and try to gather up her scattered emotions.

How was she to countenance her daughter's refusal? For all Society was continually coming to her for her opinion—not only on what was elegant, a quality which she modestly owned she had in excess, but for her advice on their own social and emotional problems! Hadn't she even been a regular correspondent with Lord Byron, as well as his wife? And had they not both put their side of their disagreement before her, asking for use of her good offices to persuade the other party to stop the wild accusations? And had she not graciously spent several nights composing letters of comfort and unexceptionable suggestions to both? Not that she had hopes of preventing the dissolution of their marriage, but that had not been her objective. She had, instead, won what she always desired—two delightful correspondents, who emptied their hearts to her so fully, she was never at a loss for conversation at her saloon. The Prince Regent had similarly sought her opinion about his wife—who, he claimed, was currently conducting more foreign affairs in Italy than did his ministers. And Lord Byron, cursing all his advisors, had devotedly turned to Lady Leonie, since she alone had urged against his and, indeed, marriage in general. "The Muses meant you to be wed only to them," she had written the poet. "Content yourself, rather, with *temporary* human sur-

4

rogates." She herself had been loath to embark on a second voyage on the matrimonial sea, believing in singular pleasures. "Certain select souls such as you and I," her letter continued, "must remain free. To us 'unions' are nuisances that tighten into nooses." She flattered the Regent by including him in this membership of select souls, along with herself, Byron, and the Viscount Wynnclife (although the latter was to be preemptively dismembered now that she had need of him for her daughter).

Presently both poet and prince were penning her their desires to be at liberty to take new liberties with new partners. She encouraged both to do so. Yet when the Regent took her literally and attempted liberties with *her*, she questioned the soundness of her recommendations. It was scarcely flattering to be on that long list of royal loves that not only included the exiled princess, but Lady Jersey, Lady Hertford, the untitled ladies, and the original morganatic wife.

Her ladyship's well-worn refusal was the one she always used for men of rank. So elegantly phrased, it always left the gentleman uncertain whether he had been rejected or not, but eventually her message became clear when she was seen with another noble. The prince, to whom praises were his daily bread, and who had trained himself to avoid reading between the praises, missed the operative words. It took, therefore, several letters ere he understood he had actually been refused. Yet so much regret was delicately entwined in that elegant refusal that even His Highness could not take offense. Lady Leonie would never dream of condescending to plain speech.

And, to have her own chit of a daughter demonstrate so grossly her not having inherited even a twinge of her elegance was demeaning and downright demoralizing.

On second reflection, Lady Leonie was even more outraged, for she deserved, she told herself, more than style from her daughter, but actual obedience! Was it not every young girl's duty to accept her mother's choice? Certainly she herself had accepted her father's choice and never lived to regret it.

A smile of reality interrupted her justifications as she recollected that actually, she had regretted marrying the Honorable Mr. Manfred Marlowe rather more often than not. But she had learned how to get around him and make do with her situation. Fortunately, they had had rather a short life together, his having come a cropper over a rather low fence, riding out his choler at his first child turning out a girl! If one were to put a fine point on it, their disappointing daughter had led to his demise. And here Emmalie was attempting to bring her mother down as well! Dash it, that young girl had another think coming if she expected Lady Leonie to so easily cock up her toes! No, indeed!

And with that oath, her ladyship was instantly on her feet to prove how little she was affected, after all.

Yet, in truth, she was vastly amazed, for she had not only assumed her daughter would be dutiful but, actually, she expected her to be overjoyed by the arrangement. Although generally against marriage, her ladyship felt single blessedness was allowable only if the girl had exhibited some singularity, and that could never be said about Emmalie, who was clearly common. Indubitably she was a garden variety weed that must be given singularity by being attached to an exceptional plant, such as the viscount. Faith, it was essential the girl have someone else to lean on, for her continually clinging to her mother was threatening to turn both of them into a social joke. That had become obvious at the last assembly when Countess Flemington jested that Emmalie was her mother's "accessory." Annoyed, Lady Leonie spun round and actually saw her daughter following so close behind, it seemed she was seeking to hide under her gown! In an instant, it brought back her irritation when the child-Emmalie had literally peeped from behind her skirts at anyone approaching, necessitating her having to be plucked forward to face up to the visitors. Similarly now, Lady Leonie had resorted to the same tactics of pulling her daughter off the wall—so to speak—and forcing her to accept only the greatest gift in all Society. Or the prime Corinthian of their set. The veritable pink of the ton. Reggie, himself.

And how Lady Leonie had worked to achieve that miracle—no one but she and Reggie knew. Weeks of preparing him for the suggestion by hinting that time was getting away from him. Weeks of mentioning how other gentlemen who had been in his class at Oxford were now proud papas and secure in their succession. Then, she had occasionally remarked on the thinning of his hair, which was not quite so, but undeterred by the facts, she hinted that "from the back, there were definite indications of coming sparseness."

To this he had merely replied, "As I have very little occasion for viewing the back of my head, it has my permission to become as sparse as it wishes. Indeed, as I only turn that view to those for whom I have the least regard, I need not be unduly concerned." And he was not.

Lady Leonie was in a pucker at being unable to influence him, and when subsequently spotting a knowing glint in his eyes, she knew instantly all stratagems should fail, except for the greatest stratagem of all—the truth. That always had the advantage of a surprise attack, forcing the opponent to admit part of the truth himself, just to keep up with the weapons chosen, which gave her ladyship a decided advantage.

Therefore, she quickly admitted to the viscount that she was attempting to set him up with her daughter. And upon acknowledging with amusement that he suspected as much, she continued to do so in perfect guiltless ease.

"I have my daughter's interests at heart, of course, but yours as well. For of all women, *she* is the most perfectly suited to you, Reggie dear."

"My dear Leonie," Reggie responded, with one of his languid glances and the beginning of his slow smile, "with that glint in your eye, I suspect that I am about to bear witness to one of your well-known paradoxes. And I am scarcely up to it so early in the morning. But if you insist on inflicting it, I best equip myself with a tablet to take it down for posterity!"

"There is not the smallest need to reach for your quill, my dear boy, I mean merely that since what you most wish is no woman at all, Emmalie comes as close as one could hope to fulfilling that elusive criteria. She would cost you nothing in money or attention, never having demanded either from me. Actually, she has to be forced to purchase a new gown and will wear the same dress two occasions in a row and simply not be aware of that repetition. Nor did she ever trouble herself to learn any instrument—neither the pianoforte nor the harp—so you need have no fear of having to sit through those endless recitals to which other young ladies continually subject their acquaintances in order to justify all their practice. No, nor is Emmalie known for her needle—she neither embroiders nor tats, so you need not have to shudder while displaying her efforts on Malbern's hallowed walls. Further, it goes without saying, but I shall say it nonetheless: Emmalie rarely speaks."

At that, the viscount raised his eyebrows, and Lady Leonie quickly inserted the explanation: "Oh, a word or two of necessity, one must expect, and a bit more one might pry out of her after much effort, but generally it is as if no one were present. As for appearance, she has not taken after her father and his dark good looks, nor after me and my somewhat well-praised fairness— no, she has somehow turned out a bland amalgam of both of us. What Emmalie really blended most appropriately with," she continued, "was the air about them. And therefore, you should for all intents and purposes, not have a wife at all to perturb you; yet you would, to

8

everybody else, have the appearance of being a married man.''

''You have given your daughter a remarkable character—or rather, no character at all. Surely even an ant must have more individuality than that you have ascribed to your only child! And yet, perhaps you are speaking the truth, after all. For although I have visited you often enough in these last few years, I do not recollect ever having met her. Or worse, I have met her and do not recall the introduction.''

''Quite. You see how perfect a wife she shall make you! For indeed, you have met her several times and even dined with her at table, and yet she has not made the slightest impression on your mind. Did you not tell me often enough that your main reason for not wedding was not being able to bear having a wife constantly in your presence? Well, Emmalie alone can perform that feat of being in your presence without your ever being aware of it. Within a week of your nuptials, I expect, you shall have totally forgotten her. And yet, with the smallest effort on your part, you'll have provided for the succession. As for Emmalie, she'll be contentedly living in her own apartments at Malbern, never needing any Society. Fill her apartments with books, and none shall see her for months on end.''

''Ah, she reads!'' the viscount said in exultation. ''There! Unknowingly you have given her a bit of personality, after all. Careful, Leonie, soon she shall become a person, and I shall have the perfect reason for refusing her. Actually, now that you mentioned that one flaw, I feel it cannot quite be gotten over. You know I cannot abide women with 'improved minds.' I do not believe anything should tamper with a lady's natural ignorance.''

''And a gentleman's natural ignorance?''

''Ah, we men are protected by our egos, nothing can get past them, so we are naturally immune to any knowledge whatsoever. Ladies, unfortunately, are always willing to be taught, and then it goes to their heads, and they insist on spreading it about to the men in their lives, when they should know we are hopeless cases.''

Leonie not only laughed, as she was expected, but stood up and hit him lightly with the closed tip of her fan. He grabbed at it and held it tight, pulling her toward him. ''Never start a duel if you are not willing to continue it . . . blow by blow.''

''Behave yourself,'' Leonie chided, taking back her fan but appreciating the intense look he directed her way; it quite gave her the feeling the years were shedding off, although she was only about eight or maybe ten years older than the viscount. ''I am quite aware you are trying to distract me from the topic at hand, and I shall not so easily be put off. Going back to my daughter,'' (she raised her voice over his groan) ''you mistook me. Emmalie does not read moral texts, and if she does, they never moved her to improving lectures. A young girl who has long since accustomed herself to having *me* as a mother shall not find you too wearing. Even if she should so forget herself as to attempt to speak, neither of us would listen. All both of us need, my dear lord, is an occasional reply, preferably a 'Yes,' or even an 'Indeed.' But a simple nod shall do. And that is Emmalie's forte. She excels in simple nods.''

''You are deadly, indeed. But I refuse to be linked with you in your state of garrulousness. I *have* been known to draw breath. Usually while the rest are applauding my witticisms. Further, if my words are fewer, they are more to the point. My words about marriage were that *someday* I should think of setting up my nursery. I did not say I was presently prepared to do so.''

''Ah, why wait? As Hamlet said, 'If it be not now, yet it will come: the readiness is all.' ''

''Why the devil should Hamlet interfere in my life, when he made such a bloody botch of his own?'' his lordship exclaimed with a grin, but then seriously added, "Nevertheless, my answer to both you and Hamlet is, in my own words: I am not ready."

"You shall never be ready, if left to yourself. Come, now, if a thing is to be done, it is better if it were done quickly. The more distasteful, the quicker one should get it over with."

"You sound curiously like my old nurse when she was attempting to get me to swallow some evil-tasting medicine."

Lady Leonie bristled at the aging comparison but would not allow that to deflect her from her set purpose. "Like medicine, indeed, you must resign yourself to swallowing my prescription and be all the better for it, before it is too late."

The viscount now was very close to exasperation. "I am not yet in my dotage! I have quite a few more years to wait before it is too late for starting a family."

"Fiddle! You are just at that point where to wait even half a year longer should have you settling into a preserved state of bachelorhood, when you shall find even the thought of children and family fatiguing! Own up— do you not feel yourself slipping into that state?"

The viscount found the conversation slipping into a harangue and was prepared to make his departure as soon as civility would allow, when Lady Leonie looked him in the eye and whispered, "I fear I shall have to repeat a confidence, after all. I had hoped not to have to betray Her Majesty."

The viscount was all attention.

"Our most beloved Queen mother was good enough to speak to me last week. She let fall that the young Princess Charlotte has developed a decided *tendre* for you. She was speaking of mentioning the matter to the Prince Regent himself. And you know how *he* is once something gets fixed in his mind—like a bulldog and a bone. He shall gnaw at you and gnaw, and then take offense if you do not do exactly what he wishes. Why look you what happened to Beau Brummell for simply making one injudicious remark!''

''I do not believe I am at the same level as that valet's son!'' the viscount objected, but he had abandoned his bored expression.

''Hardly. Yet, neither are you, as the Beau was, his most bosom companion. Nay, you know what can happen if both the queen and the Prince Regent decide you are perfect for the princess! You shall not only find yourself married to royalty but, more fatiguing, become one of the *family*, which must of necessity oblige you, for the rest of your life, to be constantly in *royal attendance*!''

The viscount felt all the horror of that, and instantly he walked toward the fireplace and nearly did not stop at the grate, so nonplussed had her words left him.

''I must admit this news does give me pause,'' he whispered, turning back to stare at her ladyship. ''Good grief!'' he expostulated. ''I must indeed be married at once. Nothing could be more debilitating than to spend any more time than absolutely necessary in the royal presence. Stab me, it is all my fault! Last month at Almack's I was so injudicious as to pick up the princess's fan. Could that have done me in? Faith! I believe I recollect her giving me quite a saucy look over it, and subsequently she dropped the fan again, but I merely assumed that a sample of the natural clumsiness which runs in the royal family. And indeed, it was! But not of the physical variety! Merely her awkward attempt at setting me up as her flirt! Hell's bells, I am, sans doubt, in prodigious danger!''

''You are on the very precipice of your imminent downfall,'' Lady Leonie assured him, with quite a straight and sympathetic face. She even went so far as to pat him on the arm for comfort, meanwhile slipping him the letter she had received from the queen. While he was reading it, she added more goads, whispering, ''And for a lady not in prime twig, as is whispered the case with our gracious Majesty, to so put herself to the trouble of this message speaks of the urgency. Note where she asks me to 'subtly feel you out'—before *she* does. That actually is what I have been doing—tactfully, tactily.'' And she ran her long fingernails across his dark blue cutaway coat that fit him to the inch (clearly showing him to be not only fashionable but slap up to the echo). Despite his preoccupation with her words, he had a moment's additional alarm that she would crease his apparel, but she left off to conclude: ''And as uncomfortable as you have found it at my hands, how much worse should it be at the queen's august dactyls!''

The viscount put the letter down. Yet, the face he turned to her ladyship, she was discomforted to see, had returned to its usual indifference. Or possibly, hopefully, it was manly resignation to his fate. His next words joyously allowed of the latter interpretation. ''The prince recently spoke to me in his usual roundabout fashion, but I was not in the mood to give him the necessary attention required to decipher his mumblings. Now, it appears, I should have put myself to the trouble.''

''I daresay you should. Actually, the only possible way, at this point, that you *can* be saved is if I instantly replied to the queen, informing her of your having a long-standing engagement to my daughter. I declare, nothing tends to nip a declaration of love in the bud faster than a marriage announcement to another. Of course, that does not assure Her Majesty might not order you to cry off, claiming they have the royal prerogative of first choice. Especially since nothing has been sent to the *Gazette*. Further, they might suppose, as your friend, I am temporarily sacrificing my daughter for your convenience . . . or even, faith, that this is all a ploy on both our parts to rescue you from the princess—who not only tats and embroiders, but even plays the piano, and finally, dare I say it, has been heard singing in glees, as well as a cappella performances of entire concerts. In Italian!''

"That is quite enough! I shall never survive that." Reginald's voice was strained, and his usually sleepy eyes were wide open in apprehension.

Lady Leonie put in the final nail. "No indeed, nor would you ever again have the comfort of your own thoughts. I have met the young lady, and she continually asks one, 'What are you thinking?' ''

The viscount had turned pale before, but now his face was red with choler as he stood to take his leave. "I am all gratitude to you, Leonie. Unquestionably I must be wed at once, and your daughter is the perfect shield . . . eh, choice. I pray, do not delay a moment. Send the notice to the *Gazette* this very evening. I myself shall let the news be known among the prince's Carlton Set this very night at White's. Do not fail me. My future is in your hands.'' And with a bow, he was gone, leaving Lady Leonie once again marveling at the perfection and smoothness of her tactics. No wonder she was called "Lady Guile"—a term first meant in opprobrium, but which she herself had taken up and turned round to one of approbation, and truly, now more often it was replaced by "Lady Style."

But whether as Lady Guile or Lady Style, her ladyship did not, as the viscount had requested, send the notice to the *Gazette* that evening. Rather, confident of her powers of persuasion, she had had the foresight to have sent it before her discussion with the viscount. And her being beforehand had her already receiving letters of congratulations ere the queen could attempt a countermove. Among the flood of congratulations the following day, her ladyship received a cold note from Her Majesty, informing her of the princess's sudden interest in the Earl of Spencer. A face-saving device Lady Leonie was delighted to accept—wondering only how the poor princess had been made to do so. Every feeling must be offended, not to mention one's sensibilities at the thought of that squatty nodcock in exchange for the elegant viscount!

The congratulatory notes were of various complexions. A few begrudging, some merely doing the civil, but most were in great delight at the finish of such a formidable gentleman-bachelor. Lady Leonie even received several visitors who spoke of the end of the "Wynnclife Era," as if a great champion had fallen. So many remarks like "When comes such another!" and "The Incomparable is taken!" And so much awe was there generally exhibited that Lady Leonie's triumph was obviously of grander proportions than even *she* had anticipated. Eventually her ladyship herself was quite fatigued with being praised and left off her usual orchestration of it. Yet everyone was demanding particulars, which forced her to consider them herself—such as a wedding date. She was musing over that and menus and had even already made arrangements to visit her favorite seamstress for the fitting of the mother of the bride's dress, when she bethought herself of a minor detail: the need for a wedding gown, which must of necessity require her daughter's presence. And then, she stopped in at Emmalie's apartments with the happy news.

Unaccustomed as Lady Leonie was to listening to her daughter's replies, she did not immediately hear the young girl's small no. And when Emmalie drew breath and emitted her full sentence of refusal, it had to be repeated before quite penetrating her mother's volubility and then awareness. And subsequently, the tiresome girl refused to enlarge on that sentence. One sentence, and that repetitive, was more than a lady of her known intelligence could bear!

Yet, however expressed, there was no possibility that she could countenance the rejection. The connection was too universally known at this point for it not to appear as a slip on the shoulder for either the viscount or, worse, herself! Infamous of her daughter to have put them all in this position. Heartless! Inconsiderate. Severely mortifying! Shockingly shag-rag!

After pacing through her entire apartment and finding no alleviation in any corner, Lady Leonie rushed down the marble stairs to the portrait gallery below to face her husband with her plight.

What had they done to deserve such a child? she addressed her late mate. He did not reply, which actually had been his usual response in life; therefore, she did not think to remark on it now. The portrait had his dark eyes fixed in a permanent glaze of astonishment, which again had been his normal reaction to his wife. Wishing to blame him for his daughter's taciturnity, Lady Leonie had to acknowledge that Mr. Marlowe, though not necessarily glib, could, when desired, make himself understood, speaking as a sensible man should. The honorable gentleman showed no pleasure in that compliment, just his continual surprise. The complaints from Lady Leonie continued unabated. Every feeling revolted at the reflection that such a daughter could come from their union!

What could they do with such an obstinate girl? Lady Leonie had run out of patience. Surely the gentleman must be in high dudgeon at his hurly-burly daughter—whose want of conduct could not but give him disgust, if not leave him dumbfounded. Obligingly he looked so, in fact, quite knocked acock! Placated, Lady Leonie returned to her apartments. Her late husband continued his staring after in surprise until the candles were snuffed out, allowing him finally a privacy of his well-oiled thoughts and reminiscences.

began all from her position, that made her secretary...
very...began that Wynncliffe could choose whe...
After passing through her entire vocabul... and finally to return and...
...

CHAPTER TWO

THE NEXT MORNING THE DAWN'S LIGHT BROUGHT NEW enlightenment to Lady Leonie as she realized that perhaps her daughter had been caught unawares and had replied in panic. Indeed, upon reviewing the situation she concluded that she had not used sufficient finesse with Emmalie. Having proven the powers of her persuasion with the viscount, she could have, undoubtedly, better managed that young chit. It was simply that she had not felt the need to extend herself, when what she had done was so clearly to Emmalie's advantage!

Why did people have to have the benefits of a situation explained to them? She was extremely fatigued with having to point out the obvious. Very well, she would deal with Emmalie with a lighter hand. For certainly it should not do to have the viscount arrive and find his bride unwilling! The Wynncliffe pride was too well known to withstand such a blow.

Lady Leonie's first course was to request the presence of Emmalie's governess, Miss Spindle, for a brief conversation. No longer needed as a governess, yet Miss Spindle stayed on and had been allowed to graduate to a state usually filled by better-bred spinsters or that of a ''dear companion,'' which left Lady Leonie feeling herself owed a full portion of gratitude.

That dear companion reported before Lady Leonie in such a state of fidgets that her muslin cap was all askew. An order to straighten it (for Lady Leonie could not bear anything or anyone not in prime order) left the woman even more in a quake, dropping her shawl and having to pick it up twice, unable to grasp it perfectly with shaking fingers.

"Oh, do sit down!" Lady Leonie exclaimed, forgetting her stratagem of polite persuasion. But in the next moment she recollected it and smiled steadily, even patting the place next to her on the sofa. It was an honor the older woman had not thought would come to her. To be sitting next to her ladyship! She hesitated so long, her ladyship had to grimly repeat the offer and pat the sofa hard enough for some dust to rise before the ex-governess would be seated.

Without further preamble, Lady Leonie explained her wishes for Emmalie's future in the most glowing terms and, when finally still, waited for the woman's reply. But the governess just stared, causing her ladyship to suspect her as the source of her daughter's laconic style. Yet, upon enlarging further on the honor and joy awaiting Emmalie, Miss Spindle was quick to redeem herself by not only agreeing but subsequently becoming quite voluble about the viscount himself. Without doubt he was the solution to any young girl's dream. Such a leg, he had. No spider-shanks he! And such shoulders! No need for his tailors to use buckram wadding, when nature had given him such delightful proportions.

That was going a bit far. Approval had been expected but not with such appetite! And her ladyship had to struggle to keep a straight face at her thoughts of the viscount's reaction to this governess's personal comments. Yet her getting carried away boded well for the finalization of the match. Surely if this faded old ape leader could be roused to life again by just the image of the viscount, would not her young daughter eventually begin to see him in the proper light? Especially if this lady were to add her persuasions to her mother's. All might not be lost. Therefore, she added a bit of flattery to her command, taking the older woman by the hand and saying earnestly, "My total dependence is on you!"

"Oh, your ladyship. I shall do all I can to make Malie see the match in a more favorable light. With such a romantic figure, how could it be less than ideal? Could you perhaps divulge some of the details to me . . . that I might be able to pass on in their most entrancing form? For instance, has the viscount been in love with her from afar for some time?"

Lady Leonie frowned. "I do not think we need go quite into such intimate particulars. His lordship's feelings are just what a gentleman should feel."

"Ah! I knew it. He has hesitated to put the matter to the touch for fear you should not give your permission. Exactly like Romeo and Juliet!"

"Not quite."

"No? But surely, although it cannot be his position that stands in their way, possibly he fears you might not quite like the difference in their ages?"

Lady Leonie was no longer finding humor in the situation, for the woman had actually picked out just the flaw in the romantic picture. And she replied with more distance, both figuratively and literally—dropping the governess's hand and standing away. "The viscount is just the perfect age for matrimony. And remember, Emmalie is not in her first bloom—although I do not believe she ever achieved that even in her teens, Miss Spindly."

"Spindle."

"Ah, yes."

"And if your ladyship will forgive me, Malie is only one-and-twenty, and she is still in her first bloom."

"Precisely. It just must have escaped my notice."

"She is not a showy blossom, but she is so very dear, like a violet."

"Eh . . . indeed. I have often thought so myself, and I believe the viscount would think so as well. Spindle, between the two of us, we must cultivate this match to bring it into full bloom!"

And thus botanically, as well as romantically, inspired, Miss Spindle went directly to Emmalie's bedroom. Her usually sedate steps all but skipping; her voice breathlessly dancing as well.

"Your mother, in great affection, has sent me to you, Malie dear!"

Smiling, Emmalie put away the book she was reading and said fondly, "She could not have sent me anything I would more willingly receive. Indeed, her giving me you as my governess is the only kind attention I have ever received from her."

It appeared that outside of her mother's presence, Emmalie could indeed speak.

The governess smiled at the young girl and gave her a hug. "It has been my happiest time to be with you. And you know I speak only with your interests at heart always. You cannot avoid marriage forever, as I was fortunate to do. You are not in the social class that would permit that. Your mother has been kind enough not to force you into marrying one of the many fortune hunters, as another might have, just to have you wed. But all Society would consider her totally heartless if she made no attempt to provide for your future. She has been very selective. She has waited and chosen for you the very best. The Viscount of Wynnclife is no ordinary suitor—he has title, power, personality, charm. He is even polite to his inferiors. Witness his refusing to sit last week until a chair had been found for me."

"I knew that little attention would win you!" Emmalie scoffed. "It was just common civility."

"I beg your pardon. Civility to one of my class from one of yours is not all that common—and I speak from experience. He is very nice in his manners to all. And he has been a particular friend of your mother's for years."

"Precisely," was all Emmalie would say before her face closed up again.

"Ah!"

"Yes. I refuse to take her *leftovers*!"

"But, my dear, there has never been anything of *that* sort between the two. It would be known among the staff if there were. They are friends of the spirit not soma."

"Soma?"

"Remember your Greek, Malie dear. Soma means body. And keeping it in Greek, they have a platonic friendship—which means eschewing anything physical for a more elevated union. In short, they are simply spirit-chums."

"That makes it even worse. It is my mother's cruel spirit that has so daunted me all my life. She thinks me . . . spiritless. You are well aware of that. And thus, he shall think me as well. I could scarcely bear to continue this painful existence all my life—extended from mother to husband and perhaps even unto children. Being continually undervalued and . . . *unseen*."

"Oh, my dear, dear child," Miss Spindle cried out from her heart, embracing the young girl. "And if they would but look, they would see a girl of great depths and sense and intelligence—not to say kindness. All the staff loves you . . . down to the gardener. Is that not worth anything? All your teachers and I, your friend and governess, value you and care for you so—is *our* account of no value?"

Emmalie assured her it was of very deep worth to her, and they both commiserated with each other and concluded that in all probability her mother would not press the issue, now that she was acquainted with how definite were her daughter's feelings. "After all, she never concerned herself with me before. I do not suppose she shall be overly insistent. I shall soon be forgotten once again."

Yet the next morning Emmalie was made aware of

how foolish was that assessment, when her mother had sent along on the same tray with her morning chocolate the fateful edition of the *Gazette*, formally announcing the glad tidings of her engagement. While tossing the newspaper away, she upset the chocolate and was much concerned with cleaning up the mess, during which diversion Miss Spindle arrived and picked up the edition.

"Ah," she said, hovering ineffectually.

"Hopeless," Emmalie said softly, staring at the stains.

"Nonsense, I have seen worse stains re . . . ah, you mean . . ."

"Yes."

"Oh, dear. I nerved myself again last night, upon leaving you, and went straight back to your mother. Recollecting *Macbeth*, you know . . ."

"You killed her?" Emmalie asked with a straight face.

"Malie!"

"Well, how else am I to read the *Macbeth* context?"

"You are to recollect that Lady Macbeth speech we went over: 'Screw your courage to the sticking place, and we'll not fail.' "

"And you?"

"Failed. I did all I could to acquaint her with the depth of your feelings against the gentleman, but she refuses to take your refusal seriously."

Emmalie, never having had much hope of Spinny's influence, turned and concentrated on changing into her morning dress. It was the same brownish shade of her hair and declared her to be as prim as her expression. She brushed her silky ash brown hair that was long enough to sit on and thick enough to be a cloak. One hundred strokes were dutifully finished, during which both were silent. Then, gathering up its abundance, Emmalie pulled her hair back with a clip at her neck— neat and properly presentable at last. That image of herself in the cheval glass seemed to comfort her. For it was the usual Emmalie. And with so many unusual things occurring, there was some ease in the assurance that she herself was the same.

Turning to Miss Spindle, the diminutive Miss Marlowe said positively, "Obviously I must take matters into my own hands."

"And that means?" the fond lady asked anxiously.

"That I shall just have to give my refusal in person to the viscount. I do not believe a man of his starched ways would relish being publicly rejected. He must agree to our asking for a retraction from the *Gazette* and our universally denying the report."

"Oh, dear, dear."

Emmalie faced the agitated lady and said kindly, "Do not fret. I shall make it crystal clear to Mama that you have done all you can to persuade me."

"Oh, posh! Do you actually believe I am concerned over that? You know how I care for you, my dear. And I worry that though you are intelligent, you are not *au fait* with the world. In this instance, there is no possibility of there being a request for a retraction when the notice was sent out under your mother's own name and signature. It would only be viewed that something had been discovered of a questionable nature about *you*. And heaven help us, it shall be *you* who should be universally disgraced. And your mother as well. Surely you know her well enough to understand she would never stand for that!"

Emmalie agreed, pursing her lips and thinking. "Well, if I can't do it that way, I must do it another! Perhaps Mother can go on a holiday to Vienna or Geneva. She often travels when she is bored. Let her do it now till the talk is not so current, and when she returns, she can have so many stories to tell her friends, and perhaps bring back a new cicisbeo to get their tongues wagging, that *I* should be forgotten and allowed to remain here undisturbed."

"But is that what you wish for your entire life? To

remain the daughter in her mother's house? No standing of your own? Constantly seen as of less importance? In your own home, my dear, with your own children, you should be of first importance. Think of that. Think, Malie dear, of your mother's coming to visit you, and, as a viscountess, you would have *precedence* over her.''

"Yes, that would be pleasant indeed,'' Emmalie agreed with a giggle, stopping for a moment of pleasure in that image, but then she shook her head. ''But not pleasant enough to have to accept the viscount in the bargain.''

Miss Spindle stared at her for a very long time, and Emmalie, at last, turned her head and acknowledged, "To save you the indelicacy of putting that question into words, I shall be open with you. Yes. It is the viscount himself that is the obstacle. It would be impossible for me to accept him . . . because I have a shameful secret in regard to him. I have more than a *tendre* for Viscount Wynnclife. . . . Rather, he is and has been, all along, the very core of my fantasies.''

Blushing, Emmalie was silent for a moment. But now under her governess's compassionate gaze, she felt free to, at long last, admit all. ''I have felt this way ever since he first began calling on my mother—eight years ago. I was thirteen and looked, if you'll recollect, about nine because of my small stature and Mother's desire that I never mature—apparently her will always has its way. I am still small for my age. Well, I first saw him at a moment of some alarm. I had gotten caught up in the maple tree trying to get Boots down. You haven't forgotten Boots, have you? She was that little Persian that kept climbing up tree after tree and then meowing pathetically, too frightened to ever come down. At times, she was a jolly nuisance. I had ripped gown after gown. This time, however, instead of coming to me, she climbed higher and higher, and I went up as well till we had both risen too far, and then with her in my arms, I was unable to climb back down. His lordship was walking by, and I, in diffidence, remained silent. But he heard Boots (who had no such delicacy) and looked up; and almost without breaking stride, he pulled himself up the trunk of the tree and had us both down in a trice, as if he were helping a lady out of a carriage. And he even bowed, as if I were a lady, and asked my name. I thought he asked the kitty's and said, 'Boots.' And the next few times I saw him, he winked and called me 'Boots.' And from then on I could not stay away from him, till one day Mama became annoyed at my constant presence or my staring at him . . . or both, but she whirled round and claimed my face was dirty and that I should leave to wash it, and he, without even looking my way, fully laughed with her at me and replied, 'We must have my valet take a strap to this ''Boots'' and shine her up, eh what?' And Mama kissed her hand to him. And the two were rollicking with mirth at my hurried exit. Well, I stayed out of his way from then on, watching from afar, but always watching, until I realized that even if I were directly before him, he would not see me. So I tested that theory, and it was so. Oh, he saw other people—Mama, of course. And when he was occupied kissing Lady Darlymple's hand, he saw her, I expect, at least enough to whisper in her ear. But never me. I was and am invisible to him! Why then should he suddenly wish to *marry* me? Unless he is being forced to by Mama or, or unless I am to be used as a screen for his union with Mama. And, and *that* I could not bear!''

Emmalie began to sob.

''That is too horrible to contemplate,'' Miss Spindle exclaimed, but then pursing her lips, she did contemplate that possibility—after which she shook her gray hair beneath her cap. ''No. It is not logical. I taught you to weigh probabilities. Consider. Why should either need your presence—if they wished to be together? Neither is married. Nor with His Highness, the Prince Regent, having made it the fashion to have lady companions of more advanced years than himself. . . . Why should Society find that sort of liaison at all remarkable?''

Emmalie looked hopefully at Miss Spindle. ''You think not? That possibility has really had me in a taking.''

''Nay, no need. I told you. They are not that way involved. Your mother, I am very certain, is concerned with settling your future. She always chooses the best for herself and for you—from the most respected needlewoman for your clothes to the most sought-after gentleman for your husband-to-be.''

A short laugh from Emmalie caused Miss Spindle to insist. ''Indeed, she always chooses the best for you, for she chooses her own preferences, which naturally always turn out to be, because of her superior taste, the superior choices!''

''Yes, she has inundated me with *her* preferences. Her style of clothes. Her friends. And then, one wonders why I always wind up wearing clothes that transform me into a smaller, more inferior version of herself. Or that I must marry the man she would have chosen at my age . . . and who has chosen me to please *her*. Yet, dear God, where am I in all this transaction? I am nowhere. Nothing. And so I shall ever be if I accept this final obliteration.''

Her voice caught, and as Miss Spindle could not quickly devise a more face-saving version of the facts, she could only take the young girl in her arms and try to console her with what everyone offered when stumped. ''Take your *time*,'' she urged. ''Time is on our side. Yes, yes, they must need grant you time to adjust if you agree to the marriage. Ask for a long engagement. And the more of a wait there is, the more likely there shall be a reversion to past habits of forgetting your existence.''

''That's it!'' Emmalie exclaimed, jumping up and hugging her governess all at once. ''I can set terms!

26

Ah, why have I allowed myself to sink into the blue devils? If they do not accept my rejection, they must be willing at least to accept a condition for my acceptance—no, three conditions, just as occurs in the stories we always read. I shall say he must *win* me!''

Aghast at the way Emmalie had enlarged her small suggestion, Miss Spindle countered, ''But what if he has no wish to . . . to win you?''

''Even better,'' Emmalie exclaimed jubilantly. ''He must then jolly well cry off! And Mother shall leave me alone in my disgrace for the rest of my life.''

''But what conditions did you have in mind?''

''None readily come to mind, actually. Yet generally I feel they should be not too outlandish, albeit they must be impossible to comply with.''

''Difficult.''

''I daresay.''

''But before we become entangled with particulars, I still have not quite understood why he must pass tests to win you. I mean, it is more likely he should assume you would have to pass tests to win him. Recollect whom we are talking about—this is Reginald, the Viscount of Wynnclife, and the most sought-after lord in our kingdom.''

''Perfect. He shall be so appalled by my undervaluing him, that he shall be delighted to work with Mama to find a way to cancel our nuptials. The more I insult him, the more likely he shall become our coconspirator for voiding this contract.''

Miss Spindle shook her head till her cap was loosed and falling. ''Recollect, my dear child, obviously he has *agreed* to the engagement. And once his lordship has given his word—it would hardly be the thing for him to break it. Honor is now the question. Having pledged his word, he must keep it. Therefore, in all likelihood he should do all possible to overcome your challenges. And since he is known for his wit and strength, it should be rather difficult to stump him.''

"*Spinny*! Why must you keep dashing my hopes? Very well! I shall take a moment to consider your objections." And Emmalie actually went to the window of her apartments and contemplated the lake in the distance. She had grown up paddling in that lake, and when Spinny was occupied, she would slip away on her own and had even taught herself to swim in it. No one assumed such a frail child could do half the things she found herself strong enough to achieve. And this time, as well, they should all be surprised by what little Emmalie could accomplish. And that should be the bringing of this almighty viscount to his knees. And her mother alongside him. Both bowing in defeat before her. All she must do is continue to surprise them. Surprise was her battle plan!

"I shall use their assumption of my weakness to defeat them," Emmalie exclaimed, turning and facing her anxious governess. "Three tests is what I shall insist on, *but* the first test shall seem so inoffensive, they shall be quite willing to humor me. And once they do, my trap shall be sprung. Indeed, the first shall be a test of his wit, which he will easily pass. And that shall set up both in their conceit. And the second shall be of his strength, which will be somewhat more difficult, but which again he will pass. And the third . . . that shall be of *endurance*."

The young girl's hazel eyes glowed with golden lights as the imp in her took control. "And *that*," she said with the intensity only her governess had ever heard in her colorless voice, "he shall *never pass*! For neither Mother nor he have had to learn the lesson we lesser mortals have had to—that of patience and endurance!"

Miss Spindle, knowing her charge, felt confident that this little thing could indeed do just what she promised and was at ease for the first time since entering the room. And after more discussion in which the particulars were sketched out, both ladies were widely smiling and well satisfied.

* * *

On the day when the viscount was to be presented to his unwilling bride, unaware of her reluctance, he arrived and had been seated in the morning room by the butler while Lady Leonie was looking over Emmalie's attire and throwing her hands up in despair.

"Gracious! You must have a finer outfit than that white, wilted crepe. It appears to have been your boon companion for several Seasons!"

"It is a comfortable dress, Mama. And I feel in this uncomfortable and strange situation, I must strive for something that is familiar."

"Well, it is of little matter. Come along, and quickly, he awaits us." And as the two ladies ran through the halls, her mother said under her breath, "Fortunately he accepted you sight unseen."

Blushing in the discomfort at this total dismissal of her worth, Emmalie newly swore to herself that she would insist on her conditions.

After languidly making his bow to mother and daughter, the viscount drew out his quizzing glass and stared through it at the young girl who was to be his bride. After having seated herself against the white cushions of an overpowering settee, she was almost invisible. He felt vastly reassured. Her mother had not spoken falsely. She was all her mother had said—a little minus of a girl. The viscount turned away, and from then on, neither he nor Lady Leonie felt the need to involve her in their conversation—which lasted upward of half an hour and concerned the amusing reaction to the marriage notice. To which not only did Emmalie not contribute a single syllable, but not even her attention. She was rehearsing her planned recitation to herself, and when she felt she had that down pat, she drew in her breath and attempted to get their attention by standing up. It had no effect. She found it necessary to walk deliberately in their line of sight. The viscount rose and walked around her to continue his bon mot. She moved again, more in his path. This time he saw her. He looked questioningly at her mother. Lady Leonie said impatiently, "Don't be tiresome, Emmie. Can you not see we are conversing? What do you mean by disrupting us in that manner?"

"I wished to get your attention, because I have something to say, and if necessary, I shall stand on the piano."

Lady Leonie, not bothering to react, simply signaled the viscount to continue their chat. Emmalie realized the need for a bolder move. She stood up on the piano and hit the keys with her heels. That silenced them at last. They looked her way.

"Thank you for the courtesy of your attention," she said rapidly.

The viscount advanced toward her, laughing. "Well, little one. What's ado?"

"I have read an interesting item in the *Gazette*. If it is not a misprint, I understand you have asked for my hand in marriage."

"Don't act as if you have more hair than wit!" Lady Leonie exclaimed. "You are aware . . . that is, I informed you of the viscount's kind offer."

"And did you inform him of my kind refusal?"

"What's this?"

"It is Emmalie just being prankish. Really. I do not believe you are necessary here any longer, my dear child. You are excused."

But Emmalie would not be dismissed. She continued addressing his lordship. "I must speak to you, Viscount. I have refused to be your wife, steadily, since the offer was first made to me. If you have any pride, you would not wish a reluctant bride and shall allow me the privilege of crying off."

"*Good God!*" The viscount was all astonishment. It was as if suddenly a mouse walked in and spoke up. "And this is the young girl that should be of no trouble to me at all—of whom I should scarcely be aware of her presence!''

"I am at a loss, Reggie. You have my profoundest apologies. And hers!'' Then turning to her daughter, she said, "You bad girl. Apologize this instant! What shall your intended think of you?''

"Obviously just what he said—that I am not what he intended. And that is the truth,'' Emmalie responded softly, beginning to leave the room. "I can visit my distant cousins in Yorkshire while you two settle how you shall cancel this agreement—best for all parties.''

"I'm afraid that is not possible,'' the viscount said with a frown. "There are reasons why I must not cry off, nor can I allow you to cry off—or I shall really be in the suds. So while I may not be your ideal, it would be quite impossible for us to give a lie to this situation. But I shall attempt to be as little as possible in your way, as I expect you shall in mine. We shall carry on tolerably. Don't allow it to concern you.''

Frowning, Emmalie raised her small voice again. "Tell me, your lordship. Just how do you intend to get your intended down the aisle, if I refuse to go? Shall you have me dragged by your footmen? Not quite the image for a man of your pride, what? I shall *not* wed you—unless under *restraint.*''

"*Odd's blood!* Here is a deuced of a pickle. Certainly I shall allow you to cry off. Never let it be said that I forced an unwilling bride. Dash it! Never happened to me in all my life! Never even been refused for a gavotte! And this . . . this affront . . .''

Lady Leonie was in a flame of anger. "Emmalie! How dare you continue to make such a cake of yourself, disgracing not only yourself but your father's memory, who should turn over in his grave if he knew what a hoyden his beloved daughter had turned into! It appears I shall have to send you abroad indeed. To Madame Belvoit's School, where you can study German and learn to be proficient in tatting—and never have a

31

moment's freedom of thought. Certainly novels shall not be permitted you there. Further, *Miss Spindle's services* shall no longer be necessary.''

"There really is no need to wring the child's withers! Egad, never thought one would have to threaten a young lady with German to accept me. But one lives to learn and be humbled.''

"Make your decision," Lady Leonie said impatiently. "There is much to do in either case. I must either write a letter of recommendation for Miss Spindle and a letter to Madame Belvoit, or you can come with me to London and purchase your brideclothes.''

Emmalie was silent.

"Very well," Lady Leonie said with a satisfied nod. "It appears Emmalie is now returning to her natural silent state, and we can arrange for the brideclothes.''

"Excuse me, Leonie. But instructive as it is to discover how one can control this young lady—one just threatens her with German lessons—I cannot believe I can accept such a sacrifice. Rather, I shall accept the princess—at least she has an inclination in my favor. Not that I expect adoration, but I must at least have *tolerance*.''

"This is not to be believed!" Lady Leonie fumed. "And for you, Reggie, this is hardly the time to demonstrate your delicate sensibilities. You are no longer in a position to accept the princess, for if it becomes known that you were turned down by my daughter, the queen would never accept you secondhand!''

This aspect of the situation not having been grasped by either member of the couple, they both stared in amazement. Emmalie, in fact, giggled in delight that the viscount was in a worse situation than was she herself. But on second thought, his dilemma made it imperative for him to be accepted by her. Her mother's face as well was in such a mask of affront that Emmalie realized if somehow the situation were not resolved to her ladyship's satisfaction, never again would she have one moment's peace. Nor was she cruel enough to want to so totally cast down the viscount, who had, in his favor, at least once done her a kindness. In any case, they were now, she judged, in enough of a quake to be fully alive to the importance of accepting her conditions. And the young lady prepared to throw in the midst of their foundering the safety net of her bridal terms.

While the viscount was exclaiming and refusing to force her hand, despite what it would mean to him, and Lady Leonie was insisting that he take a reluctant bride as his only course, Emmalie's soft voice strove to get their attention. Once more she resorted to theatrics—this time taking up the Norwich shawl (which had been draped over the piano) and waved it wildly about.

"You wish to speak again?" the viscount said with some amusement, even though his patience was sorely tried.

"Yes. Thank you for your attention. Which is the point of my intervention. Your attentions. I recollect that the viscount once did me a singular service, and while that does not mean I shall accept him, I am willing to lessen the severity of my refusal by . . ."

"What service?" the viscount demanded.

"You rescued Boots."

"Are you fantasizing again?" her mother asked in disgust.

"Oh, I say, you are Boots! The dirty little urchin and the kitten."

"Yes. That is, the cat was Boots. I am Miss Emmalie Marlowe. And if you wish for my hand, you should at least know my name."

"Emmalie, you have gone your length! Don't try my patience too far!"

"Very well, *Miss Marlowe*, if you give me leave. And what now? In recompense for my having rescued that scruffy little ball of fur, I am to have the pleasure of your acceptance?"

"I should scarcely think that small service was worth

the sacrifice of my entire life. But as in the fairy tales—
in German, Mama—when the young girl has been
cursed by fate, a beautiful good fairy always appears,
and while she cannot quite remove the spell, she can
mitigate it. And thus, I shall mitigate our situation by
giving you a test. And if you pass the test, I shall accept
your proposal. But mind, it is a difficult test—threefold,
and only a man of great resources and strength shall be
able to triumph.''

So often in the last few days had Lady Leonie been
astonished that now she had only a small gasp left. Not
so the viscount, who had immediate recourse to his
quizzing glass to fully look at this presumptuous hoyden, and then with the devastating coldness that had
caused many a challenger to lose his nerve, he said,
''Could you possibly recall we are not living in a fairy
tale? It should give our exchanges some degree of tolerance.'' Then turning to her mother, ''It appears,
Leonie, that your daughter's wits have been addled by
an excess of reading.''

''I believe I shall have to make it a fourfold test after
all,'' was all Emmalie would reply to that. ''Let me
know what the *two* of you decide, since apparently, Viscount, you are not man enough to make decisions on
your own, nor to pick a wife on your own!''

''You have gone too far, young lady,'' the viscount
said with quiet wrath. ''A wife is scarcely of enough
importance to require my undivided attention. That is
why I accepted your mother's assistance. Now if it had
been a really serious matter such as a selection of my
boots—that would be quite another thing.''

''Very well,'' Emmalie said, with as haughty a tone
as his. ''You may use my mother's offices in this unimportant matter, but I remain firm on my conditions.
It is up to you—or rather the two of you jointly—whether
you wish to meet my conditions and save the viscount
the humiliation of my refusal being universally known.
Surely the lesser of the evils is simply to meet my chal-

lenge. However, it is only fair to warn you, my lord, that in this test I shall not allow you to have my mother's assistance. For it is to be *your* test, after all. I already know all I wish about my mother's character and depth of affections. I need rather to discover your mettle. If you are daring enough to accept being tested— that, in itself, would reveal there is more in you than is generally, superficially displayed.''

And with that as her last word, she let fall the Norwich shawl that she had earlier swung about—very like a bullfighter who drops his cape and turns his back on his opponent. And head high, she turned and walked out without a backward glance.

Alone, the nobles stared at each other. The viscount absently picked up the shawl, then after looking at it for a moment, pointedly waved it about, exclaiming, ''And *this* is the invisible girl you offered me? Good God, in not above half an hour she has shriveled my pride and cut my character into ribbons. What kind of dance shall she lead me as a wife? The last thing I wish now is to marry that chit! And yet—the last thing I apparently can do is *not* accept her challenge!''

''Calm yourself, Reggie. There is no difficulty here. You have only to win her over, and she shall be, as all the young ladies have been (not to mention the older ones), totally pliable in your masterful hands. Simply pretend to accept her challenge, and meanwhile you have a secret challenge for her. Against your well-proven charms, I expect it should be not even a fortnight before she is as besotted as the rest of the females who have known you. Nay, not even that long—a sennight at the outside!''

''Hmm. Yes. *That* is possible. But I am not in the mood to put out lures. I have played that game so many times. It is all so tiresome.''

''This time there is some difference. Firstly, she is my daughter—which puts her ahead. Secondly, you must marry her to save your face in Society. And thirdly, she has given you a challenge, which in all conscience no man of any pride could see fit to refuse. That is not ordinary. There is some interest there, surely?''

''The devil-a-bit! But what can one do, after all? We are in such a dashed-hobble! I shall have to do as you request. The only question is—did the young chit think of all that on her own, or is she another pawn of her fascinating mother and just repeating well-rehearsed lines?''

Lady Leonie laughed, fluttering her fan with which she had been cooling her reddened face. ''Ah, I would take credit if I could. But I was not aware of the kitten you had rescued. We apparently owe this entire adventure to your having first appeared to my young chit in the guise of a rescuing knight. It does not seem to me that it would need much from a man of your address to further that guise into a full knight in shining armor. You simply wear her favor and pass the test. There,'' her mother said with a smile, indicating what he was still holding. ''You already have her shawl. You may keep it to wear a piece on your helmet, Sir Knight.''

The viscount could not be as amused as her ladyship, and he found himself quickly dropping the fringed item and responding, ''I sense a decided lowering of my position, not only from viscount to knight, but from adult to child. Spare me these romances. But if I must woo the young lady, I must. However, I expect you to be on hand continually to spice up our encounters—lest I find myself sinking into extreme fatigue. Devilishly tiring playing Prince Charming . . . yet rather amusing to enact that role to a lady who so little resembles one's version of a fairy princess.''

''Nevertheless, you shall take on the challenge? Shall I tell her so?''

''Oh no, we must play this game correctly from the beginning. I shall write her a letter accepting her conditions myself—and such a letter it shall be, I shall halfway have won my battle. Shall I go to such lengths as to include poetry and a poesy? Or would that be going too far? No, for *that* young lady too far would scarcely be enough! Yes, I shall depart immediately to begin my composition!''

And with some surprising relish for the adventure ahead, the viscount departed.

Lady Leonie was doubly flummoxed—not only at the new personality she had discovered emerging from her daughter's slight form, but at the viscount's so forgetting her, in his reaction to Emmalie, that he departed without engaging in their usual game of gallant hand kissing. For the first time ever, her ladyship had been left unsaluted. Affronted and all afield, Lady Leonie began to suspect that though all her life she had been the leading player, she shortly was to be relegated to a mere onlooker in what promised to be a most interesting game.

CHAPTER THREE

ALTHOUGH THE SEASON HAD STILL NOT BEGUN AND London would be rather thin of company, Lady Leonie wished to be in the thick of the thin and ordered her household to immediately depart. Then, too, although her Richmond estate was not a significant distance from town, with the astonishing behavior of her daughter, she deemed it best to be within a few minutes of the viscount's Piccadilly address for proper coordination.

Upon arriving at her Regent's Park domicile, her ladyship was about to inform the viscount of her presence, when Emmalie was beforehand. She demonstrated that by holding out two letters as she stood before her mother.

"I have completed the first test of the riddle and received the viscount's response," she said softly.

Lady Leonie flushed. "Are you informing me it was sent without my prior perusal?"

"He has passed it," was all Emmalie replied, but that did a great deal to mollify her mother.

Her ladyship oft wore long gloves, even informally, for her gestures had been compared to the grace of a swan, and gloved to the shoulders extended the fluidity. But now, forgetting grace of movement, those gloved hands eagerly reached out for the letters. Quickly skimming through both epistles, she read the conundrum aloud: " 'A negative conclusion fits my first. My second—struts with a uniformed display to spare. But together, this naught and this equivalent make a matchless

38

pair.' " Huffing, Lady Leonie said in exasperation, "He needs not have overly stretched his gray matter to reach the solution. For it is himself. A nonpareil."

"Indeed, it is," Emmalie answered, unperturbed. "But self must always intrude, and while he finds himself there, it is also myself, in that I am suggesting that what oft seems of negative value, upon closer observation, might be inestimable."

"Hmm," Lady Leonie said, forgetting her usual stylistic gesturing as she giggled behind her gloves. "And the riddle also sends him the message that *together* the two of you could form quite a rare combination?"

Her daughter did not disavow that, and her mother was pleased. There was something behind Emmalie's stratagems, after all. She took up the viscount's response and observed with delight he had quickly grasped all, for he expressed satisfaction that Miss Marlowe was beginning to view their coming union as a "matchless pairing."

As Emmalie had predicted, the ease of the first test had both his lordship and Lady Leonie exhibiting more tolerance to the young lady's game. Further, the viscount felt in rather high leg at this proof of Emmalie's lacking her mother's wits. For it assured not having to put himself to above tolerable exertion through the entire courtship. Stored in his idea pot he had a convenient cache of compliments for all occasions. He need no more than languidly dip in for the appropriate phrase and sprinkle the young lady with all. And he did so, expecting the usual show of considerable regard and received instead a show of considerable restraint. That necessitated his unleashing his prime pretties, remarks that never yet failed him. Which as well fell flat. Strike him, there was something about Miss Marlowe's direct gaze that stifled the words on his lips and had him henceforth courting via correspondence. Yet the several pages already composed, at some fatigue, he must say, had not dented that flinty little heart. They included his usual prize quote of Byron's: "man's love is of man's life a thing apart; 'Tis woman's whole existence," and she'd had the nerve to return it with a marginal response next to the quote, "Depends on the woman!"

So much for Lady Leonie's prediction of his having Miss Marlowe in his pocket in a sennight! Yet the viscount continued with his proven tactics. He'd had over a decade of success with them and saw no reason to make the smallest change for this small miss. Except, possibly, for the reason that they were not succeeding. For she continued rarely replying. Although sparing him the fatigue of reading her efforts, Reggie was still miffed at her failure to appreciate his prime offerings. The ton's favorite poet was Robert Southey, and his lordship sent her a collection, suitably inscribed, assuming she must at least acknowledge it. Rather she returned the volume itself with a note stating her preference was for the *newer* poets, such as Shelley.

That was the one blow too many, and his lordship must seek her on his next visit to her mother and exclaim in some dudgeon, "You refer to those cockney school representatives! *Blackwood's* found them objects of humor. I should blush to read anything so ill reviewed!"

"Perhaps you should trouble yourself to read more than the reviews. Perchance you might discover value beyond what is currently *commonly* accepted. Sometimes, as I have attempted to prove to you, the uncommon is better."

He made one of his envied bows, but her impudent response had his lordship pokering up and for the rest of the evening treating her as one of Lady Leonie's invisible domestics. Therefore, Emmalie left the lord and lady alone, assured they were not even aware of her exit. Miss Spindle informed her the next day that the viscount was expected for dinner. To which Emmalie cried, "Since our arrival in London, we're never without his presence! It is as if he were already part of our family!'' And forthwith she decided not to even make token appearances. Yet Miss Spindle continued to report his lordship's activities. He was currently exercising his new grays. Emmalie had a fondness for all animals and had heard a great deal about those prime horses. Indeed, accompanying him on this outing would have been the one thing she might not have refused. But he had not given her that opportunity.

Nor had he given it to Lady Leonie, who, considering that Reggie would be in the Park during the hour of the Grand Strut, felt being in the viscount's high-perch phaeton could not but add to her consequence. She was further peeved, wondering who then he would be so obliging as to take up. Certainly with the notice in the *Gazette*, he would not dare ask any of the ladies in their first Seasons. But he would surely not be prohibited from thus favoring a recent matron eager to attach him as a cicisbeo. That possibility had her near to recommending Emmalie be taken along for a much needed airing but stopped herself, recollecting that neither Emmalie nor the viscount would appreciate such blatant direction. Nor was such obvious maneuvering Lady Guile's forte. Instead she insisted her daughter report for dinner, waving away her excuses, and prior to his lordship's arrival made her privy to this advice. It was possible that Reggie had taken up in his phaeton some lady, best described as a ''bird of paradise.'' Every young lady should know her proper reaction in the eventuality of observing one's gentleman in such a situation.

''I shall ignore them both,'' Emmalie said obediently.

''Naturally, but you must further give the impression that you assume the befeathered lady had landed at his side by *chance* and he too much of a gentleman to shake her off, even from his arm.''

Watching her mother's amused face, Emmalie could not help but ask, ''And that is to whom Viscount

Wynnclife is presently demonstrating his prime cattle?''

Pleased at this mite of interest in Reggie's doings, her ladyship merely looked enigmatically, saying everything by saying nothing.

Abruptly Lady Leonie noticed her daughter's gown and was horrified the young chit had not changed, immediately sending her off to do so. Heavens, her ladyship concluded, she herself had to manage every step of this arrangement, for her daughter was giving her precious little help. Thank goodness she was so phenomenally capable!

Lady Leonie was not a stranger to self-congratulation—being constantly giving herself sufficient of that in her thoughts. But she particularly preferred her praises being said aloud, which meant she needed an audience—usually her black Persian cat, Negus, named for her favorite wine beverage. This pampered feline had earned his role due to his unequaled record of never betraying one of his mistress's confidences. As well, Negus offered unswerving attention and not a word of opposition. He was, in truth, a capital listener, except for his usual capricious yawn whenever Lady Leonie soliloquized about Emmalie. This time Negus went so far as to instantly doze at her ladyship's mention of her daughter, which brought on a rare reprimand. ''I tell you there's more to Emmalie than in a cat's eye. Ungrateful puss! Who always remembers to remind me to order your favorites? Who bought you that delightful wooden mouse? All forgotten because Emmalie rescued the garden birds from your clutches. Correct?''

Unresponsively Negus's yellow eyes stared back, and then he imperiously nudged her with his nose, which indicated he wished to be petted and made much of.

''Typically male,'' her ladyship concluded, yet obliged him.

When Emmalie entered the drawing room in another dress, which was not materially superior to her previous one, Lady Leonie could only sigh while Negus hissed.

"He is dashed spoiled," Emmalie said. "Unlike Boots who ran around and played and cuddled and was a total darling. Negus just sits."

"No one does it better," her mother said with pride. And indeed, black, massive, and majestic, Negus sat grandly and in whichever chair he chose, pushing anyone else off. Usually it was Emmalie he so deposed. Further, Boots had been so good, eating whatever was put in his plate, but Negus would not deign to stoop for his sustenance. He had to be fed directly into his mouth. If Lady Leonie was occupied, that duty fell to a maid or more often, young Lord Melwin, her ladyship's cicisbeo. At the thought of him, he arrived. Always accommodating. Promptly, he took from her ladyship the onerous task of petting Negus. Lady Leonie gratefully greeted this relief with an exclamation of, "Dear Pug." She had christened Lord Melwin "Pug"—both for his snubbed nose and since he seemed rather like an additional pet. The change of his hand for Lady Leonie's was done with extreme care, for Negus, to assure sufficient petting, operated on the principle of punishment for pausing. To mark his displeasure, he would either deeply scratch or fiercely nip a derelict hand. Emmalie, Pug, and even Lady Leonie herself had learned not to stop stroking until given leave to do so by Negus himself—by his moving away.

Now relieved of her task of stroking, Lady Leonie looked at her court and evaluated them. There was her daughter, Emmalie, renowned for her silence. Then Negus, who occasionally gave a meow of either satisfaction or objection. And lastly, Pug, who did most of his communicating through imploring eyes, while sitting silently at her ladyship's feet. It was a source of amusement to all that Lord Melwin had chosen as the object of his total adoration not only a woman older than himself, but one who prided herself on her gift of speech, while he scarce had a word to say. And when he did speak, he drawled and lisped so extensively, one word became a full comment.

"Why is it that I am attended by such a silent court?" she asked them, her eyes sparkling. When directly addressed, Pug was quite willing to respond with an appropriate compliment. "Becauthe, my delight, you are thociety's moth valuable thepeaker."

"Voluble," Emmalie corrected with a twinkle.

Lady Leonie was amused by that and replied with her famed tinkling laugh. "I expect I am both." She ceased smiling when the viscount was announced, hurriedly taking Emmalie aside to whisper an admonition not to inquire whom Reggie had taken up in his phaeton. "I shall do it for you," she concluded.

While indifferent to that affront, Emmalie was not to the viscount's actions upon entering. He had an aside for Pug, a kiss for Lady Leonie's hand, and for her, a barely imperceptible bow, as if she were an afterthought. After which Emmalie could hardly resist her subsequent act.

Admittedly her training as a lady cried out for her to desist! It spoke in her mind in Miss Spindle's voice, but Emmalie ignored it and went directly toward Negus. With much resolve, she lifted him. It needed not much of a pretense to drop the feline's prodigious weight, but she did maneuver her position next to the viscount and aim directly for the astonished lord's lap.

"Am I once more performing a signal service for you and your cat?" he asked with his usual languor, and his eyebrow lifted at such a height, she lost all her hesitation, especially since he confused Negus with Boots.

"He is not *my* cat. That is Negus, Mother's cat. And I suggest you quickly pet him to prevent his feeling offended at nearly being dropped."

The viscount had a vague recollection of the black Persian at her ladyship's side. Not being a cat fancier, however, he had never been formally introduced to the animal nor had occasion to become familiar with its tendencies, but as a gentleman, he complied with the lady's request and gave the feline a few perfunctory pats. Upon leaving off, Reggie was attacked. "What the devil!" he exclaimed, jumping up and letting Negus slide to the floor. A deep scratch marked his hand, and the viscount wiped it with an oath. Negus meowed his oaths of indignation and ran for comfort to Pug, who knew enough to calmly pet the animal until it had sufficient and slunk away.

The scratch was accepted with some tolerance by the viscount, but as a fashion dandy, he was seriously alarmed at the black fur clinging to his creaseless beige coat and matching pantaloons. While vigorously brushing his attire back to its pristine state, he turned and caught Miss Marlowe's look of "innocence" and was convinced in a trice that that hurly-burly girl had schemed his discomfort. Lord Melwin's shaking his head at Emmalie and commenting, "Thuch a bad little girl," made it a certainty. And as Emmalie hurriedly excused herself, Reggie did not miss the twinkle in her eyes as she glanced back at him. Actually, he suspected she was laughing aloud the moment the door was closed.

That assumption would have been verified if his lordship had followed the lady to her bedchamber. Not that he would dream of intruding there. Part of Miss Marlowe's delight was that she had not had to stay for dinner with her mother's group, after all. Although the conversation would have been of some interest to her, for the viscount turned it to Negus and his idiosyncrasies, inquiring, "Then it is well known that the animal shall strike if one ceases petting it?"

"Thertainly," Pug said with a look of commiseration. "I have many thcars."

Lady Leonie merely laughed and said, "Naughty puss," and it was not clear whether she was referring to Negus or Emmalie.

"Naughty, indeed," the viscount said softly, and there was no question to whom he referred.

The following day Emmalie revealed the second test. It could not be said that her announcement put her hearers out of their suspense, for both had almost forgotten there was to be another—rather, two others. But due to the ease of the first, there had not been the smallest trepidation. Which lack of alarm was soon justified. The second test was even less difficult than the first. The viscount was to show his physical strength by carrying Emmalie up the stairs of the Tower of London.

His lordship was more than willing to meet the terms, feeling he had strength enough to carry such a small girl twice that distance and not be winded. But Lady Leonie was prodigiously disappointed, exclaiming with some peeve, "Why not have him swim a certain distance of the Thames, pulling you in the boat—something that should have him properly *challenged*?"

"I am not assigning a Herculean labor to test his strength as a laborer. Rather, I am reducing him to a beast of burden in relationship to myself, while I, as a lady, am carried about."

Once more Lady Leonie was astonished at the hidden depths her daughter possessed. A faint smile hovered around her lips as she realized that carrying would bring the courting couple into closer physical proximity. "You relieve me of all apprehension," she began but, unable not to add her touch, said, "Would it not be more efficacious if the test encompassed carrying you *down* as well? For on the journey upward, he shall rather be striving not to pant and not pay you heed, but downward, more relaxed, shall have him more aware of you in his arms."

Emmalie saw the wisdom in that but was prepared to refuse simply because the suggestion was her mother's, and she wished this contest to be entirely hers. Aware of her reason for the hesitation, her mother tactfully inserted, "Even a *master* playwright's effort, I am told by my good friend, Mr. Kemble of Covent Garden, can be improved by an experienced actor's suggestions.''

The use of the term *master* playwright in regard to herself somewhat lessened Emmalie's reluctance. Indeed, she was totally mollified. Even more so, for it was the first compliment of such a superlative nature ever received from her mother, and being so pleased with it, Emmalie would not ruin the perfection of the moment by obstinacy. ''And down, of course. I had meant that as well.''

''Of course,'' her mother replied.

The viscount, awaiting Emmalie's and Miss Spindle's arrival at the White Tower of the London Tower complex, did not find the addition to the test such an obvious matter of course.

''And *down*!'' he expostulated, rather vexed.

''Unless you do not feel yourself up to the descent,'' Emmalie added with such solicitude the viscount insisted he could take her up and down ten times over.

''Really! Then ten times let it be,'' she conceded sweetly.

Properly dished, Reggie stared at the innocent brown eyes, beginning to detect a golden impish glint within that Spinny had often remarked on and been wary of.

''Twice,'' he compromised shortly, ''shall be sufficient to assure our being proper objects of amusement. Any more will have the gapeseeds gathering in groups.''

''You'll note I did not included the 114 steps descending to the dungeon,'' she whispered kindly, and he merely bowed and led her to the foot of the Tower stairs. Having brought his valet with him, his lordship, with an excess of formality, removed his coat and handed it to that stolid-faced man. Emmalie could not resist turning to Spinny and, adopting the same hauteur, removed her pelisse and handed it and her muff to that dear lady, who accepted both with a hiccup of a giggle.

Aware of Miss Marlowe's mimicking him, the viscount had to restrain his desire to shake the young lady.

She increased his peeve by softly explaining, "The removal of my pelisse shall lessen the burden. And, if you wish, I shall as well remove my bonnet."

"There is not the slightest need," he snapped. "I expect I can bear that small feather atop of your feather weight."

Nodding, Emmalie did not remove her new bonnet. Bought her mother, it was not in Miss Marlowe's usual staid style, especially not the rather aggressive ostrich feather that sprouted up as if in surprised exclamation.

With a bow, Reggie approached and firmly lifted the young lady. Thus, silently the two began the ascent. As Lady Leonie had predicted, the viscount carried her up the flights with a tolerable degree of composure and formality. Rather like a footman, or chairman. Not one word was exchanged between them, not even when, without being the slightest bit winded, he had brought her safely down and began the second ascension. This time inexplicably the feather of Miss Marlowe's bonnet seemed to be more in the way, for it bobbed with each step, tickling his lordship's chin. He attempted to rise above that vexation by raising his head higher than its usual elevated tilt and found himself actually navigating with his head thrown back, which gave a certain uncertainty to his steps. And yet the feather was inexorable—hailing his every third motion. And each time the feather hit, Emmalie had to press her lips tightly together.

Feeling rather than hearing her giggling, the viscount said coldly, "I perceive I have fallen into the vulgar position of becoming your source of amusement."

"It's my feather," she whispered. "It's tickling me that it's tickling you."

Unbending a bit, the viscount smiled at that and was immediately subjected to the feather's tickle once more, which had his lordship saying dryly, "I daresay I should have accepted your offer to divest yourself of the bon-

48

net. I perceive a feather can be a lady's most deadly weapon.''

Whereupon Emmalie removed the bonnet with one grand motion and threw it up into the air where it arched and went tumbling down the stairs.

"A gesture worthy of your mother." He approved, relieved of its pokings, but that comment rather pokered her up. She became more and more listless in his arms and suddenly went so limp, she was decidedly more difficult to carry. That swooning attitude caught the attention of a guard. He was a Yeoman Warder in his Tudor red coat and pie-shaped black hat. Nearing, he solicitously inquired whether the lady was in need of medical assistance.

"She is not. She is merely fatigued and wishes to be carried," the viscount said shortly and dismissed the guard with a disdainful wave of his hand.

"You have a very solid grip," she observed. "Not since my stable hand, Danny, have I felt myself in better hands."

He was forced then to look at the young girl's face close to his. "Are you equating me with a stablehand, egad?"

"Or a chairman? Or a footman? You are performing your function with perfection that could only be envied by the best-trained flunky."

So close, he was able to observe the yellow imps in Emmalie's eyes. And for a moment the viscount was fascinated and nearly missed a step.

"Ah, I see, I praised you too soon," she commented.

"The devil," he muttered, and increased his speed till both were winded. At the top he took a deep breath and after a small pause started the final descent. In a few steps, he was fully stopped by a well-meaning lady, offering the use of her vinaigrette for the young lady's condition. The viscount resorted to the never-failing raising of his left eyebrow, but the lady, albeit reduced to temporary incoherence, stood her ground. She would not be fobbed off.

"It is most generous of you, madam," Emmalie interrupted, "but I have not lost my senses, except to permit this bounder to be bounding me down these stairs for his amusement."

"Good heavens!" the old lady exclaimed. Much alarmed and overflowing with justified indignation, she turned to the viscount and at full voice demanded, "Unhand the young girl, sirrah! Or I shall be forced to make use of my umbrella—with which I am never without!"

Ere his lordship could sufficiently explain, the old lady's shrieks brought forth not only another guard with lance, but several visitors, all of whom formed a circle about the sputtering viscount.

Whispers of abduction went flying round. "Unhand her!" was the universal demand.

"Not till I have achieved my purpose!" the viscount replied, in annoyance, and pushed the interfering commoners aside.

"Oh *ho*!" the yeoman exclaimed. "Did you hear that? Not till he has achieved his fell purpose, the blackguard!"

"Scoundrel!" the old lady called out, and made ample use of her umbrella to hit the viscount on the head as he attempted to slip downward.

With the guard on one side and the old lady and her umbrella on the other, they succeeded in stopping the viscount.

Chagrined, his lordship gave the most fulminating glance to Emmalie, who smiled sweetly and whispered, "We appear to be the cause of some vulgar attention, after all. Pity. Was not that just what you wished to avoid?"

"Unhand her, villain!" The old lady was crying now, coming down to their level in a rush, just about to catch her breath. "I shall not allow a young child to be molested in my presence, sirrah! I am Mrs. Thorngton and have sufficient influence in Society to see that such atrocities are not committed in my presence. Certainly not in an historical edifice! You bring disgrace to its memories!''

"Rather in keeping with its history, I daresay,'' the viscount continued, and attempted to evade her and her umbrella, which was by now landing blow after blow on his head and arms, causing his lordship to finally exclaim in high dudgeon, "Madam, restrain yourself! She is my intended!''

The guard and the old lady demanded the young girl answer if that was the case. Emmalie hid her visage with her hands and through that said, in a smothered voice, "He has been insisting I wed him, but I have refused, and yet he is demonstrating figuratively that I shall henceforth be forever in his arms and at his command.''

The fear in her little girl's faltering voice was sufficient to decide the entire audience, noticeably enlarged beyond the first group of onlookers. "Shame! Fiend!'' was fully voiced throughout the many layers, all closing in. The old lady refused to desist from making use of her umbrella, until the viscount was bleeding profusely from a cut on his chin by one of the broken stays.

"Set her down immediately!" the guard ordered.

"I shall not!'' the viscount replied. "Not till we have reached the bottom of the stairs.''

"Oh, heaven protect an innocent girl,'' Emmalie cried out to her gasping audience. "Take me from his arms—he is touching me with a familiarity no lady can ever countenance.''

That cry could not but be met with instant action. Half the men and all the ladies in the group crowded up to her. And with the old lady and her umbrella leading the charge and the guard, now pointing his lance, the young lady was scraped out of the lord's arms. Forthwith several men laid hands on the struggling lord, keeping him well back; while, with the aid of the elderly lady and several other ladies, all pushing vinaigrettes under her nose, Emmalie was escorted and supported back to Miss Spindle, who was waiting for her at the foot of the stairs. Too shocked to question, Miss Spindle allowed herself and her charge to be bundled into a summoned hack. And only then did the lady with the umbrella desist from her protection. It was a moment of sweet triumph for all to have rescued a young innocent from the hands of a libertine who had been so bold and knavish as to attempt to have his way with her in public view! One rarely achieved such total victory over evil forces, and the old lady was never to cease talking of her grand deed and even subsequently kept her shattered umbrella mounted, as some knights of old kept their lances—as a symbol of her victory.

Alone in a hired hack, Emmalie and Spinny, with conflicting emotions, stared back at the crowd of guards now holding the viscount under arrest.

When Emmalie turned forward, she allowed the laughter, bubbling so long within her, to have its way. She was in positive whoops. "Did you see his face? Oh heavens, he shall never forget this humiliation."

"What did you do?" Miss Spindle asked, aghast.

"I? Why do you assume I did something? I was merely rescued by a crowd of well-wishers from the arms of an overeager suitor. I could not resist the opportunity. The situation presented itself, and I simply aided the outcome. If he was not capable of handling such a well-meaning interference from the outraged citizenry of London, with the leader being a mere elderly lady, he is obviously not competent to handle me! You see, Spinny, I have been worrying for naught. He has lost the second condition on his own. He is simply not up to snuff! Not up to the standards I have set for him!"

"Indeed," Miss Spindle agreed. "You are quite a handful. If nothing else, today's adventure shall teach him that." Miss Spindle gave a large sigh. "But I own it is with some reluctance I relinquish my dreams of your happy marriage.''

Emmalie turned away from her governess.

Both ladies sunk into a reverie. The only sound in the carriage was that of the horses clip-clopping them homeward. Emmalie's overwhelming sense of disappointment so surprised, she must needs explain it away as what a knight in battle would have felt at felling his opponent in the preliminary blows. One expected more of a challenge! And then, she gaily exclaimed to Miss Spindle she would shortly have the satisfaction of informing her mother that Reggie, her favorite, had been so little up to snuff he had been checkmated in the first few moves. A sham suitor, indeed!

''It shall be as you wished, Malie dear. You need not see his lordship again,'' Miss Spindle said, with such a knowing glance, Emmalie could not help but protest.

''Heavens! You think I am disappointed! That I was *enjoying* his attentions!''

''Yes,'' Miss Spindle said, taking the girl's hand and squeezing it in commiseration and adding softly, ''Were you not?''

''Yes,'' Emmalie admitted, unable to continue a pretense before her closest friend. ''Oh, Spinny! Why was he such a weak opponent? Indeed, I cannot but think that if he really wished to win me, he would have made more of an effort!'' And she sniffed and was quiet.

The next sound was one of alarm from both ladies as a passing coach edged their hack to the side of the road and brought it to a stand. Before Emmalie had a chance to inquire of the hackman what was amiss, she found herself being dragged out of the vehicle and dropped unceremoniously into the waiting coach, while the viscount turned his team to the veriest inch and back the way they had come.

''Why do you not simply admit you have lost?'' Emmalie cried out, as the acceleration of the carriage had her straining to hold her balance.

"I have not," the viscount threw at her and increased the speed of his horses. As a known whipster, he demonstrated his finesse time and time again through the whirl of London's traffic, while unchecked and undaunted he posthaste returned the lady back to the Tower.

"You little spitfire. I am in total sympathy with Henry the Eighth's methods of settling with disobedient wives, and we are approaching the appropriate setting! To extricate myself from the pretty tangle you left me in, I had to resort to use of my title, which I am generally loath to do, and I need hardly say the entire experience was beneath me."

Emmalie, with a satisfied smile, said, "As usual, my lord, you hide behind your station in life. But that shall not work with me. You have lost the test. And me."

"The devil I have," he muttered. "Your test was simply that I carry you up the stairs and down. You had no proviso about interruptions. I was carrying you down without hitch until you, through your pathetic ploy, interfered with that successful conclusion. Nevertheless, I intend to repeat the procedure!"

Emmalie did not have time to question his intent further. For they had returned to the Tower, and he had her back in his arms. This time, there were several yeoman guards waiting and bowing when he entered with her. They held back the gaping crowd and allowed him to be the only one ascending the stairs. Nodding to them, the lord began racing up the stairs and continued down. And then once more ascended. All along, with steely resolve, he never once even looked at her, resisting Miss Marlowe's attempts to distract him.

"Unhand me! This no way to win my hand. I allowed no provision for a repeat test. One failure is final in my view," she exclaimed.

"Be quiet, you are disturbing my stride." And he increased his speed—like an Olympic challenger.

"*Help!*" she cried out.

"You are being repetitive! That ploy shall not work this time," he informed her, between clenched teeth and with all the dignity possible in such an impossibly undignified situation. "No one shall help you, by gad, and, if you do not stop wiggling I shall drop you on each stair to test your breakability!"

"Your heart is beating loudly against my ear; it is most disconcerting," she countered in disdain.

"Pardon, but I expect that is a sound, as my wife, you shall have to accustom yourself to."

"You are shockingly indelicate."

"You are shockingly aware to think I was being indelicate," he whispered, and as they had reached a landing between floors, he paused for a moment and looked at her fully. Both of them felt a need to get their breaths. Her hat having long been disposed of, her long brown hair had come loose and was swaying in all its glorious length around them. Her delicate little mouth was open and panting, which altered the vexation of having her in his arms into a sensation of some interest. Remembering his objective was to arouse in her a *tendre*, the viscount allowed himself to give way to his inclinations and kissed her fully. And while carrying her down, he gently continued to do so: step by kiss by step by kiss, until the yeomen on the bottom landing came into view, and then the viscount slowly set the lady down on her feet, where she took a moment to regain her balance.

"I have won," he said, his eyes twinkling, and he seemed to be saying that he had won two battles that day.

"You have played false," Emmalie said, reclaiming her pride and her breath at the same time. "The old lady with the umbrella was correct, you are a blackguard."

And turning on her heel, she signaled a hack, but the viscount would not allow that.

"You are unescorted," he said. "Do you think I shall

allow you to travel without protection through London?''

"Indeed? You fear I shall be subjected to some gross act of indelicacy! What more liberties could be taken than you have already attempted?'' Emmalie claimed, her small voice rising, while she continued to signal for a conveyance.

"Have you no sense of decency?'' his lordship protested, waving away the slowing hack. "My carriage awaits us with my valet to give you consequence. The daughter of Lady Leonie shall not become the subject of a scandalous *on dit* while in my protection. I daresay your mother would never forgive me. Kindly remember your upbringing.''

Those words and his disdainful air succeeded in fully rousing Emmalie to exclaim, "Recollect it is *you* who besmirched my respectability, not only by losing poor Spinny, but by making me the public object of your advances. I shall find my way home alone, my lord. Remaining with you is sadly subjecting me to comment on the thoroughfare!''

Nevertheless, the viscount had his way and returned both Miss Spindle, who had been safely in the custody of his valet, and Emmalie to her amused mother's arms.

Both were so preoccupied giving each other fulminating glances, Lady Leonie exclaimed, "Heavens, which one of you lost? Which one of you won? It seems, actually, from your expressions, that both of you have both won and lost.''

No response. Apparently neither the viscount nor her daughter were in the mood for light banter. One bowed. One just turned on her heel. Each one departed in a huff.

Left waiting and unanswered, Lady Leonie sighed, but she was not seriously discombobulated. She had her own way of finding out whatever she wished to know. And before the evening candles were lit, she had wheedled sufficient out of Miss Spindle. Naught from Emmalie, however. Having begun to respect Emmalie's reserve, as she had begun to appreciate Emmalie's stratagems, Lady Leonie congratulated her daughter—silently.

CHAPTER FOUR

IT WAS THE VISCOUNT OF WYNNCLIFE'S BELIEF THAT no true member of the nobility need jolly his servants into performing their duty of dedicating themselves to his comfort. That doubtless was his staff's reason for being. Therefore, when Finley, his butler, who had been with him since Reggie was in shortcoats, brought him the newspapers, properly turned to the Society section, and a glass of brandy with a plateful of his favorite shortbread treats and had stoked the fire to the proper level of blaze and paused to inquire if aught else was required by his lordship before retiring for the night, Reggie did no more than incline his head in gracious permission for his departure.

Only cits or nouveau gentry, whose lineage had a distinct smell of the shop, or Lady Leonie broke that rule of maintaining a proper distance. Of course, her ladyship always decreed herself an exception to every rule. From chambermaid to footman, all were aware, even while she was smiling and asking the state of the health, morals, finances, and amours of every family member that she was merely conferring a favor, and none presumed on her interest. Actually, it was essential for Lady Leonie's peace of mind to know everything about everyone within her perimeters. And thus she could be their judge or their good fairy, depending on her mood.

Not that the viscount was unaware of the concerns of his subordinates. The pensions and yearly bonuses were of excessive generosity. Moreover, he had arranged for Finley's son to be taken into service by his closest friend, Lord Lanadale, and Finley's daughter was a maid at one of the viscount's country estates. But all was done with an assumption of disinterest that fooled only himself. His staff was devoted to his every whim. His comfort, their first objective. Finley especially sought to anticipate an order before his lordship put himself to the fatigue of voicing it. As now, while sitting down to his brandy, the viscount discerned its dosage exceeded the usual—indicating Finley's sensing his lordship being somewhat out of curl.

After several sips, however, Reggie felt in finer fettle and contentedly looked about. His London establishment personified the elegant Grecian style of his Society. A great many of the other domiciles of his set, particularly Lady Leonie's, had been overrun by Egyptian, not to mention Chinese, decor following the excesses of the Prince's Brighton Pavilion. Everywhere Mandarin screens were popping up, hiding good English woodwork. And one could scarcely sit on a chair without observing with dismay its gilded claw feet as well as those on the table alongside. But most appalling of all were the menageries of statues of sphinxes and cats. Her ladyship had fallen prey to the latter, probably in tribute to that feline fiend, Negus. Involuntarily he glanced at the mark of Negus on his hand, forming a closing scar. That and the bruises on his face, emblems of his battle at the Tower, were courtesy of one and the same person—that little insignificant miss whose misconduct not only aroused misgivings about their relationship but even thoughts of misogyny.

Several sips emptied the glass, which had the viscount frowning. Apparently Finley had not accurately measured the state of his discontent, and his lordship was put to the bother of having to pour himself a refill. On his return to his chair, he almost tripped over the small table that always held an open copy of *Peerage*.

There was not the smallest need for the viscount to ever have to peruse that volume, since he was perfectly aware of the heritage of everyone that mattered. Yet, it was customary to have one available, and the viscount eventually did what was expected of him. Just as he belonged to the correct clubs no matter how excessively bored he'd become with the same faces. And just as he always won the favor of each Season's most prized young lady, no matter whether she appealed to him or not. Witness his allowing himself to meet the height of everybody's expectations by agreeing to being leg-shackled. Not that the lady of his choice would have been the choice of the ton. Indeed, their whispers were spoken aloud by Lord Lanadale. "One understands obligations to friends, but, old sport, marrying to please the mother is surely going beyond the pale!"

"There is more to Miss Marlowe than meets the *general* eye," Reggie replied with dignity. "Accustomed as you are to a Society with people who *look* everything and are nothing, you cannot appreciate one who is the reverse."

Pleased with his riposte at that time, the viscount was even more so now on rethinking it. Food for thought, he decided, which reminded him to feed himself, and he took a bite out of a shortbread treat on the tray. Lifting up his crystal glass, refilled with brandy, he caught the light from the chandelier above in its honeyed depths. Peripherally his attention was snagged by the scrolls and polyanthuses carved into the ceiling. They taunted with a memory. Dashed elusive. And then, Reggie pinned it down and smiled. It was of another ceiling in the state room of his country seat, Malbern, that he, as a halfling, had had the jolly good time of flecking off the gilt with his slingshot. Finley had caught him at it. But when questioned by Lady Wynnclife about the deplorable state of their gilt, the old retainer had invented a tale about the humidity leading to peeling. She had accepted it, as his mother always accepted her domestics' replies, with half-attention—which was the full extent of her interest in their world. That was slightly above her concern in her son's. For Reggie recollected her ladyship mostly as passing him by in the halls, giving him a semismile of recognition that faded before her scent had faded from the air. And he would be standing there alone, looking after her. Upon her demise, Reggie had returned from Eton for the funeral and judged himself unaffected by her complete passing, until overtaken by her scent emanating from a discarded handkerchief in her rooms. Most astonishingly he had succumbed to sobbing in a disgracefully unmanly manner that would not abate. It had been Finley who had found him thus, and discreetly arranged for Reggie to be closed up in his rooms and spread the story of an attack of virulent chicken pox which precluded the young man's attending the funeral as well. When Reggie's father had stuck his spoon in the wall, it was later, and being at Oxford, there was no need of Finley's protection, for one had learned not to show emotions before one's chums. Not that the viscount had any grief to suppress, for he had become quite accustomed to losing a parent and even said as much to a fellow farouche enough to commiserate.

To himself he explained his sangfroid with the amused conclusion that his father had been considerate enough not to leave behind any memorabilia that might discompose his heir. Unless one considered his snuff collection—which was not Reggie's sort—and which led rather to a sneeze than a tear. Whatever the reason, the young man had taken to his solitary state with such aplomb it seemed his natural element and eventually became his preferred style, even when, subsequently, as the fifth Viscount of Wynnclife, he was sought by most of the ton. His lordship dismissed companion after companion with the conclusion that selectivity and infidelity were the true signs of the socially conversant. Not till Lady Leonie had the viscount found anyone worthy of his continued observance. It would be too much to say that she had the same fragrance as his mother, for she did not. Actually, her attraction was more her similes and satire rather than scent.

At their first meeting Reggie had been squiring the latest beauty, a brunette with the impossible nickname of Dodo, short for Dorothea. Looking at the young miss on his arm, Lady Leonie had inquired over the girl's head, "Are not Dodos extinct?"

And he'd laughed and promptly replied, "So is Dodo then, from my Society, especially if one has found a more lasting lady bird?" And he promptly dropped the young miss and spent the rest of the evening pursuing Lady Leonie. Afterward, the bond formed by a relishing of each other's conversation was further sealed by their joining forces to look down on all their acquaintances.

Remarks were saved to be savored together. And Lady Leonie had taken to sending his lordship the current novels or belles lettres, with underlined passages and comments in the margins, so that reading became a discussion with each other as well. After her, Reggie found all other ladies mere dalliances one escorted to be seen with. Incognitas sufficed for his passionate nature's release and required naught in return but incomes—of which he had so much he never felt the dent.

There had been times when Lady Leonie's charms had him contemplating a closer relationship, but her ladyship kept him at a distance. Her interest was simply in his mind. Never having been sought for that, neither by any other lady, lightskirt, and certainly never by any gentleman friend, it had been an exhilarating experience. He was excessively honored to become the favorite of her ladyship. For that group, the viscount well knew, included the Regent himself. In her youth, Lady Leonie Clayton had been one of the ladies who wore the prince's feather in her cap to indicate her support of the Regency Bill, giving the Prince Regent power while his royal father wallowed in his insanity. After meeting the prince and listening to his rambling royal complaints, Lady Leonie discovered considerable less enthusiasm for his cause. Eventually her ladyship learned to orchestrate conversation to revolve around herself and henceforth found discoursing with His Highness tolerable. It was soon whispered that His Highness had given her an emerald ring. More than an homage, the ring was a pledge: upon receipt of which, he should drop any current lady and give Leonie all she requested of him as well as his heart.

Lord Byron had been another one of Lady Leonie's confidants, but tall, thin, love-sick Lord Melwin, or Pug, Reggie rather suspected of truly enjoying Lady Leonie's favors. All of Society did so as well, when one of Pug's infantile poems described her bed in such detail as could only admit of its being familiar territory. There was much brouhaha about her preferring one young enough to be her son. Upon the viscount's being ironically uncivil enough to bring that *on dit* to her attention, Lady Leonie in like tones responded, "But Reggie, dear, are not each Season's diamonds rapidly becoming young enough to be your daughters?" And after that, he had not questioned her further, understanding he must accept the constant attendance of Pug, for henceforth, everywhere Lady Leonie went, Pug was certain to be—a few steps back.

Hovering behind as well had been her daughter, Emmalie. Apparently her ladyship had decided she did not need two shadows. And so the viscount was assigned his own little pug. Yet one he discovered could scratch!

Reggie had just finished his drink and reverie when Lord Lanadale arrived. Refusing to disturb Finley at this hour, Basil was offered a full decanter and told to help himself.

Lifting his glass, Basil claimed he knew not whether to toast or roast his friend, for the latest crim. con.

story was of Reggie's arrest for attacking his betrothed, in of all places, the courtyard of the Regent's house.

"London Tower, old boy. Must get your facts accurate if you are going to live up to your reputation for the greatest tittle-tattle in Society!"

"Bosh," Basil said with a grin. "A rattle, I might be, but I do not make it my profession to spread stories, unless the bumblebroth be about you, old boy. Then I am the resident expert and always applied to. Did you attack that little Ariel? You, a big bad wolf and she just a delicate sprite? Not the thing, old boy. Not sporting, what?"

"Hmm!"

"Which means?"

"Nothing."

"Hmm! back to you, then. Whenever you say, *nothing*, in that folded up way, I fear there is a barrel of nothing waiting to come falling over us all! Better spill it out, old boy. Here's Basil, ready to help you mop things up."

"You sound suspiciously like a scullery maid, Basil boy, and you're acting like a pig! Stop swilling! You've dashed near finished that bottle. I shall have to ring for replacements. Consider my domestics and restrain your thirst—and for *on dits* as well. I have nothing to tell you."

"Nothing again! Ah, that's it, then! You found the young girl to be a total nothing and wish to cry off. Unable to do so and that's why you're so blue-deviled as not to offer me any of the shortbread treats one always visits you to consume. I'm devilish sharp-set."

"I've finished the last of the shortbreads. And as for rumors, you have my permission to deny all!"

"Certainly shan't deny what you've just verified to me, and especially since you ain't offering me any treats."

"When did I verify . . ."

"Accepted the facts. Simply corrected the locale. Although I must say an attempted seduction in the prince's garden would be more in keeping with the policy set by His Highness, but at London Tower—lost your head, did you, dear one?''

The viscount was amused by his friend, and amusement was always a way to win one's way into his favor, and so with an all-suffering sigh, he not only divulged all, but also agreed to waken Finley for the remaining shortbread treats, or at least muffins, as well as Basil's favorite, Holland Water and a replenishing of the brandy stock. Several trays of the treats, as well as two of muffins and biscuits, were quickly brought; the liquor replenished, and fresh crystal glasses presented. Lastly, coffee—not requested and not touched.

Consuming all the delicacies lessened Basil's sense of delicacy as he demanded, ''Now, let me get the lay, old thing. This little one is to be won by feats of daring? Ain't that the right of it? And one feat was carrying the child up and down a staircase. . . . And you *failed*? Need a bit of a workout, what?''

''Confound you, Basil! And give me back my brandy bottle! You have your own drink. Since I've confided in you, at least get the blasted facts straight! They're dashed damning enough! I told you I had successfully carried the little minx up and down and up! But on the last *down*, a lady with an umbrella tripped me!''

''Clumsy.''

''Not a bit of it! After nearly blinding me with the blasted thing, she stuck the cursed umbrella under my feet—claiming all the while, at the top of her quivering voice, she was rescuing Miss Marlowe from my clutches!''

''You were clutching her at the time!'' Basil exclaimed, sadly shaking his head.

''I was *carrying* her! Have to clutch when one is carrying, especially if the blasted girl was wiggling. Up and down the stairs, she was a wiggling against me and breathing hard in my face!''

"Ahh! *Ha!*"

"Precisely so. Just then a guard attacked as well!"

Basil was silent for a moment while popping open another cork, and the sound had him saying, "That drew his cork, eh what? Proper mill ensued?"

Reggie threw himself into an explanation, even demonstrating the conflict. "One could hardly credit it, but the old lady was rather adroit with her parasol, popped in a flush hit under my guard. Left me wide open for a leveler from the yeoman, who was seeking to spear me through."

"Bloody battle, that."

Appeased at Basil's commiseration, the viscount collapsed back in his chair and convivially offered his bottle. "Take another swig, old boy, this whole thing is getting too dry to relate without a wet whistle. You understand, Basil, I could hardly engage in an authentic mill with a lady of my mother's age. Not sporting, what? Nor with Miss Marlowe, herself a lightweight. Not in my class. Should have paddled her. But, nobleman, you know. Merely dragged the damned chit back and carried her up and down the stairs and then kissed her till she didn't know what blasted thing was happening to her! She was panting like a puppy."

"Ah! Ha! Enjoyed her, did you? Little morsels can be quite tasty, I'm told." And Lord Lanadale smacked his lips.

"There's nothing of *that* in my feelings for the chit," the viscount exclaimed, offended. "Going to *marry* her."

"Quite," Basil said. "Well, what's ado, old thing? One notices your penchant for short things—shortbreads, et al. And the child is shortish."

"Blast you, Basil, stop calling her a child. She's one-and-twenty!"

"Is she, by Jove? Last time I saw her she seemed like a child, not even ready to have a Season. Little thing, all eyes."

"All eyes and spirit. And she looks at one as if one were going to eat her up and puts those kind of ideas in one's blasted head, when one would normally not be thinking of even touching such a child. . . ."

"Ah! *Ha*! Ha! And another *Ha*! You called her a *child*!"

"Speaking of childlike, Basil, what the devil do you mean by dribbling?"

"Am I? Must mean I'm bosky. When I can't hold any more liquor, it comes spilling out of me, as if to say, 'Full up in here. Stop, can't hold anymore.' But I never pay no mind. Just keep on spilling it in, and it just keeps on spilling out."

"Delightful," the viscount groaned. "I hesitate to reflect what shall come spilling out of your mouth when you've sobered up. All my confidences, no doubt."

"No doubt. Never did learn to keep my lips sealed," Basil confessed in frank agreement. "I say, better tell it your way first, before it comes out through me, and you become the laughingstock."

The viscount paused before he took another glass of brandy. While convinced he, unlike his friend, was nowhere near being ape-drunk, he sensed himself nearing. Basil began to give the falconer's cry, "Hillo, ho, ho, boy!" and had to be hushed up with a plate of muffins just joyously discovered under a towel.

Reggie took one himself which required brandy, after all, to wash it down. And then as he munched, he exclaimed, "Why am I blessed with such a friend and such a fiancée? It's as if the gods conspired to make me ridiculous. I, who have been so respected all my life!"

Finishing the muffin, Lord Lanadale tossed another to Reggie and said with a grin, "Here, make a cake o' yourself, by Jove. About time you were ridiculous. Ain't enjoyed yourself being so respectable, have you? Try being a gudgeon. Like me."

The viscount closely approached his dribbling friend

and said confidentially, "Basil, it is my serious opinion that you have shot the cat!"

Basil agreed to shoot any cat Reggie recommended, and the viscount offered him Negus which Basil refused being a lady's drink, and they both took a swig of brandy. "Ye gods," of a sudden the viscount erupted, "I'm the world's biggest idiot to propose to a girl whose entire purpose it is . . . is to gammon me! Me, London's prime Corinthian turned into a . . . Cod's head . . . a jack-straw. . . ."

"Cawker," Basil happily tossed along, as well as several muffins. And then added in delight, "Nodcock, gudgeon, flat . . . slow-top . . . gowk . . ."

Not to be outdone, Reggie contributed his own insults back, as well as tossing more muffins Basil's way. "Totty-headed jobbernoll . . . shag-bag!"

"Quiz . . . gudgeon . . ."

"You're repeating yourself," the viscount said with his famous hauteur of disapproval. "*And* you are littering my Axminster carpet with mounds of muffins. Look here at all these bits of baked dough! What, I say, do you intend to do with them?"

Basil picked up the bits of muffins and stared at them, and then, his eyes lighting up with inspiration, he cried out, "By Jove, order some jelly!"

And the viscount, staring at him with fierce concentration, finally stepped back and nodded. "Righto. Jelly it is. Finley! Holla! Jelly here! And more muffins!"

Since Finley was not in the room, no more muffins nor jelly was brought. The lords made do with those on the carpet, scraping them up and finishing them off along with the end of the brandy.

Reggie was still mumbling about Miss Marlowe and how he was going to make her share in his humiliation. "I've been staying my hand, due to her sex and size. No bigger than this muffin here. She looks small but throws a leveler." And he smashed a muffin flat to illustrate his intent and was wildly applauded by his friend, especially when he scooped up the flattened muffin and said, "Thus, shall I deal with her!" And he gulped down the muffin bit and Miss Marlowe in one loud swallow.

"Don't let her bite on the way down," Basil whispered, and then half-giggling, half-snoring, fell sound asleep on the settee.

Reggie observed him in disgust and then, in his lordly way, lay down on the other settee, closest to the fireplace and contemplated the mess around him, symptomatic of the mess in his life, he opined. He wondered if she would bite on the way down, by Jove—and whether he might not jolly well enjoy that!—but fell asleep before reaching a conclusion.

CHAPTER FIVE

LOOKING INTO HER CHEVAL GLASS, EMMALIE CON-
cluded she had grown an inch or two from her spirited
encounters with the viscount. That illusion could also
be caused by her having lifted her long brown hair into
a mass of curls on the crown of her head. Taller yes,
but too imposing for an unimposing lady. And after a
few hours, it slipped out of its pins, as if deciding on
its own to keep to its old, long waves.

Lady Leonie had quite an ornate hairdo, filled with
ringlets falling over her ears and long curls in the back,
but Lady Leonie was tall enough to carry that off. Just
as she did all her jewels. Not that her ladyship could
ever wear all she had, for gentlemen had a habit of
constantly gifting her with them. When Emmalie was
still a halfling, upon her mother's leaving her apartments, the girl would sneak in and explore the many
treasure caskets. Quite like visiting Aladdin's secret
trove. One gilt casket was just for rings—of every
jewel—diamonds, emeralds, rubies, pearls—black and
cream. Other gilt chests were for the necklaces and
bracelets. Lady Leonie's long graceful arms, gloved or
not, were perfect for modeling the current fashion of
three bracelets worn on each arm—one at the wrist, one
at the elbow, and one on the upper arm. And somehow
the more bracelets she wore, the more gestures she contrived to flaunt them all. In effect, she so orchestrated
her conversations that everyone enjoyed her motions as
much as her meanings.

Just two of Lady Leonie's rings on Emmalie's hand dragged it down and were quickly removed. That had her recollecting her mother's *on dit* to the viscount about the prince's wearing such a quantity of rings and bracelets that his fingers actually numbed—necessitating prodigious use of Colonel McMahon, His Royal Highness's private secretary. The latter even wrote the Regent's most personal letters to Mrs. Fitzherbert, his abandoned commoner wife, assuring her of his continued regard.

"Not enough regard, I collect," her mother had concluded, "to risk his numbed fingers to write on his own."

"Let that be a lesson to you," Reggie had replied with a twinkle. "For shortly I shall be expecting your marvelous letters to be dictated as well. One bracelet more, I daresay, shall do it. Such as this."

And he brought out another bracelet for her mother's collection—it was made of cameo heads on solid gold. That weighty piece of jewelry had fallen off Emmalie's delicate wrist whenever she attempted to wear it in her excursions into her mother's jeweled world. There, too, was the emerald ring from the Prince Regent. So oft had she heard that story, Emmalie could quote his Royal Highness's exact words, "To bind still stronger the brotherhood which we have always claimed."

Another chest had Lady Leonie's head jewelry—mostly tiaras. Emmalie would oft try on the coronet, part of her mother's court attire. Another distinctive headpiece had classical cameos of agate, undoubtedly the inspiration for the viscount's matching bracelet. More delicate than the tiaras were diadems. Lady Leonie wore two, sometimes three at a time—one over the brow and the other two farther back.

Emmalie had a preference for the diadem with a delicate laurel leaf design; it gave the young girl just enough height without overwhelming her. That was the first item she wore on entering those treasure troves.

The last item was the mourning ring that had graced Lady Leonie's finger for a sennight after her husband's death, decorated with his initials woven out of his own dark hair. With her lips Emmalie would touch that in a farewell salute. Her real father hardly ever showed her as much of an acknowledgment. But since his demise he'd been conveniently replaced by an imaginary father who visited her rooms on her birthday or just prior to a ball to offer uplifting words, such as "Good show" or more often "Capital!" And it was to that father's ring she made her obeisance.

Recently Emmalie had come nigh to having a ring of her own. The viscount had attempted to ascertain Emmalie's favorite stone in order to procure an engagement ring. That was a consideration she had not expected, assuming he would ask her mother for *her* preference. Emmalie had, of course, refused the ring as being premature until the conditions for her acceptance were met, and in that unlikely event, she preferred an amethyst—which of all stones was the least obvious in its coloration.

"And of the least value," her mother could not resist inserting. A pause followed, during which all instantly equated that minor stone to Emmalie herself. The viscount's gallantry rescued the awkwardness by his concluding each jewel, as each lady, had its own individual beauty.

No such courtly remarks, however, had come from the viscount since the Tower affair, for he'd simply not waited upon either Emmalie or her mother. "Sulking," Lady Leonie had concluded with a laugh and assured Emmalie he would come about.

Yet Reggie did not come about until a full sennight, and even then his every gesture indicated he was still somewhat in a miff. He kissed Leonie's hand in the most perfunctory manner and seated himself some ways from her, stretching out his long legs, as if that explained the need for distance. The presence of the black ball of fur next to her ladyship might also explain his reluctance to come near. After having marked a man, Negus always remembered him as an enemy, especially if no peace offering had been made, such as the presentation of a chicken giblet. Lady Leonie was forced to soothe both by ringing for shortbreads and giblets—respectively. Man and beast were somewhat mollified, and after joint imperious nods, fell to. She further appeased his lordship by giving complete attention to his comments on her daughter's defects. Which were so numerous, he said, he was justified in picking a bone with her.

"And I with you. Your backbone in fact, for I understand you had difficulty in meeting the test of strength!"

"Did that blasted hoyden tell you that?"

"Certainly not. Nor would I ask her for particulars which can be so easily derived from this." And she handed him the *Gazette* which hinted about a certain peer that had found himself close to arrest on the Tower grounds—upon grounds of committing a gross indecency.

"Drivel!" Reggie expostulated, but now understanding several pointed looks in his direction.

"Emmalie's doing?" Lady Leonie asked solicitously, pointing to the bruises on his face.

Stiffly he denied that. But after sufficient suspense he announced the culprit. "It was a fiesty crone with an umbrella."

Unable to restrain herself a second longer, her ladyship's musical laughter filled the room. So infectious was it, at long last the viscount allowed himself to grin. Being made acquainted with the whole, Lady Leonie shook her head in disbelief. "The Viscount of Wynnclife, who could capture any female regardless of her age, defeated by a mere girl and an elderly lady with a parasol!"

The viscount attempted to put a good face on it all,

but his good nature was sagging under her banter. He did not mind being roasted to a light golden tone, but this was doing it too brown. And thus he reverted to his toplofty tones.

"One expected more delicacy, more charm, more pedigree from your daughter!"

Lady Leonie's blue eyes turned jewel hard at that, as now her own pride was being touched upon. "I collect one overestimated you, my dear Reggie. One wonders how much your reputation had to do with your being the Viscount Wynnclife and owner of so many landed estates? Obviously this is a true test of your *personal* mettle. For Emmalie is not interested in position. One must win her by one's own merits."

"Good grief! Do you know your daughter at all?" the viscount exclaimed, showing hackle. "One cannot win a lady who has been brought up with no awareness of the manners and maneuvers a gentleman and lady can exchange. One says to her, 'The flutter of a bird's wings is very like the flutter of your exquisite lashes when I am close to you.' Faith, that simile has never failed me, it has caused generations of ladies to flutter like wild birds! But what did Miss Marlowe do instead? She flatly stated that she never fluttered her lashes at gentlemen nor swooned nor hid behind fans . . . that those were all devices. 'If you wish to court me, you best do so honestly and with some awareness of whom you are addressing.' Impossible twit. I should have compared her to a sparrow—brown and common."

"Come, Reggie, I have never seen you so down pin. Is my young miss such a formidable opponent? Surely not for a known exponent of the science of fisticuffs. Is it not true that you have never received a flush hit? And that you have an arsenal of maneuvers: such as feints, dodges, not to mention levelers?"

With some modesty he acknowledged the truth of that, and in a short time, her ladyship was maneuvering him toward Emmalie in the garden. Yet he stopped to insert a proviso in the same boxing cant. "But I warn you, Leonie, I shall no longer pull my punches."

"That is understood," her ladyship agreed and waved him out . . . and onward.

Miss Marlowe, absorbed in reading, jumped in alarm at his approach, dropping her novel from which the bookmark went flying. Gallantly he stooped, retrieving both. Handing back the silken and embroidered bookmark, its wordage caught his eye: I AM COMING BACK.

"Is that meant spiritually? Are you a believer in the return of specters?"

The young lady, not expecting to meet him, did not have her usual protective armor, and she replied in her old colorless way that it was merely to keep her place.

Sensing her lack of fight, the viscount's confidence was further bolstered, and he continued in his usual sardonic style. "It is my opinion women never know their place. And if they do, they scarcely ever keep it."

At that rapier touch, Emmalie was pricked enough to attempt her mother's form, "A true gentleman accepts a lady in whichever place she wishes to be, if he wishes to keep her."

Enjoying her more subtle response, the viscount was delighted to parry, "Perhaps a woman's, or say rather, a lady's true place is in a gentleman's heart."

"Hmmf," Emmalie said, having had sufficient time to recoil at their game and become Emmalie again. "That sounds like something Mother would have me embroider on a sampler."

Annoyed at her irony, he responded, "Actually, I was assured by your mother that you had no such lady's talents. And yet from this," he indicated the bookmark, "I perceive you embroider quite . . . acceptably."

"There is nothing *acceptable* about me!" she cried out from her heart. "That bookmark was embroidered for me by Miss Spindle. My mother was correct. I have no talents whatsoever. Except perhaps one—that I always attempt to speak the truth."

"Not a talent—that, I daresay. Rather a vulgar trait of the unfinished lady. The nobler, more considerate minds learn to embroider."

"Flummery, you mean. I believe in plain speaking. Not like the little insincerities you've sent me. Are they not copies? I expect there are dozens of ladies with those very stanzas in their albums."

"You underestimate me. Say rather hundreds," he said with his old hauteur.

"And you accuse *me* of being common. You are a complete commonplace book, indeed. And you only just met my second test through use of your title—which indicates a lack of both wits and strength. By rights I should simply demand my release as of now, but I am so certain that you shall never be able to meet my third and final test that I shall allow you to advance to that point."

The viscount took some time flicking open his enameled box of snuff and taking a sniff—whether to show his indifference or to give himself time to speak with indifference, but at last his voice was cool enough to conclude that she was all goodness, and he awaited the third test at her convenience.

That would be announced on the morrow as originally planned, Emmalie said with equal chill. To which the viscount merely bowed and left.

As the result of her sparring session with the viscount, Emmalie was spirited enough to dare include herself in her mother's evening attendance at Drury Lane Theater.

"You know my fondness for Edmund Kean," she insisted, which mention recalled to both mother and daughter their opposite reactions to that actor's first season two years ago. Lord Byron, in Lady Leonie's saloon, was discussing Mr. Kean's vivid style, quoting Mr. Coleridge's remark that watching him act was "like reading Shakespeare by flashes of lightning." And Emmalie, sitting quietly in the corner, was fired up to see

76

him, especially when her ladyship opted for the more classical style of John Philip Kemble, claiming the man Kean was clearly too short for roles like Hamlet that required Kemble's stature. Naturally, this turned Emmalie into even more of a supporter, and she arranged for herself and Miss Spindle to view his performance. On her return, Emmalie had dared to softly make known her admiration. Merely raising an eyebrow, Lady Leonie had concluded, "He shall not last."

But he had. And grown in stature, if not physically, at least critically and in his devoted audience's eyes.

Therefore Emmalie's attending a Kean performance with her mother not only was a pleasure, but a twitting of Lady Leonie's judgment and an affirmation that the physical stature of people had naught to do with their actual height! Moreover, everyone was whispering about Mr. Kean's latest performance as Sir Giles Overreach. The mad scene was of such verisimilitude that his fellow actors could hardly remain on the stage with him, and ladies in the audience could only sustain watching it through liberal use of their vinaigrettes, although, even so, many had swooned away. Therefore, it behooved each lady to be accompanied by a gentleman of the strongest nerves as well as arms.

"Reggie shall not be attending, having already seen it, if your object is to swoon for his lordship to carry you out of the theater," Lady Leonie added, hoping to dissuade her accompaniment. Emmalie responded stiffly that she never repeated herself, and, curious as it seemed, she was attending the play because she wished to see it! That was not her ladyship's intention; hers was to divide her attention between two escorts—Pug, of course, and her newest cicisbeo, the young Earl of Warshire. Emmalie's presence would force her to adopt a more severe tone with her admirers than she was want. But she would still, she expected, enjoy herself. For two gentlemen in their twenties to be so enamored of a lady in her forties could not but please, as well as add to her consequence and self-esteem. Not that she had need of extensions to either.

At the theater Emmalie devoted herself to the play, missing the byplay going on behind her in the box. Not till intermission did Emmalie notice another gentleman had joined their box and was silently staring at Lady Leonie throughout. It was Lord Sanders who suffered from a tormenting *tendre* for her ladyship. Although given his congé, he was permitted, upon agreement of not speaking nor making any gestures, to ease his pain by occasionally being allowed in her presence. Once she dropped her program, and both Pug and Lord Sanders sought to retrieve it, but when Lord Sanders moved faster and handed it to her ladyship, she shook her head with a small smile at his overstepping their agreement, and he humbly handed the program to Pug, who handed it to her ladyship.

So spectacular was Lady Leonie in her blue bombazine gown, long white gloves, golden bracelets, and cameoed tiara, one could not but wonder at Emmalie's wishing to lift the fringed drapes at her side and cover herself over. Actually, she scarce needed to hide, for it seemed Miss Marlowe had the natural ability to disappear from everyone's sight, as none sought to converse with her or acknowledge her presence. The viscount's recent awareness of her and reacting to her words had been a first and had made her forget her previous invisibility. Now it was painfully recollected and became a warning for her future.

The last act took away all thoughts of self. It was Edmund Kean's great moment—portraying Sir Giles Overreach going stark mad, before all. As if on signal, the ladies opened their reticules and reached for their vinaigrettes. The gentlemen sat forward. Scream after scream reverberated through the theater from the maddened man onstage. In response, screams were heard from the audience. The entire theater echoed with alarms. Emmalie was silent, but she held tightly onto

78

the arms of her seat. Lady Leonie's hands were both grasped by her admirers—although it was not clear whether they were giving comfort to her or demanding it, for Lady Leonie's face was composed, if not a bit amused.

When they rose to depart, she was heard to mutter, "Rather melodramatic, what?" Immediately both gentlemen agreed, although both were still shaking from the performance. As was Emmalie, who could not rise but simply sat there in her brownish gown and pelisse, blending with the curtain—a small bundle of terror, recovering from her emotions. When at last she opened her eyes, there was another terror of discovering she had been forgotten.

Rising quickly, she soon was made aware that her mother's carriage had long been called for, and the party had left. Rather than being thrown into a quake, Miss Marlowe simply informed the theater attendants, who were quick to procure her a hack, and she was driven home without any further mishap.

Her peace, however, was all cut up that night—partly from the leftover effects of the performance and having herself become a leftover . . . and partly from being out of patience with her resurrected invisibility. Surely it would be better to be married than to continue being so unnecessary in her mother's life. Yet possibly she would merely be exchanging her domicile and not her conditions. To own the truth wouldn't one lief be ignored by one's mother than by one's husband?

If only she had a third choice. And while thinking thus, Emmalie had a splendid revelation—or as Spinny was want to say, "an eruption from her idea pot." So strong was it, she rose out of her bed and rushed to her desk to put down the particulars. In all this testing where was *her* prize? She should insist on a codicil being added to their agreement that regardless of the outcome of her challenge, she should never again be forced to live with anyone who did not really want her.

Hence, on the following afternoon, so anxious was Emmalie to spell out this new stipulation that the moment Spinny whispered his lordship was in the drawing room, she quickly raced there, rather than waiting to be sent for, only remembering herself at the door. There, she was brought up short by a not very common sound of raised voices. All curiosity, she stepped in.

Unlike the viscount's recent actions of respectfully rising at her presence, this time he missed Emmalie's entrance. Last night's events were prophetic; apparently she was rapidly sinking back into nonexistence. Indeed, she found herself standing there a full five minutes and was still not perceived by either her ladyship or his lordship. Their somewhat testy discussion had both a bit out of curl.

"What's in the air of late . . . with myself countenancing a refusal and the Prince of Orange having previously been rejected by the Royal Princess? Dash it, are all our ladies seeking a single state?"

"Not quite. Actually due to our quick action scotching the princess's prior feelings of warmth toward you, now, happily, Her Highness is to be given to another."

"I say, you slipped that in rather smoothly," the viscount inserted coldly, his eyes narrowing with suspicion. "Whom is Princess Charlotte contemplating accepting? And how *long* have you known?"

Opening her fan, Lady Leonie languidly gave herself a moment's delay before she answered whom ("a minor princeling") and ignored the how long. The viscount was not so easily fobbed off, insisting on more information, and her ladyship was forced to name Prince Leopold of Saxe-Coburg and further own there had been some interest in that direction for some time, but the Prince Regent had opposed the insignificant connection, which allowed other names being suggested. "Yours among others."

"Among others! Egad!" the viscount exclaimed, his face flushing. "How different is this from the picture presented me earlier! If I were a mere candidate among many, there—confound it—was no urgency for me to . . . that is, I need not have jumped into a parson's trap myself!''

''Excuse me, I never urged you to jump into matrimony, if that is what your vulgarism implies! And recollect, if you would, that the queen had a decided interest in *your* direction. I have shown you the letter to that effect. Actually, only when you were not readily available were other names rethought! How strangely selective your memory, forgetting entirely the fate that hung over you. A close connection on that level would have meant constant court attendance! I need hardly say more. And as for the lady herself, the princess is known to be as flagrantly silly as her mother and as much of a blatant buffoon as her father. A combination devoutedly to be missed!''

''In short, eliminating all your extenuating clauses, there is to be an announcement.''

''Indeed. The Prince Regent has relented. We shall therefore be dancing at a royal wedding ere the Season is over. Once royalty has laid claim, there is no time given the gentleman for adjustment. Unlike yourself who should be grateful to Emmalie for not only giving you time, but for making such a delightful game of it.''

''An infantile game,'' he said with a touch of asperity. And he stonily stared into the fireplace, poking it with the iron, as if engaged in fencing maneuvers. The light of the fire was reflected in the glow of his burnished hair and warmly outlined his Grecian features, whose perfection was ruined by an abrupt grimace. ''Oh blast!'' he groaned. ''If I am to be riveted, I'd as lief it were over—to forget the entire event!''

''What a charming, loverlike speech,'' her ladyship said with a humph. ''No wonder you are not making headway. Emmalie is a romantic—and you are definitely not. I begin to think any woman makes a mistake in agreeing to marry men of your stamp. Look at poor

Lady Byron, her letters complaining about her husband's infidelities have reached such a level, one has to skip through the charges to maintain one's complexion!''

Since they were off his affairs and onto those of their friends, the viscount relaxed and seated himself, falling into their old, delightful exchanges of *on dits*. Reggie's contribution, strictly *entre nous*, was that Byron was giving a double showing at Drury Lane: backstage with the actress, Miss Cookes, and in the audience with his sister, Augusta Leigh, who, he gathered, had been privy to many such *private* performances.

Lady Leonie laughed. ''You are snocking! My letter from dear Byron denies all!''

''You were always on that blasted libertine's side,'' he chided softly.

''I have a weakness for blasted libertines,'' she said with a smile, giving him a most pointed look.

He bowed but continued, ''You'll recollect that I am a single man and have never *knowingly* destroyed a lady's peace of mind.''

''*Knowingly* being the convenient word.''

''Come, Leonie, admit it is ladies who are trained in the art of toying with a man's peace of mind. Have you not passed it on to your daughter? Truly since our first meeting, Little Miss Marlowe has robbed me of all my peace. But she overplays her games. At least with you, m'dear, one enjoyed the preliminary sparring.''

As he approached Lady Leonie, she, although pleased by his remarks and slightly red in the face, fended him off with the novel in her hands.

''Behave yourself, Reggie. Why will you gentlemen never accept when a lady has refused them? You have the bullheadedness of the Prince Regent. Be content with your acceptance as my son-in-law.''

His voice low, he said, ''And if I am not content with that position, can I aspire to higher claims?''

Once more her ladyship made use of her novel to

push the importunate lord away, which caused the volume to fall. Laughing, he retrieved it, recognizing the bookmark with the embroidered motto: I AM COMING BACK.

"This—from your daughter?"

"Yes. When I first received it, I took it to be just what it was, a rather inane way of holding one's place. But since discovering there is more to Emmalie, I suspect a double entendre. Even a threat—meaning that no matter how I attempt to marry her off, she shall always be coming back to reside with me for the rest of her life. And this fact looms as more of a certainty since I, apparently, have not chosen a gentleman with enough allure to entice her away."

"Nor one," Emmalie interrupted, "who is observant enough to know when I am even in the room." Unlike previous occasions, she was gratified to note both reacted to her presence. Her mother merely smiled, but the viscount, although showing a flash of anger, stood up until Emmalie had seated herself.

"Are you prepared to offer us the third and final condition?" he asked, with somewhat of his old aplomb.

"Yes."

Emmalie was back to her laconic way. Eventually, at their impatient expressions, she elaborated, "It is a matter of some delicacy, so I expect Mama shall excuse herself."

Lady Leonie's eyes went wide. "In a matter of delicacy, *I* am not to be present?"

Emmalie merely smiled. "I expect the viscount shall tell you all, since the two of you exchange your every thought, but I wish to have his reaction without the protection of your motherly concern."

Lady Leonie rose and, staring at her determined daughter's face, nodded. "Very well, as you wish, my dear."

Yet Emmalie delayed her with a gesture, taking the bookmark from the viscount's hands and handing it to her mother. "Here's something to read while you are waiting. Or you may leave it here as *your* threat to us."

Her ladyship, unlike her usual self, merely flushed and left the room, taking the bookmark with her.

CHAPTER SIX

Warily, the viscount stared. It was as if one had accustomed oneself to having a kitten for a pet and then being told by an animal expert that she was of a wild nature and could strike for the throat. And yet, she seemed so small and sweet.

Which reminded him. He offered her the comfits he had brought.

"Trying to turn me up sweet with sweets?" she asked in her forthright manner, dropping them on the table and hurrying on with her stipulation. "I should deem it most obliging if the wager between us was . . . sweetened, so I should at least win something." Her hackles had risen to some height from my lord's and lady's exchange of remarks—so irked, she proceeded directly to her point and hammered it home. "If you win, you have the reward of my hand. If I win, my prize is *not* having to wed you. Yet that is pure gammon, for now I collect with the announcement being made, I can achieve that by simply holding fast to my refusal. No, I believe you should elevate, eh, raise the stakes, as they say, by including as *my* incentive your castle in Cornwall and a yearly stipend to continue its upkeep."

Totally aghast, his lordship exclaimed, "What the devil! You have overstepped!"

"Why? Does property mean so much to you? It is known you are wealthy as Croesus, not even aware of all your estates! Fortunately I am mercenary and willing to settle for a mere castle. In olden days when such challenges were set up, a gentleman either won the maiden or lost his life. Authentic champions were willing to go to those lengths to win their loves.''

"But since I do not love you, it seems I shall lose either way,'' he said coldly, forgetting his scheme to win her heart.

"For shame. And to think of all the lovely love poetry for which you have been wearing out quill after quill! Infamous of you to have been indulging in such sham sonnets! Never mind, it has given you practice, which you sorely needed. Another benefit from this association for you! Indeed, with a background of being so petted and cosseted, you have grown rather soft of will, and my challenges have given your character much needed exercise. Very like an athlete who through several helpful sparring sessions rediscovers his muscles. I daresay I have helped you uncover many hidden attributes. I flatter myself I have already gifted you with the greatest boon known to all mankind—one the ancient Greeks thought worth carving on their temple: 'Know Thyself.' Certainly that is worth more than one measly castle.''

"Blast you, if you believe that self-knowledge is the same as loss of self-consequence! Since getting to know you, I have never been so undervalued . . . so demeaned.''

"Pity. I expect you'll come about though, and with the benefit of having understood how the rest of us have to live. Ah, there is no end to what I have done for you!'' And Emmalie's soft mouth smiled as she concluded with airy equanimity, "Indeed, this third condition shall give you the ultimate in strength of mind and spirit and body. Going beyond the first, a test of mentality, the second, physicality, this last is a test of *spirituality* through endurance!''

Whereupon she informed the astonished lord that he was to wait a full year for their marriage—during which entire time, he must lead a totally celibate life.

"I have not heard you correctly," the viscount said coldly. "I expect you have misspoke yourself or are not aware of the meaning of that word. Certainly a lady would not use it in a gentleman's presence." So shocked was the viscount by her indelicacy that he looked around for assistance, nearly rushing to seek her mother.

"Very well, if the word 'celibacy' offends you, I shall use a more delicate analogy. I wish you not to have any relationships. And if you break that vow once, even with one of your many ladybirds . . ."

"Odd's blood, that is another thing you should not be saying!"

Emmalie huffed. "Which word offended you now?"

"I shall not repeat it. This entire conversation is beneath contempt. You might as well be tying your garter in public."

"Why are you so offended by plain speech? I thought you were not so pompous."

Staring at her innocent eyes, the viscount laughed of a sudden. "You are correct. I shall accept your speaking plainly, since apparently you are not really aware what you are asking."

"Dash you, I am very well aware. I wish you to remain celibate for a full year, which means you must instantly dismiss all your many incognitas, lightskirts, or whatever words you wish to use to refer to them, and if you do not—you have failed the test of endurance, and our marriage-agreement shall be instantly suspended."

At that point viscount began to see the humor of the situation. "I say," he said with a grin. "How would you possibly know if I were faithful or not? Ladies never know what their gentlemen are doing in private."

The self-satisfaction on his face was too much for Emmalie. Yet undaunted and determined to achieve her objective, she returned a reply that had him totally flummoxed.

"But I shall simply ask you. You are too proud to

win a bet by a falsehood. It is one thing to cheat on a wife, quite another to win a wager that way. That, in our set, is the one thing never done, for it would bring in question a gentleman's honor. Isn't that so? In any case, you agreed to meet my tests. And this is the third and last one. If you feel you are not able to meet it, you have an easy recourse. Simply refuse the condition . . . and me, and we shall both be free.''

Staring at the triumph in the young lady's face, the viscount ejaculated, ''You are the very devil of a chit! That is exactly what you wish me to do—but I shall not release you so easily, blast you. I accept your challenge, and may we both be damned!''

The viscount had stiffly bowed and had almost completed his departure when Emmalie sweetly called after, ''Do not forget the castle in Cornwall as my winnings for this wager. . . . I expect I shall be moving in within a fortnight.''

He muttered something but closed the door on it with a decisive snap. Emmalie sank down on the settee in relief and was just wondering whether he had stopped to convey all to her ladyship, when Lady Leonie proved he had not by hurrying in and wishing to be told all.

In keeping with the viscount's decision for privacy, Emmalie, after a few civil but unresponsive words, retired.

Scarce had Miss Marlowe arisen on the morrow when she found a note on her morning tray and feared it might be from his lordship.

It was.

Then she feared it would be a refusal to include the castle in the wager.

It did.

But rather he was giving her the castle *beforehand*. Emmalie's heart jumped, and she followed after. Was this a total capitulation?

Miss Spindle was waiting in alarm to hear the contents. Her lace cap was askew from bending down and picking up the note Emmalie had let fall from her hand. Asking permission with a look and being answered with a nod, Miss Spindle quickly perused the missive and then, in perplexity, read it aloud.

"My dear Miss Marlowe," it formally began. "Much as I wish to meet all your requests, I cannot in good conscience encourage your tendency toward gambling by turning our arrangement, already of the wildest sort, into one to be recorded in the Bettor's Books at White's. Therefore, my estate and grounds in Cornwall shall not be included in the challenge between us. Rather, as a reward for your graciousness during our combative time together, I shall immediately offer you, gratis, the estate as your own. Naturally with an income, as you so wisely specified, for its upkeep. May you have many happy years behind its moat, although I hope that wish shall soon be a moot point, indeed. Your most humble suitor, Reginald Lancaster, Fifth Viscount of Wynncliffe."

Upon concluding, her companion anxiously queried Emmalie, "Have we won or lost?"

Sitting back on her bed, Emmalie touched the fringe of its curtains that she oft strummed, hoping for a noise, although it, as always, remained soundless. As did she, still thinking.

"Well?"

"It is a strategic move, I collect," Emmalie concluded. "He thinks to disarm me by this gesture. Doubtless he and mother, and even propriety itself, expect me to refuse a gift of such magnitude out of hand and demand it remain the prize in the bet. Then he shall be free to refuse it as such on moral grounds. But," and of a sudden she hugged Miss Spindle, "I shall toss propriety to the winds and take his castle! Yes, that shall be my countermove. And I shall demand it be put completely in my name, so Mother can have naught to do with it. For living here I must constantly be involved in Mother's little affairs, and I use that term in both instances. Her assemblies and dinners must inevitably include me, and I must creep in and play my role of watcher through another evening of homage to her. To not appear gives the impression of resentment. But, if I no longer am domiciled with her, I shall be free. Free from all obligations and humiliations. And *persuasions*! Equally, having the castle beforehand frees me from the viscount's presence, which increases my chances of total victory!''

In high jig, Emmalie was dancing round the room, stopping before a yet confused Spinny. "Don't you see, my dear one, I have accepted the castle. It is mine as of this moment. Never again shall *your* position be used to force me to . . .''

"That must never weigh with you, my sweetest Malie! I have told you, I am not so old that I could not find a living to support both of us.''

"That is yesterday's concern!'' Emmalie exclaimed with a satisfied grin. "Not understanding his opponent, the viscount has been overconfident in his play. But I, awake upon every suit, have captured his castle! Not only shall I forthwith accept it but ask for a speedy transfer, so we can promptly change our locale. He has been caught indeed! Once having offered, as a gentleman, he cannot take it back. His only escape would have been if I had acted as a lady and refused. But I am too desperate to play by a lady's rules. Ah, think, Spinny, what further follows from this! The viscount is so accustomed to a social life here in London, it is scarcely likely he shall travel such a distance to an estate once his and no longer—just to see me!''

"Yes, it is not likely he shall do so, indeed,'' Miss Spindle said with a sigh. "Which means we shall not be seeing him. Perhaps not ever again.''

"So much the better,'' Emmalie declared with some pride. "Rather that, than his coming here to see Mother and my walking in on their little tête-à-têtes. Bosh to them both, and may they continue their little flirtation on their own! I have given him a third condition impossible for a gentleman known for his petticoat ways. Actually, I heard him once confess to Mama that he always 'perched on the nearest branch,' and, much amused, she said, 'You are a flighty one, indeed.' In response he sent her a yellow bird in a gilded cage. Which was to be used illustratively, for he took it to the terrace, and amid her applause, set it free. Symbolic of his lordship's free and flighty ways. No thought for the bird, which was near caught by Negus in one snap. But I tell you this—as much as he venerates his freedom, so do I! And by my act I gain freedom for both of us, *from* both of us. I'll write him a letter eventually from my castle and ask him directly whether he has kept the third condition, and he must needs respond on his honor, and once he does, our engagement shall be terminated.''

"Hold off the wafer," Miss Spindle cried as Emmalie was sealing her letter and fate in one gesture. "Consider, why settle for one castle when you could have dozens *and* a gentleman of the viscount's perfections?"

"You know why!" the girl said fiercely, stamping the wafer on with a punch.

"If you would only give the gentleman more time to . . . appreciate . . . you."

"I have given him years being near, and he either has not seen me or finds it, of late, a chore to play my games, which apparently lack the finesse of the delicate dueling he so enjoys with Mama! Nay, I cannot continue to live as someone's regret. I would as lief be riveted to a . . . a footman—if he had genuine admiration for me!"

"Hush! The footman might hear you and get ideas above his station!" Miss Spindle exclaimed, glancing fearfully about. No footmen lurked by, but in high jig, Emmalie discombobulated the elder lady by promptly summoning one. Upon his arrival, much to Miss Spindle's relief, she did not make any untoward proposals to the venerable servant, who had known her since she was a child, rather handed him her note. Then, turning in satisfaction, suggested to Miss Spindle they cease dallying and begin preparations for transference to their new abode.

Several streets away in Piccadilly, the letter was received by his lordship, just as he was about to be shaved by his valet. That had precedence, and only upon its conclusion and the brushing of his hair to an arranged nicety did he advance to Miss Marlowe's note. Perusing the contents, he frowned.

In truth, he had not expected this response. Rather he was confident his maneuver of offering Miss Marlowe the castle beforehand would have been an effective checkmate. Not that he overly regretted the castle, although it was one of his favorite properties. He had oft had several of his friends there in its moated seclusion for what the locals whispered were orgies but were rather just jolly good fun with an orgiastic bent. His ancestors had been wild men with the ladies of the neighborhood, which might explain the rustics' apprehension. But they need have no fear of the viscount who had his fill with Society ladies and would scarce settle for lowly local fare. One had one's standards, after all.

What use that little lady would have for the huge place with all its dungeons and towers and huge Gothic windows Reggie could scarcely imagine! Further, there were wall hangings with some rather explicit scenes that should be replaced before the young innocent entered. He should dashed well not remove the statues of leering satyrs in the priory yard, which sculptures were quite a rara avis. Albeit witnessing Miss Marlowe's reaction might be worth a trip there, he thought with a grin. And then, in a flash, he concluded—by Jove, he *would* be there! While the legalities were being completed, he would escort and acquaint her with her soon-to-be property. That should outjockey her!

It was always a particular delight for the viscount to

turn what others assumed was his defeat into a victory by simply not acting as expected. Actually, his giving her the castle beforehand would demonstrate his magnanimity. Its massive size alone would incur a rather monumental obligation. Ergo, all that must materially lessen her combativeness and lead to an earlier marriage date—an objective devoutly to be wished. For egad, it was not a few days into his celibacy, and the viscount was finding keeping his oath dashed difficult. So personal was the third condition, he had not felt it behooved him to acquaint any of his friends of its demeaning, not to mention infamous, restriction. Certainly Lord Lanadale should not be given further cause for roasting him. Nor indeed had the viscount told his current delight, the actress Miss Kitty Jones.

Capturing such a prime article had added much to his lordship's consequence. Her following comprised the most noble young bucks who filled the pit at her every performance. At each of the blond beauty's entrances, it was the custom for the entire pit to rise and meow in delight. She would then give them her usual feline stretch which provoked wilder purrs and some catcalls from the authentic theater devotees, resentful of interruption. Nothing, however, disturbed the placid puss; she merely curtsied to that group as well, showing a generous glimpse of her assets. Good God, the viscount had thought upon first observing her onstage and especially after taking out his quizzing glass for a closer look, he should have that game pullet, if it cost him a fortune. And it had. Beginning with a carriage-and-pair to a house in town and always a generous shower of jewels. And after beating the competing nobles all hollow, he'd been dashed if he'd give her up! Nor was Miss Kitty easy to fob off. She kept demanding his attendance. This leaving for Cornwall would lessen the chances of either the glorious Kitty or any of his set discovering his abstinence. Indeed, leaving for his castle with Miss Marlowe—where one would not likely have the slightest temptation—was just the ticket.

Once decided, his lordship acted immediately. And removing the inkpot, sand caster, and a variety of pens from his sterling silver standish, he wrote a reply to the lady of his choice if not his heart.

CHAPTER SEVEN

WITH MORE HASTE THAN EITHER MISS MARLOWE OR Miss Spindle could have anticipated, they were seated in the spacious carriage the viscount had provided for their journey south. As they approached Cornwall, the mist rose and gave it a mysterious air. In his own curricle Reginald was riding ahead arranging for their comfort at the proper inns and at the way stations for changing horses. Neither lady had ever traveled in such style. Liveried footmen were perched on the outside of the carriage, handy for ascents and descents and for lighting lamps when the dusk settled over. Within, the crested carriage was not only upholstered, but it had a sheepskin mat upon the floor and a rug they could wrap around their legs when the Cornish air came through. There was even a selection of reading material for their amusement.

They had been in Cornwall for some time ere the mist cleared and Emmalie could at last view the huge cliff walls that seemed like natural castles open to the sky, preparing her for the grandeur of the viscount's castle to come. His lordship had already informed her that Windsrest was in some state of disrepair (that due to his being somewhat remiss) and the region wild (that due to nature's being somewhat remiss—he added, his eyes twinkling). Gallantly, Reggie offered her the exchange of a compact and convenient estate, near Lady Leonie's own Richmond holding, called Wit's End, to which he had oft resorted when in that state, but Emmalie opted for the castle. Since first hearing his description of Windsrest to her mother, it had seeded itself into her imagination. Hopefully, it would not cause her as much surprise as had Lady Leonie's reaction to her

departure. Unexpectedly, upon being informed of the arrangement, her mother had made every attempt to persuade Emmalie to remain until her marriage. So sincere had she seemed, Emmalie rescinded her planned departure remark: "Now you no longer have to fear I shall ever be close enough to tread upon your gown."

There had even been tears in Lady Leonie's eyes as she bade her daughter farewell, and but that Emmalie concluded they were for the viscount's benefit, who was standing by to hand her in, Emmalie would have had tears in her own eyes as well.

Yet on the journey the young lady was pleased with the decision and herself, very like when she'd run away from their Richmond estate of a summer morning to secretly swim in the lake. The viscount's attendance she did not take, unlike dear Spinny, as an indication of his being unable to bear their separation. In a moment of conveniently rearranging the facts in her mind, Miss Spindle had convinced herself she was witness to a great romance and did not need Lady Leonie's taking her aside before the departure, reminding her of her duties as chaperone.

"Indeed, my dear lady, I shall not falter in protecting dear Malie from his advances. I am well aware that gentlemen cannot be trusted to withstand temptation at close quarters." And she winked and pressed Lady Leonie's hand for added emphasis.

Her ladyship, taken aback and moving back from the lascivious gleam in the woman's eye, simply repeated that all conventions were to be strictly observed.

In full volume Emmalie had laughed when told of both Spinny's and, surprisingly, her mother's concern. "Oh, that is famous! I daresay my innocence could not have a stronger protection than his lordship's indifference."

In the young girl's opinion the viscount was merely accompanying her to do his duty as a gentleman, and further to assure that his servants remained true enough to him to report the arrival of correspondence from London that might alert her to *his* town doings. And thus, previous to their departure, she once again repeated to the viscount her lack of intention of resorting to spies and such—his word must always be enough. And he answered dryly that her harping on the "condition" seemed to indicate she had it continually on her mind, while he himself had scarce need of such relished repetition! That effectively ended all her references, if not her speaking to him at all.

Turning on her heel, Emmalie left the room, giving her mother and the viscount an opportunity for the conversation they so clearly wished—as was obvious from her ladyship's lifted eyebrow and other signals that would have been readable even to one who had not spent most of her adult life responding to them.

Actually, the nature of the discussion between his lordship and her ladyship would have much astonished Emmalie. Lady Leonie—not being aware of the third test, no one having informed her of it—was recommending that the viscount use his famous address and in the loneliness of Cornwall take "every opportunity" to rouse her daughter's emotions. To which the viscount asked bluntly, "I hope you are not suggesting I take advantage of the poor girl in a carnal way—for I have never in my life forced myself on a lady of any station and certainly not one whose innocence so shines in her eyes. Blast it, I should be the greatest blackguard."

Her ladyship naturally refused to admit she had indicated such a gross act, she was simply hoping he would find every *gentlemanly* means of assuring that his suit prospered—which must be immeasurably helped by the setting and the lack of distractions, such as yeoman guards! "Reggie, our delay in announcing the wedding date is giving our dear friends delightful expectations of something having gone amiss. We cannot continue to thus entertain them. It is essential you and Emmalie advance beyond your present terms of common incivility, so that I may schedule the wedding festivities post haste!"

With unshaken sangfroid, Reggie replied, "It appears that Miss Marlowe is, deliberately or as a side benefit, testing *your* patience as well."

"Trying my patience, you mean."

"Both," the viscount had responded. A further testing of his lordship's and her ladyship's patience came upon Miss Marlowe's advancing toward the carriage, holding a gilded cage in which the viscount's yellow bird was happily singing. Immediately he asked, "Had I not set it free?"

"Indeed, and right into Negus's jaws—if I had not moved with alacrity!"

"Naughty Negus." Lady Leonie had laughed. "He is so well fed, surely he was merely playing with the bird."

"He ripped one of its feathers ere I stopped his sport. And tore into me."

Her ladyship shrugged, allowing, matter-of-factly, that Negus was a fact of her life and accustomed to ruling his roost. "And now he and you can reign in peace," Emmalie had said, handing the bird cage to the waiting Spinny.

"I shall miss you dearly," Lady Leonie had whispered and kissed her daughter, who dutifully responded with a curtsy and an uncertain smile and left her mother and her mother's home in her usual manner, without saying quite all she had planned.

Windsrest neither surprised nor disappointed. As the coach neared, she and Miss Spindle saw everything expected by devoted readers of Gothic novels. At the front there was a narrow moat noted for its stagnancy and superfluousness—since the castle could easily be reached by land through the rear and sides. Nevertheless, it was a tradition to lower the drawbridge, and so tradition was followed. Tradition being an honoring of things one might more conveniently do without, yet the keeping of which expanded one's notion of oneself. So with all required pomp, the slow descent of the drawbridge began, evoking in the new owner an ascent of emotion—part ancient pride, part anticipation. The lady of the castle had arrived.

On an easy incline the carriage continued up the stony driveway. The distant cliffs momentarily caught one's eye as they rose perpendicular and menacing and then sharply dropped off into the sea. But then in a few more paces, the castle was all one wished to see. The weathered stone gray walls rose like Goliath to her David. Further atop were squared turrets, reached by stone-balconied walkways. Then the coach stopped before a massive oak door, and the liveried footmen were waved aside by the viscount who did the office of handing Miss Marlowe down. Emmalie caught her breath at the breadth before her. All that, every stone, every Gothic window, every crumbling terrace belonged solely to her! The viscount was addressing the butler and making introductions which Emmalie attempted to carry off with Lady Leonie's ease but was too delighted by it all to refrain from smiling. Smithers's set face momentarily formed something akin to a grin before resuming his retainer's impassivity, but allowing Emmalie to feel she was not wholly resented.

The viscount was speaking to her. Emmalie forced herself to listen. "That way one comes to the sea. There's a small beach that leads to a fogue or cave as a child I called my pirate's den. In the summer one might even risk an invigorating dip in the sea, but with the undertow here, I should not, of course, recommend that course to a lady. Beyond, in that direction, is a larger cove and sailboat, now yours as well. But I advise allowing Burton to take you out, he is quite experienced. Taught me to sail as a youngster.''

Emmalie had a moment's twinge, fearing she heard regret at the loss of all this, until she recollected his several sailing yachts and estates in the Isle of Wight. And then graciously he was continuing, ''Devil's Wood beyond the moors is rife with Druid Oaks that might bear exploring. Within an easy walk is the abbey with its several impertinent statues in the garden that a lady might find . . . offensive; and if you do, I'd as lief you not have them destroyed but rather allow me to transport them.''

The size of the castle and my lord's civility as he played guide sunk Emmalie back to her natural silent state. Now, indicating the top of the castle, he added, ''The Cornish mists swirl about that small turret room out of which one can look and have a sense of living in the clouds. . . . Shall we enter?''

It took a moment for Emmalie to realize he had come back to ground and was indicating the oak door being held open by Smithers and a footman. All three gentlemen bowed her in. The hall continued Windsrest's intimidation with its thronelike stone staircase, directly in the center, parting halfway up to an east and west wing. While walking toward it, Miss Marlowe passed several six-foot-high carved wooden candelabras holding torches. And then a large dog sprang by her to flatten the viscount, which could not but please, until Emmalie observed his lordship obligingly wrestling with the animal. Grinning, Reggie rose up, somehow less of the viscount than ever before; he even forgot, heaven forfend, to smooth his prized golden locks back off his forehead into its famed and much imitated arranged waves. He looked younger with a prodigious amount of the hauteur knocked out of him. But, in the next instant, the viscount had regained his noble airs and was nonchalantly directing Emmalie to her choice of rooms—

one in each wing. First, of course, must be the master bedroom, and they adjourned there.

After looking about, Emmalie and Miss Spindle exchanged discreet looks of dismay. All was dark and hung with crimson velvet drapes of a heaviness that Emmalie could not but feel weighing on her heart. The viscount called her attention to the paintings of his ancestors, assuring her more of the same could be seen in the formal gallery. To which Emmalie could only reply, "Delightful." Next she turned toward the generous fireplace which was undeniably smoking. Before it, the large mastiff was stretched out, having preceded them. "Gnasher," the viscount said loudly, and Emmalie was uncertain whether that was the dog's name or orders for her demise. But as the dog waved its tail, she understood it was a formal introduction and nodded, offering another all-purpose "Delightful." Her glance continued on, attempting to overlook the mahogany four-poster, larger than her entire room at home. Helpfully the viscount drew her attention away from it by pointing out the window. "From here," he said, sounding suspiciously amused, "the abbey is blatantly visible . . . with its statuary previously referred to."

An awareness of his enjoying her discomfiture made it increase. Indeed, coming closer to him, she perceived a muscle twitching at the corner of his mouth, and she refused to oblige him further by peering out. Rather she merely passed by with another "Delightful."

Bumping into her governess, Emmalie was aware that Miss Spindle had not taken her attention off the bed, assaulted by its size, it not having sufficient decorum to recede from a lady's sight. And Emmalie, as well, at last had to face it. She could not resist wondering why its curtains, equally of heavy velvet crimson, were closed. Was is possible that someone or something was within? Edging closer, Emmalie dared to reach over and slowly peek through.

"There is no one awaiting you in there . . . *yet*," the

viscount said lazily, coming up behind her and whispering, "Although if there were, one should undoubtedly discover that the most delightful of all!"

Put to a blush by both his remark and her own action, Miss Marlowe froze. No one had been within, after all. But the width of that bed was so scandalously broad, one could scarcely rest easy without constantly wondering who was sleeping at the other end!

Moving away, she said primly, "It wants . . . airing."

"It wants . . . *something*," the viscount solicitously agreed and directed her toward the second choice of apartments in the west wing. An addition to the happy group going westward was Gnasher, who appeared to imagine his opinion on the two rooms was sought as well, no matter how much the butler attempted to discourage him from that notion.

Stepping into the second apartment, one immediately noted the difference. It appeared bathed in light—which was actually coming from a huge bay window with a pillowed and cushioned window seat the lady and Gnasher could not resist running toward. Sitting there, petting the by now fond canine, Miss Marlowe looked below. Beyond the cultivated terraces, rocky ledges were visible—stone slabs, like giant steps, successively leading directly to the dark green sea. And farther off, it was all sea, bound within the stone arms of the tall cliffs, the two amorously blending, like lovers.

At that thought, she was astonished to once more feel rather than hear Reggie's presence behind her. "This was my mother's room," he said softly, staring out at the waves. "Obvious, is it not—her love of the sea. The sitting room, through there, has a balcony that overlooks the gardens. She grew tropical plants and herbs not often found in England. Everything she touched flowered and rejoiced—all she would touch, that is."

Emmalie gave a quick side glance and felt a decided difference in him that became more pronounced every mile away from London. Even his dress no longer had its complete-to-a-shade perfection. Gone the pantaloons and Hessians, replaced by top boots, breeches, and a looser coat. But most evident was the change in his neckware. He'd left off his famed cravats of monstrous proportions and donned a simpler mode which allowed his head ease of turning. Even Reggie's voice had abandoned some of its fashionable languor—taking on the crispness of a Cornish sea breeze. Lastly, one could spot a rare full smile, as now when he said, "This is another world, is it not? One can hide away from life . . . or *find it.*"

Like a young lady in her first Season, Emmalie quickly lowered her eyes and turned back to continue her evaluation of the room. The bed here was of a sensible size with open drapings of the lightest blue muslin and lace. A graceful pedestal in the corner held a fully foliaged plant that Gnasher took a fancy to and in one bound overturned. Smithers was ordering the plant to be swept up and its holder removed when Emmalie softly ordered, "Leave the pedestal. I'll place my bird cage there." She had chosen.

The viscount did not smile until he returned to the master bedroom, which he had previously ordered prepared for himself. Foxworth, his man, had even concluded the arranging of his clothes and was now donning gloves to remove the viscount's top boots. After which, Reggie took a flying leap between the curtains into the wide bed.

In there he stretched out, allowing the curtains to close him in, and only then permitted his amusement full release. Miss Marlowe's peeking between the curtains continued to delight him. Whom or what had she expected to be within? Egad, the girl's blatant yet embarrassed fascination with it should undoubtedly give him enough amusement to last through the first sennight. Rolling about, Reggie realized with pleasure there was enough room here for several ladies, and if they were all of Miss Marlowe's size—perhaps a good dozen!

CHAPTER EIGHT

On the following morning, Emmalie set out to further explore her property. If the viscount wished to show her about, she should be civil enough to accept his escort. If not, she should direct the steward to do so, just as she intended, subsequently, to view the interior of the castle with the housekeeper who was already in cozy collusion with Miss Spindle. That part, thankfully, Emmalie could leave in her capable hands. In essence, a similar message saying she was to leave the castle's business in *his* capable hands had been left by the viscount before he and the steward had gone riding to oversee the needed changes. His note was politic enough—assuring he was doing all for her comfort, but Emmalie thought no reason sufficient for being overlooked. She had had too much of *that* in her life and did not mean to begin thus in her new domicile. Rather, she should have interviewed the steward herself. Or at the very least insisted on being a participant to this morning's conference!

As Miss Marlowe passed through the castle, the footmen opened the doors with a degree of servile obeisance to which the young lady was quite unaccustomed, being for so long merely the daughter of the house. Alone in the garden, the new mistress had a similar show of respect from the new budded daffodils, bowing their heavy heads before her. Lest all this go to her head, Emmalie was quick to grin and admit the plants were succumbing more to the March wind than her new dignity. Yet even so, she gave them a gracious nod, turning, and in the same proprietorial mood, looked up at her entire castle. Its imposing yet brooding air gave her rather a shiver. One could easily assume a lady being imprisoned in one of the tower rooms and the viscount having ordered such, under the sanguine assumption that he had arranged all for her convenience. She could just anticipate his comments: Was it not delightful living in the clouds? . . . And surely she was refining too much upon the window bars and locked door. "Stuff!" Emmalie said loudly to herself with a giggle, thus clearing the air of all her apprehensions. Even if one were to assume the viscount bore her ill will for loss of his castle or had any other reason for executing such restriction upon her person, she had Spinny here as a protector to object and inform her mother. The latter should doubtless arrive and effect her rescue by the simple expediency of ordering a footman to direct her to her daughter's dungeon and open the cell's door. Whereupon her ladyship would inquire of Emmalie why she could not have done as much.

These thoughts demonstrated, Emmalie concluded with a sigh, how sadly disordered her nerves had become in reaction to Miss Spindle's tales last night of the dungeons beneath the castle that still bore skeletal remains! To reassure her companion, Emmalie had flippantly claimed, the dungeons now being hers, rather than either of them being sentenced there, more likely she should order those who displeased her to be imprisoned. Not excepting the arrogant viscount! At which point, the ambivalent Miss Spindle demanded her word of no such untoward designs on his lordship, which would not at all be the thing, unless he overstepped himself! Then Spinny would stand buff and protect dear Malie from his evil designs!

But apparently in the bright daylight, Miss Spindle lost all fears for her charge's virtue, for she was left, unchaperoned, to wander about. And now having reached the end of the stone walk, as well as the dirt road, Emmalie lifted her skirts and stepped out onto the cliffs themselves. Here, they were a mere four feet above the sea. But circling out from this point, they graduated in height, eventually looming several hundred feet high. Also adding to the starkness, there was a noticeable lack of trees, with the exception of those one would call survivors: the hardy lot left after bouts with the fierce winds coming off the sea. The Atlantic storms in the winter months were powerful enough to crack stone, yet these single trees had held firm. But their slanting postures showed the quality of their battles, for some were almost parallel to the ground—tenaciously rooted, as if only their dryad spirits kept them alive. One oak of exceptionable size grew at the very edge of the cliff before her and hung over the sea, like a gentleman in a perpetual bow. Below, the ocean tempted the gentleman to dive in, but he remained eternally petrified in his act of taking his leave.

Unable to resist, Emmalie curtsied to the bowing tree and then, emulating its angle, leaned perilously over till she could discern steps in the cliffs below, leading to the beach. Difficult to attempt with a long dress, but a gentleman might assist her down, she was thinking.

"You should doubtless slip on the lichen and be washed out to sea, and I should then reclaim my castle," a soft amused voice said next to her ear. Whirling, she came up against the viscount and his teasing light eyes. She moved a respectable distance away.

"Unfortunately for your expectations," she returned with a similarly composed tone, "I should trust to your gentleman's code and request your escort in descending, and thus I should land unscathed and still the possessor of Windsrest."

Laughing, he bowed to her like the gentleman tree and extended his hand. She took it, and he, despite the ungallant breeze, escorted her down the slippery steps as if he were taking her into dinner, until they reached the sand below. There, he stood back and watched her eagerly running toward the dancing sea and then, running from it, laughing. And he, too, slowly smiled.

During the following days the viscount had to own himself considerably astonished at the degree of enjoyment derived from escorting this lady on neighborhood excursions. She was a bruising little rider who never flinched, throwing her heart over any hurdle. And she had the same pluck in handling her new responsibilities, discussing details with the steward and himself that would have bored any other lady of his acquaintance. He found himself naturally sharing memories with her, about the time when he was a youngster and had hidden in the fogue.

"Fogue? Sounds awfully like a pudding of sorts."

"Rather an out-of-sorts pudding," he agreed with a grin. "Or how one feels when having had too much pudding. But it is actually Cornish for cave."

She formed an instant attachment to the word, repeating it several times and concluding they must dashed well immediately visit a fogue and picnic in it! He did not wish to seem poor spirited, he exclaimed, for although the winds were mere whispers of their winter selves, still one should find it rather a wet experience due to the tides. They settled on the morrow at the driest time and brought along a hamper of food, which Gnasher was obliging enough to overset and proceed to eat most of the provisions. Rescuing some, Emmalie was delighted to discover a chicken leg for the viscount which was, she claimed, perfectly edible, if a bit pebbly, for the residual sand could easily be washed down with the ale. Forgetting his formal London ways, Reggie could not but agree that the leg was unexceptionable and both partook with appetite. Unlike most ladies, she had not a whit of their repelling reserve, Reggie concluded with satisfaction, and there upon permitted himself to suspend his own starched air, which stiff perfection he had so long labored to perfect.

To Emmalie's wish for seeing all of Cornwall at once, he was nothing loath. And they galloped across the moors each day to a new site. The first had them dismounting at a narrow brambled path where he chivalrously held back the branches in her way. Several of which bare limbs, especially in the clearing, were decorated with colored bits of cloth. Reggie went directly to the stone font that was filled with water from the spring behind it and drank water with cupped hands. He then cupped some for her to drink as well, which she was pleased to do.

"That is the ritual. We have now fulfilled it. If there is anything you wish cured or solved, it has been granted you by the spirits of the trees and spring. And one rewards them with these cloth bits to decorate their home." And from his pocket he withdrew a crimson silk handkerchief and hung it on the nearest branch.

Enthralled by the ritual, Emmalie could not restrain herself from splashing her hands in the font, liberally spraying the viscount.

"That is quite sufficient. You must not mock the spirits, who apparently have already made you spirited enough!" the viscount insisted and restrained her wet hand. "For I daresay while they can cure, any disrespect, and they might also inflict!"

Emmalie shook off that admonition along with the water, claiming, "They shall not inflict aught on me. I am a woman like themselves, and I love them and their trees and streams . . . and, indeed, all of Cornwall!"

And although smiling at her presumption then, Reggie soon began to concede Windsrest's new lady was becoming the very spirit of the country. Anything Cornish was certain to win her favor. So he took her to the most renowned Cornish phenomena: the quoits. These giant stone slabs balanced across others of five feet in height.

"But they must be tables for giants!" Emmalie exclaimed. "Everything here is prodigiously large: from the steps leading down to the beach to these quoits, to the cliffs themselves. A race of giants must have lived here. I expect I have definitely grown several inches!''

''I have noted that,'' Reggie said, with a soft smile. ''But you are correct. Here giants dwell . . . and giant feelings. Nothing here is cribbed or confined.''

Another excursion took them to the Merry Maidens— quite an unmerry grouping of nineteen stones. ''These,'' Reggie admonished with a twinkle, ''were nineteen maidens, seduced by two pipers into committing the gross impropriety of dancing on the Sabbath and instantly punished by being turned into stones.''

''And the pipers as well?'' Emmalie asked hopefully.

''As well,'' the viscount said grinning, showing, further, two taller stones or menhirs.

''Then that's quite all right,'' Emmalie said in satisfaction. ''So oft it is just the ladies who are punished for the pleasures of both.''

Reggie eyed her with lifted eyebrow. Another example of her delightful anomaly! Childish one moment and then totally worldly the next. Just what one would expect of one brought up in seclusion but by the sophisticated Lady Leonie.

Unable to resist, he tested her degree of worldliness by doing what he had been anticipating—bringing her before the collection of grinning satyrs in the priory church grounds. She minutely examined one after another, while he kept expecting her any moment to exhibit her outrage or perhaps even fall into a direct swoon. At the least, she ought to be put into a blazing blush. Instead she calmly called for the gardeners.

Assuming her objective was to have these wicked stone men hauled off, Reggie was totally flummoxed at her actual order. The lovely nymph statue in Windsrest's gardens was to be brought and placed here a respectful distance from the satyrs, yet directly in their line of sight. ''To give them something to dream about and reason to reform their evil ways,'' she said with a twinkle. And even the workmen were amused and quick to follow her command.

As for Reggie, he threw back his head and laughed aloud. And when subsequently the transference was complete and they viewed the results, the viscount owned himself prodigiously astonished to note the satyrs themselves seemed to have undergone a transformation—appearing decidedly happier and less evil. Or was that in his own mind's eye? Or even was it rather as a result of the ameliorating presence of his own little nymph applauding the effect?

"But have you considered what the proximity of all these rakes shall do to the poor nymph? Are you not concerned about her dreams turning into nightmares?" he teased.

Looking at the demure lady holding her urn, she answered, "I expect she's tired of holding the urn and now has hopes that one of these . . . eh, gentlemen, shall be sufficiently rehabilitated to take her burden from her. Besides, it is always elevating to be the good example for men of such stamp."

"Is that what you are to me, little nymph? Are you under the impression that having reformed my evil ways by turning me celibate, I shall be elevated to lift your burdens?"

"But you already have done so by deeding me Windsrest. And by being kind enough to stay here and show me such a nacky time!"

"There's your blasted honesty again. A lady does not own as much to a gentleman, lest he presume. But you are clearly not up to snuff!" And in exasperation at her trusting, he exclaimed, "What is one to do in defense, but be honest in turn? I have stayed here to make you want to marry me earlier than your year's time. I am attempting to seduce you, little one, just as surely as these satyrs would if they could reach their nymph."

"Rather you have been like the brother I never had.

I expect even satyrs had sisters and were friends with them."

"Again you are putting my honor to the test, I presume," he said with a bow.

Incorrigible girl, he thought, and as the days passed he neither made attempt to seduce nor to leave, merely allowing the pleasure of their time together to continue. The most enjoyable of all the sights, he discovered, was Miss Marlowe herself. She had a way of throwing back her head when she was happy and holding out her hands, as if basking in the feeling; and surprisingly he felt himself experiencing the happiness with her. Then there was her soft brown hair, unbound now and spreading in waves round her, and the big brown unguarded eyes, open to the moment whether sailing or riding or simply racing each other around the statues. He was dropping years every day he spent with her and picking up a light heart.

But the nights presented more of a difficulty. Both of them retired to their respective wings, companioned only by the pleasures of the day past. That mutual solitude was suspended late one evening upon their encountering each other in the library. She was reading a *Monk* Lewis epic, and he took up the volume and read aloud: " 'Wretch! Hell boasts no miscreant more guilty than yourself! Hark, Ambrosio! while I unveil your crimes.' "

Fearing he would laugh and insult her taste, the viscount abruptly stopped.

But she waved him on, exclaiming with glee, "It is delightfully excessive, is it not? Ambrosio did not commit the common crime, such as insulting a lady's feelings, which stains many a gentleman's record. Rather he violated his own sister and murdered his mother, which, not wishing to seem judgmental, does tend to give one rather a distaste of him. But, actually, he is quite suited to Windsrest and its shadows. One is constantly expecting a revenging monk to near, lift his cowl, and reveal . . . a skeleton!'' And they laughed together at that conclusion. ''Indeed, that is what has just occurred. Read on, please!''

And he did so, till shortly, half-laughing, half-caught, they had gone deep into the novel. After that, in unspoken agreement, they met regularly. Miss Spindle, perfectly agreeable to unsupervised afternoon jaunts, felt that evening exchanges, just by that very nomenclature, must inevitably lead to a falling from grace; therefore, she insisted on joining the readings, bringing her workbasket and sitting at a discreet distance. But there.

At the conclusion of *The Monk's Tale* which had earned many a shudder and smile, sometimes hard upon each other, all three eagerly consulted the viscount's library for the next selection. A heated discussion ensued, each eager to recommend his favorite. But when Emmalie and Miss Spindle concurred, his lordship bowed and allowed himself to be introduced to one of Miss Austen's comedies. *Pride and Prejudice* was gone through in a trice, during which Emmalie hinted of a relationship between the characters and themselves. With scant favor, Reggie denied a similarity to the top-lofty Mr. Darcy.

''You flatter yourself, my lord,'' Emmalie responded. ''I implied a resemblance between yourself and Mr. Collins whose self-consequence was so prodigious he could not accept Elizabeth's refusal—assuming every lady must accept him. Does that not sound familiar?''

''I, Mr. Collins! Egad, you have wrung my withers, indeed!''

So affronted was he that Emmalie relented enough to allow the similarity was merely in their attitudes, since Reggie was personally superior. In fact, he had one trait that lifted him above all else, making him truly a nonpareil.

At that, he was not only mollified but at full attention for an enlargement of her point; and she, nothing loath, holding up another book, concluded, "You are a first rate, first oars, absolutely capital—*reader*!"

An experienced courtier who had been praised by ladies so oft he thought himself immune to flattery, Reggie was remarkably pleased by that conclusion. For, actually, he dashed well was having a capital time reading aloud. It became even more of a jolly good show when she agreed to spell him. For Miss Marlowe, it developed, while silently observing her mother's circle had learned everyone's expressions and mannerisms so perfectly, she could not resist using their personas to depict her characters. The outrageous little mimic had him doubling up with amusement. As for her impersonation of her mother that indeed had him in such high jig, he wished it to be included in every reading and even urged a full depiction of her ladyship. Although Miss Spindle objected, begging the viscount not to encourage her, Emmalie immediately complied and pretending to don long gloves, she called for the footman and began speaking to him in just precisely her mother's manner of airy inquisition, putting forth to the impassive man exactly her sort of delving, personal questions.

"Davis, are you the one with the three children? I hope they have sufficient reading material, if not I shall speak to the butler to provide it. Oh, you are unmarried? Well, that does not necessarily mean you do not have children. . . ."

The viscount was quick to dismiss the footman and insist that Lady Leonie was not quite so intrusive. "No," admitted Emmalie, "she has no need to be, she would already know exactly how many children he had and their names and probably had offered her suggestions on their christenings."

In glee, the viscount had to admit that as well. His prime favorite was the elegant, mellifluous tones of Lady Leonie as Lady Macbeth, especially the washing of the blood off her hands and saying, "Out, damned spot!'' which became rather a fastidious lady's annoyance at the soiling of her garment. To counter that performance, Reggie cast the Prince of Wales as Macbeth and adopted his august, although rather high-pitched tones. But he used some license by adding the Regent's favorite phrase, ''Odd's blood,'' and thus Macbeth's line became ''Odd's blood, is this a dagger which I see before me?''—which while particularly apt had them laughing rather than falling into the dread of the drama.

From there they went on to *Romeo and Juliet*. At first the viscount attempted it in Pug's lisping ways, but when countered by Emmalie's playing Juliet with sincerity, reading her lines so naturally, he found himself not only moved but answering Romeo's lines in his own voice and with his own heart.

Staring at the large brown eyes with their golden lights gave him pause. Oft of late did he find himself bemused by her face that had once seemed plain and now was like a blooming flower, opening petal upon petal under his concentrated gaze. That analogy seemed particularly apt one morning in the garden when he handed her a bouquet of the first spring daffodils, and, unlike other ladies who would modestly accept them and call for a vase to make a neat arrangement, she pushed her face into the blooms and wished aloud that she were one of them. And he felt she was. She was everything that was real and of the highest nature.

Whatever the mood and moment, they moved together and found they were well fitted in all—from riding to sharing dreams to continually laughing. Ere long, he began to suspect she could read his mind. For they oft spoke in concert.

So strong was this sense of union becoming the viscount found himself unable to view it with equanimity. It seemed to minimize his control of his life, and he had long since prided himself on his basic separation from others. In self-preservation, therefore, he abruptly acquainted her with his philosophy of life, expounding it in his social languorous voice, "To *be*, one must constantly seek change. I expect there is no other way to conquer the void . . . a fresh place to travel, a fresh challenge, a fresh lady. . . ."

To which Emmalie merely responded, "But are you seeking variety or repeat versions of the same?"

"We are all versions of the same."

Before Emmalie could deny that jaded view, Miss Spindle, whom both had forgotten was present, could not resist inserting that his lordship had merely been searching for his *true* love, and once found, he should be content. She made her point even more blatant by eyeing Emmalie significantly, causing a prodigiously awkward pause, which had the effect of suspending the evening's reading earlier than usual, as both Emmalie and the viscount felt the need to instantly retire.

Yet the viscount's remark did not fail in its objective, for it caused Miss Marlowe to review their relationship. Clearly his lordship was warning that he was merely sipping of the fresh sensation of *her* existence before going on to another. Once more revealing himself as a bird that flitted from branch to branch.

A timely reminder, indeed, for she had forgotten he was the perfect representative of her mother's social world and begun to see him rather as she'd always felt him to be—the other half of herself. Quickly, she donned the reserve ladies were required to wear at all times, which she had so foolishly dispensed with. She even excused herself from their daily ride on the morrow. Yet although he had been the one to call a halt to their growing closeness, he resented being deprived of the fruits thereof. And when Emmalie continued through the rest of the day to treat him with a want of her usual openness, Reggie stiffly demanded whether she felt his presence was fatiguing her. She responded with a speaking look but not speaking what she felt. Pressed to disclose her thoughts, she guardedly replied she suspected it was time for him to flit onto another branch, after all.

"Are you trying to urge me to break my vow," he demanded, showing hackle, "so our nuptials shall not go on?"

"Do you still hold fast to that object?" she cried.

"By Jove, it has been my avowed object since the beginning. I have made no bones about that, now it is my pleasure, as well."

"You are a practiced courtier," she said sadly. "But why do you continue to court? It is no longer necessary for you to be married. You are safe from the princess. We have become friends enough to remain friends. . . . Have we not?"

But his lordship was not content with that, nor was friendship his objective in coming here. And he took Emmalie's hand suddenly and said, "Do you not wish to go on one more expedition with me, Miss Marlowe? We have been having delightful times, but they are naught next to the discovery of love. You cannot allow yourself to live your whole existence through without ever knowing the pleasure of two people enjoined. Two hearts so close they seem, indeed, to beat as one," he finished softly, and moved her clasped hand against his own beating heart to illustrate his point. "Feel it— here," he whispered, pressing her entire person against their hands at his chest. "So close can two become that, indeed, a separation should feel as if one's own heart were being ripped out of one's chest." And he abruptly broke away from her, even dropping her hand, so that the separation was thus fully demonstrated. And both were left, feeling in that moment, shaken and alone.

But Emmalie, albeit in a whirl of emotions, resented his resorting to his obvious courtier's ways and retorted, "Is that the way you act with all your ladybirds? And the young ladies on the Marriage Mart? For shame! I am quite content with my heart beating its own quiet steady beat on its own."

"Are you certain of that?" he whispered. "Enough to put both our hearts to the test? You, who so love testing others, are you willing to test yourself?" And he pulled her back into his arms and kissed her so thoroughly, the time on the Tower Stairs that she had been reviewing since was nothing in comparison, and she allowed him to kiss her several times before realizing that she was failing his test; and she must either agree to all his terms and all his actions, or she must break away. And swiftly she did the latter.

The next day, Emmalie allowed, with a quiver to her voice, that they had forgotten themselves yesterday and insisted both dismiss that entire exchange and continue on in Cornwall simply as happy companions. Reggie having made significant inroads was loath to agree, but as a gentleman and openly requested to do so by a lady, he could do no less. Yet, henceforth he waited for subsequent moments of her weakening. Which he encouraged by choosing plays of the most amorous nature and no longer allowing her to turn their readings into comedies. Rather, he made use of the greatest poets to do his courting for him. Dashed obliging of those fellows to come to his aid. And aid they did, for again and again Miss Marlowe would begin a reading stiffly and then become swept away by the compressed emotions of the writers, wearing at her reserve, forcing her to tremulously declare sensations never openly owned by a lady. And but for, at times, sensing an equal danger for himself, Reggie would not have had the slightest qualm about this tactic. Yet the intensity in that room would reach such a pitch, even an expert, such as himself, could not but be at risk. And oft he found himself being whirled about in it. Hoist with his own petard, in effect. Where was the amused Reggie who always stood outside of all his seductions, making ironic asides? Overwhelmed by the emotions he himself had unleashed. And he must call a halt to their readings, claiming hoarseness or fatigue. Only to chastise himself the following day and, armed with a thicker protective coating of renewed sophistication, risk the battle of amour once again. And there, under the soft candlelight and firelight of the library, he would once more permit the words of love to flow over them and pull them down, down, until they both were near to drowning in them.

The stanzas of poetry had a somewhat different effect upon Miss Spindle. Viewing all the rhyming as an intellectual exercise, she was eased enough to fall into the arms of Morpheus, while the two others attempted to hold themselves off from falling into each other's arms.

The barrier of other people's words and feelings, behind which they hid their own emotions, was daily wearing thinner until one particular reading ripped it clear away, and they were open to each other. That potent reading was the medieval story of Pierre Abelard, the French priest, and his soul-risking love for his student, the young Heloise. Reggie read it in its true version, or the actual priest's confession in *Historia Calamitatum*. The viscount's instant translation of the Latin original into his own English words, or sometimes his own free interpretation of it, gave it a prodigious reality and immediacy.

Indeed, he had chosen the Latin version particularly so that having to stop to translate not only kept him perfectly composed but perfectly in charge. As Abelard had been in charge of his young pupil, Heloise, the viscount was now determinedly controlling Emmalie—instructing her, until, like Abelard, his student's proximity began to teach the teacher. And despite all precautions, he felt himself taken over by Abelard, so the monk's admission, from centuries before, was shared by him as well as by Emmalie. For she was listening with such total, almost unbreathing concentration, Reggie felt himself breathing for her, especially when he reached the point of the actual confession of the couple's breaking through the "bounds of honor" thus, "Our hands went from those well-read pages before us to each other's hands instead." And Reggie reached over and took Emmalie's hand. Feeling it sufficiently trembling, he softly continued, "Our books before us, we moved from the words therein to the text of our bodies." A pause for the correct English word, but actually to look once more at the lady, so that openly it became his own feeling transmitted. "In our studies, kisses became our language until it was our daily speech. No gradation of love evaded us. The more we tasted, the less our satiety . . . as we ardently pursued our love . . . to its . . . final . . . expression."

And with that last translation, his voice silenced, and he allowed Abelard his way in him. And Emmalie-Heloise was obediently waiting for him as he moved closer to her on the settee and, very slowly, very educationally, taught her the gradations of love. And she, with a sinking of her heart, allowed him to teach her all he wished and would not have said him nay for whatever he wished, experiencing, like Heloise, the delirium of kisses and the binding of two souls till they were cut through by a mighty snore from Miss Spindle. And then all four partners broke clean away.

Thoroughly awakened, the good lady sat up and cheerfully exclaimed, "Well, have we done with our lessons for the night?" They had indeed.

Whereupon Emmalie, with the relief of laughter, accompanied her companion to her bed, leaving the viscount in such a state of fidgets, he was soon set to wondering whom these tactics were seducing—the young girl or himself! The devil take Miss Spindle and her untimely snore!

The next night Emmalie was circumspect enough to seat herself next to Spinny, some distance from her Reginald-Abelard, hoping therefore to screen herself from the heat of both the story and the storyteller. Yet that evening apparently Miss Marlowe had no need of any protective devices; for the conclusion of the tale of Heloise and Abelard was filled with such punishment the girl could only tremble and regret all her prior feelings. So sobering was the lesson of the ending—more morally rehabilitating than even the sight of Merry Maidens turned to stone for dancing! Indeed, the culmination brought a decided calcification throughout her body. For the lovers were not only parted forever for daring to love, but their punishments were monstrously severe. Heloise, in dishonor, was sent to a convent for life, and Abelard was in some way physically assaulted by Heloise's kin. The latter nature of which she did not instantly understand until Abelard concluded his tale by philosophically accepting his fate with the exclamation, ''I was revenged in that part of me that had pleasured most.'' Then did Emmalie turn red and glance toward Spinny in alarm, only to breathe in relief at Miss Spindle's undisturbed slumber.

Yet that night the girl was nigh onto requesting one of Miss Spindle's oft suggested composers, for she could not dismiss the effect of all that retribution. Surely the shocking revenge of castration was coming it too strong!

As is usually the case when one is frightened, one reverts to concern for oneself, and Emmalie, fearing the consequences of the growing passion between herself and Reggie, sought the safety of her mother. And thinking of her, she could almost hear Lady Leonie's elegant voice responding to that shocking means of revenge: ''Not very British, that! Surely not the sort of thing a lady orders, or most importantly, *acknowledges*!''

And then Emmalie was able to laugh away all her quakes, feeling comforted by the assurance that as Britishers and nobles, nothing of that uncivil sort could ever happen to them. And she was able, at last, to sleep the sleep of the reassured.

But the next day, the young girl sensed the viscount

had himself not had a satisfying night's repose, and when they were walking by the seaside and he reached, with some emotion, for her hand, she allowed him to hold on. It was quite obvious he needed her comfort. So tormented, actually, did his face seem, she allowed him to come close to her, indeed! Her poor Abelard, she thought secretly. and upon his calling her "Heloise," she could not protest, nor stop him from seeking the ease of her kisses as the sea pounded and echoed their senses.

An expert in seduction, the viscount at once knew he had brought the lady to the correct point, where one need merely carry on a jot more, and she would be his! Further, it would, he opined, scarcely be a dastardly deed, since they by all understanding were set to be riveted for life. Yet now he had a new obstacle thrown in his way and by all people, himself! For he was hearing the clear call of his own sense of decency, telling him to desist, asking that she be spared.

At first he did not recognize that voice, it coming at an inconvenient time. But he bowed to it, as an old friend he could no longer cut.

Yet, ambivalently, he cursed his previous reticence. If erstwhile he had acted with more push, by now she would have long been his wife and he could have forgotten the chit—allowing her to fall into that realm of domesticity that wives inevitably sink into, while he went off to his life at his clubs and with new bits of muslin. But holding back, he not only failed to catch Emmalie, but he himself had been dashed well near dished. He'd been playing so deep a game, he'd dug himself into a hole. Basil would have quite a laugh at his expense and claim Reggie to have been bum squabbled! And so he was, in truth.

Egad, the viscount could not countenance having muddled such a commonplace thing as throwing out a lure. He, Reginald Lancaster, renowned for his address, had made an infamous mull of it all! A veritable green lad, new on the town, would not have found himself in such a hubble-bubble—as while seeking to catch her, he'd been caught himself!

The London viscount might not understand his predicament, but the Cornwall gentleman did. For it was here he'd allowed that long-buried self to come to life, called forth by a lady that was all the joy in life. He'd lay odds there was not an ounce of falsity in her. Indeed, the emotions in Emmalie were so genuine, he felt his tainted her because they had so oft been feigned, although less and less each day. And by the time Reggie had realized that nothing in him was sham when it came to this girl, that he had, as had Abelard, found his fated love, it was too late to retreat to formal manners. He had trained her too well.

Each morning Emmalie ran to him; and further, she naturally hugged him over such wonders as sunsets and ocean waves while they stood on the beach together and then slowly moved on, leaving only one set of footsteps on the sand behind, for he was carrying her away from the touch of the incoming foam.

Indeed, he wished no other thing, nor no other person henceforth to touch her but himself. And he must always hold her close and smell the clean freshness of her hair, cutting a lock off to wear next to his heart, and he must always have her near to watch the yellow lights in her eyes slowly encompassing him as the two shared stares and caught their breath at the shared thoughts. And shared smiles. And shared senses.

The devil! He was, for the first time, totally and impossibly in love. So much so, that the Viscount of Wynnclife realized he had only one recourse. He had to set her immediately free, while he still could.

Else he would stain her. For he was what he was. Dash it, he could pretend to change, but he knew himself enough to know he would not. Only she would, if he forced her to marry him, and that corruption he would not commit.

Taking early morning walks on the moors, with Gnasher at his side, Reggie would arrive at the castle newly confident that he could be the man she loved in Cornwall for his lifetime. That the solution was simplicity itself—he must merely give up London and all Society for her! It did not seem, at that moment, a major concession. But his resolve never lasted beyond tea time. For by then he should have received a letter from a friend or have read the delivered newspapers, and he would sheepishly acknowledge there was no possibility that the nonpareil of the beau monde would remain here forever. This storybook existence in Cornwall was just that, a relationship that belonged in the storybooks they read to each other. His real life was in London. And if he took this Emmalie back there with him, she would become again the Miss Marlowe she was before. She would undoubtedly sink into being his shadow, as she'd been her mother's, and a shadow with reproachful eyes that he would leave behind on his more and more frequent social outings. She was like a mermaid one could only live with in the sea. Take her out of this setting, where she had come to life for him, and she would be transformed back to that insipid little girl even her mother wished to be rid of . . . and whom he'd planned to marry precisely because she would not interfere with his perfectly arranged lifestyle.

No, he could not permit her to sink into that shadow that was her former self! Best leave Emmalie here with the wild storms and the castle she had asked for—knowing for herself where she best belonged.

The only drawback to that solution was that he simply could not force himself to leave. One more day, he thought. And then one more. And then there came the night when his emotions so raged, he was totally deaf to the voice of decency—pushing it away into a mere voice crying out in the wilderness. He could not totally deprive himself of ever having her sweetness. And there, on the balcony, away from the slumbers of Miss Spindle, he no longer checked himself. Only this time he was held back by Emmalie herself who, not recognizing the gentleman as the gentle man she loved, pulled back in alarm and cried, "Do not do this, Reggie. We are friends. I have waited all my life to discover a man I can truly talk to; after a lifetime of silence, a lifetime of not being listened to, you have listened to me. Do not reduce me to one of your conquests!"

And the viscount recollected himself and who she was and that he should not treat her as if she were one of his set. Pulling himself back, he walked to the edge of the balcony, and from the shadows his voice came harsh but in control again, "Very well, Malie dear, we shall just be friends henceforth."

And he was rewarded with her happiest of smiles.

He had her, but he was gentleman enough to let her go. A moment more and he should have altered all the gentle harmony between them. He had almost, almost remained too long. One night too long. He must be off and gone by morning. There was no way he could continue to be with her and not ruin her—in every sense of the word. He would have one lady in his life he could remember as unattainable and untouched. Though he should regret her all his life after, he should leave her and the memory of her as perfect as both were. Already, as he escorted her back to the library, he was smiling at her as one did at a dear past memory. At dawn, the viscount rose and, taking his valet and his curricle and one last glimpse of the castle, he departed, without even taking his leave of the lady he loved. This fashion of leaving was infamous, he knew, and not the thing and likely to give Miss Marlowe a disgust of him, and more, it was beneath a lord renowned for always making a polished bow on his every exit. But if he could not stay for love, he could scarce stay for civility.

CHAPTER NINE

ON THE VISCOUNT'S RETURN TO LONDON SOCIETY HE found it in a bumblebroth of nuptial news. One marriage was to take place between Princess Charlotte and Prince Leopold of Saxe-Coburg. And one marriage was to be displaced as a formal separation of Lord and Lady Byron was announced. There was general interest in the former and general delight for the latter.

The viscount had been prepared for both *on dits* by Lady Leonie some time past. But he was taken aback at the intimate personal details being circulated about Byron. Perhaps it was his purifying time with Emmalie, but he found the minutiae minding of other people's concerns stifling! One was not safe from the "latest" even in the privacy of one's saloon—someone was bound to call to discuss what had just been thoroughly masticated at one's club. Lady Byron made realities of all the rumors with a legal suit that threatened to name Mrs. Augusta Leigh, Lord Byron's own half sister. Whereupon Society felt itself sanctioned to turn all into a sporting match, forming teams to cheer the disputants on.

That was especially evident at Lady Jersey's assembly. Her ladyship's affairs were customarily squeezes, but with the promised attendance of one of the participants in the cause célèbre, or the exalted poet himself, one found no room for viewing without craning one's neck. Except for Pug who was tall enough to see above the crowd and report to the anxious Lady Leonie the instant Lord Byron was spotted. In diffidence or in drama, the poet was delaying his entrance, during which Lady Leonie used the opportunity to scold Reggie for socializing in this blatant manner without his fiancée. His evasive response had Lady Leonie's antenna quivering. But before she could delve further, both Pug and the viscount called her attention to Lord Byron's entrance. That moment had further titillation when it was observed he was escorting his sister, none other than the named, Augusta Leigh, herself.

Although greeted warmly by the hostess, it soon became obvious Society was not going to give the pair the comfort of pretending to be unaware. Rather, one after another of the ton deliberately cut them. Mrs. George Lamb began it with a decisive turn away; other ladies followed. But the ostracizing became impossible to ignore when even the gentlemen did an about-face. The very people who not long since had been assiduously courting Lord Byron now pretended to have never been introduced. Lady Leonie, disgusted by that hypocrisy, was the first to step up to the poet. In a blink, the viscount was behind her. After that, several others forced themselves to at least bow. Lord Byron merely smiled, amused at both those who made it a point to speak to him and those who made it a point not to.

In their converse, Lady Leonie directly came to the heart of all this fuss, letting both Reggie and Lord Byron know that Lady Caroline Lamb, one of Byron's discarded lovers, was spreading stories of her secret meeting with Lady Byron.

"Why the devil anyone would believe that seventy times convicted liar is beyond me!" Lord Byron responded, and then unable to contain himself continued, "That infamous bedlamite. Such a monster as that has no sex!"

"You were late in discovering that," Reggie remarked, hoping by his own mask of indifference to remind Lord Byron that he was the cynosure. Recollecting himself, Lord Byron took a deep breath and with languid tones dismissed Lady Caroline's having anything of note to add to the situation. Still Lady Leonie insisted on forewarning the poet, for she had personally been told that Lady Caroline had revealed secrets about Byron told by the poet himself and which Lady Caroline was claiming to be of such "depravity" as she could "no longer hold her tongue."

"The devil take her!" Byron gasped.

"Have you not already done so?" Reggie pointedly asked, and Lord Byron, in amusement, bowed to acknowledge that appellation, and thus the situation was eased for all except Mrs. Leigh who refused to accept that jest! Indeed, her face had been progressively whitening. Lady Leonie moved quickly and took Augusta aside. Lord Byron's alarm and his motion to follow them would have confirmed all, but Reggie stopped him forcibly.

"Leonie has her and all in hand," he whispered, and the next instant the two ladies were laughing at one of Pug's antics, and Lord Byron could compose himself. Making an effort at seeming unconcerned, the two lords discussed trivialities which naturally advanced them to the one delicious topic both shared—of the actresses of Drury Lane. Lord Byron twitted the viscount on his abandonment of the Miss Jones for such a period, and Reggie unrepentantly admitted his dereliction, claiming rather he had been attending Miss Marlowe, his young respectable fiancée, who was a refreshing change from all other women.

"Good God," Lord Byron inserted. "Do not allow yourself to be taken in by desire for respectability! If I had not listened to that urge, I should not have asked for the hand of the then Miss Milbanke, the epitome of goodness, and found myself being daily fed with so much of her bloody beneficence, I must perforce run to escape it into every excess! Never listen to one's conscience. It destroys not only others but oneself. Better follow one's worst instincts, they never lead one astray.''

"You have a child, do you not?'' the viscount soothed.

"*They* have the child. The lady and her group of supporters, those relatives and ministers from hell that have been hounding me and mine. No, Reggie old boy, allow me to be of some use by serving as a timely example. Never marry a young, pure lady, urged on one by well-wishers. The more 'decent' these young ladies believe themselves, the more indecent they declare us to be.''

Alarmed at that linkage, the viscount said huffily, "Miss Marlowe has merely youth in common with the former Miss Annabelle Milbanke. Recollect I warned you against that liaison. My knowledge of the Miss Milbanke's humorless conventionality urged against her! But Miss Marlowe is an original—a lady with her own sense of independence. Actually, she even refused my offer despite pressure brought by. . .''

Lord Byron was sighing and was not backward in inserting that Miss Milbanke had at first refused him, not relenting until urged on by her aunt, Lady Melbourne.

It was of prime importance to the viscount to find not the smallest connection between the two ladies. Yet Lord Byron continued with his point, asking whether Miss Marlowe had ever attempted to *reform* him, which could not but bring to Reggie's mind the stipulation of a celibate life. Ceasing his protests, he listened closely to the poet's complaints of the inconsistency of the proper ladies of their set. For instance, Miss Milbanke married a gentleman of poetry. "And I flatter myself,'' he said, "that I have some reputation in that area. Yet she was unremitting in her demands that I quit my, and I quote the lady, 'abominable trade of versifying and all the levity and nonsense which prevents one from reflecting seriously' close quote the lady.''

With some relief, Reggie actually exhaled and said jubilantly, "That is not Emmalie! She loves poetry and laughter. In fact, she has a delightful sense of fun. She is all sunshine and laughter and gentle ways. My only fear is that I am not equal to her perfection."

"Indeed?" A faint cynical smile accompanied the poet's further remarks. "Then by all means believe that. Enough to allow her to remain in her pristine state of pure perfection, untainted by your connection, and for yourself, settle for a life of pure enjoyment with the beauteous Miss Jones."

"Ah, so you advise, but not *do*. Has not your own heart been substantially conquered, which has you in your present devil-of-a-hank? Alas, one can control any woman one does not love, but once in love, then comes destruction."

And Lord Byron allowed his face, kept so long in bitter hauteur, to relax as he gazed at his sister, Augusta, approaching with Lady Leonie. "She is the other half of me. Ask rather that one not love one's own heart."

"Are you gentlemen discussing hearts?" Lady Leonie asked. "I assumed no true gentleman would admit of owning such an unnecessary, vestigial organ."

Lore Byron smiled. "It is you ladies who once having touched our hearts assume permanent ownership."

"Ah, we are back to discussing Lady Caroline? Prepare yourself for more evidence of her belief of her ownership of your heart in the shortly to be published Gothic novel that, I am told, has a devastating portrait of your lordship."

"I never sat long enough for it," Lord Byron said with a slow smile. "Rather it should be a mere sketch."

In the subsequent days, Lord Byron's advice reoccurred to silence Reggie's doubts about permanently breaking off with Miss Marlowe. Of which he had many. For although he had left Miss Marlowe's side, he kept her beside himself by carrying on their correspondence.

Never having felt so all about in his head and heart for a lady, he continued writing to her to that effect . . . yet all the while remaining in London. Lord Byron's advice had pulled the rein on Reggie's drift toward Cornwall. For there was not the smallest chance that he would countenance becoming someone's project for reformation. He was what he was. And she, as well.

Like a weather vane, there was a want of steadiness about his direction that gave him a disgust of himself. Cornwall or London? Or rather swinging between the two? Lord Byron's words pointed him away from her. Then Emmalie's letters pointed him back. A note from Lady Leonie asking his intentions regarding her daughter pointed him both ways. First, in conscience toward Emmalie, and then away, as he recollected Lady Leonie's oft quoted remark that marriage was a halter that became a nuisance for some but tightened into a noose for others. And while originally the viscount had viewed his union with Emmalie as tolerable and a mere nuisance (and had offered for her with that very understanding), since Cornwall, he'd realized she was a stronger force than any he'd ere encountered. She could have him in a noose in a trice. Especially if, like Lady Byron, she attempted to turn him away from his friends and the entire beau monde. What the viscount needed was a lady of Society, he realized, yet one he could love as much as he did Miss Marlowe. Which combination was hardly likely to be found. Not that Society, since his return, seemed all that worthy of a gentleman's fullest attention. Indeed, something was amiss or mayhap missing in him. Dare he own it was his heart? For he could not readily staunch the very large wound the very small Miss Marlowe had made there.

All was in such a devilish coil that admitted of no suitable method of disentanglement except the great Alexander's—which was scarcely a gentleman's solution. Gentlemen did not slash about one—cutting through knots, leaving dangling ends that might dashed well trip all up. Yet blast it, why not? He was at point non plus as it was. He'd just as soon toss Society and all ratiocination to the devil and claim Emmalie—clasp her to his heart of hearts—and make that the end of it! Except she'd already shied away—determined to live in seclusion in Cornwall, hiding from lovers' feelings as well. And his lordship would not force her—either into his arms or into his world.

Enough! Obviously he was procrastinating simply because he had already made the decision and could not bear putting it into effect. And then he received one of Emmalie's most trusting letters that sunk him beneath all reproach. In faith, he urged himself, he must finally and immediately set this special lady free! It took scarcely a moment to devise a method of giving Emmalie her congé. He was, after all, quite experienced in that sort of thing, having broken several scores of ladies' hearts, although he had never before, at the same time, done serious injury to his own!

Actually, the lady herself had given him the tool. He need only break the last condition imposed upon him.

And with half-regret, half-relief, he proceeded to do so.

It was mid-April, but with the bright sun full out and the winds having gentled to a breeze, Emmalie decided to take a quick dip in the ocean in her white flowing gown. With the waves having their own beat (unlike her lake in Richmond), it was difficult to keep the rhythm of her strokes. Then, too, the sea had the audacity of ballooning her gown about her and then committing the grossest impropriety of invading her person beneath the gown with its cool and delicious touch. Invigorated, Emmalie raced out of the sea, followed by the small waves gobbling up her footprints on the sand and seeking to splash up against Emmalie as she climbed the cliffs to her discarded brown cloak. Thus properly dressed, she sat a moment on the rocks and looked down at her recent opponent, smiling. Her thoughts could not help but refer back to another opponent, Reginald himself, for she had felt somewhat of the same pleasurable sensation when he kissed her as when the ocean lost its way under her dress.

The viscount had been gone a fortnight, and Miss Marlowe never believed it possible to miss someone so acutely. At this very cove he'd taught her to sail, and they'd gone out in all weather. Once a storm had caught them, and they'd reefed and sailed it out, calling each other, "matey," till they docked. Then reverting to his old viscount way, he'd changed that to "bosom mates" adding, "I should very much like to be a mate of your bosom, my dear." But when she looked astounded, he apologized and assured her he was merely jesting.

Recollecting that, she now shyly peeked at that very bosom in question. It was full for her height and could make a comfortable pillow for the viscount's head. From there she progressed to what feelings would be hers if Reggie were leaning against her there, and then her complexion went red. "My stars!" she cried at the farrago of nonsense that kept erupting out of her volcanic idea pot. She was not only foolish beyond permission, but rapidly sinking into a wanton!

Another idiocy of late was stationing herself at the open window every dusk, waiting for the postman to pass beneath, whereupon she would signal him to put the mail in her lowered basket. Clearly overfond, but she could not wait for morning when Reggie's letters would be served on the tray with her chocolate.

Unlike in the beginning of their engagement when she skimmed through his epistles with a sceptical expression, now her eyes could hardly wait to fasten themselves on the next affectionate word. The viscount's letters to her in Cornwall deserved the highest attention, for they were, she opined with a sigh of delight, the most beautifully written and sincere expressions of love ever penned. Only a few hours after his departure, the first of these had arrived by messenger from an inn and had contained the request she send him one word of love, which was a meager return for the thousands he would send her, if she permitted it. And if she also permitted, he wrote, he would sign his letters, Abelard, for the tormented lovers he felt them to be, and, indeed, she was in his mind's eye a nun locked in her castle cell, which self-imposed bars he must break through to free her and make her his.

This went a great way toward excusing the discourtesy of his departure. As did his fidelity of correspondence henceforth. He wrote above two letters a day, as if attempting to be there with her, while not being there. Having his love while spurning her, she thought in confusion. Still his missives were of such open a nature, she could not but loosen the tone of her replies. She wished now to share everything with him. For it was so delightful to have someone who would laugh at her nonsense as it was meant and not be shocked by her enthusiasms.

He wrote encouraging her always to speak everything she felt openly to him. That he had found, in her, a quality lacking in any other person—or a desire to be one with all she witnessed, whether the sea, the scenery, the words she read, or even the person she was closest to. He understood why Spinny always spoke of her as such a "dear girl." She was most dear to him.

In her last letter, she unabashedly asked him to visit her again and was horrified by her forwardness and yet, fixing it with a yellow bird wafer, sent it winging on its way. This was in response to Reggie's most unequivocal declaration of his regard having just arrived, along with a velvet box containing a golden locket, outlined in topazes—the color of the lights in her eyes, he claimed. For that lovely comparison and for finding upon opening the locket a snippet of his own golden hair, she prized the gift above all her possessions. So much so, Emmalie, from then on, wore the heart-shaped locket close to her own heart. And despite her good sense would think such totty-headed thoughts as "two hearts beating as one."

Hence, when the very next letter arrived from his lordship, Emmalie broke it open with such alacrity, she had read the short paragraph it contained ere she could blink. Reserved in tone, the letter was an acknowledgment of having failed her last condition. No longer addressing her as "Heloise," it read: "My dear Miss Marlowe—It would be dishonorable for me not to immediately disclose to you that I am in default of our understanding. Having, in effect, not passed the third test, I have lost all and must immediately, as per your orders, release you from all present and future connection with myself. Obviously I do not have either the honor or the endurance you require for your future husband. I shall inform your mother of my failure and request that either you or she send a notice to the press of the dissolution of our promised jointure."

Small whimpers were all that came out from Emmalie as she continued making several readings. Then in a maddened state, she quickly took pen in hand and dashed off a forgiveness of his lapse and a reinstatement of their engagement. But after sealing that, she tore it up instead, and tossed the pieces into the fire. And watched them burn. And then stood stonelike before the blaze until Miss Spindle entered and wished to hear the contents of his lordship's epistle. "The merest commonplace," was all Emmalie could manage and found it necessary to plead herself feeling far from well and needing to retire.

Spinny, beyond urging a cup of tea, that which nothing could be more efficacious for all causes of indisposition, allowed the privacy requested. Not so reluctant to be viewed intrusive was Gnasher who bounded into the young lady's solitude and demanded a good night's romp. Impossible to squelch, Emmalie acquiesced to grant the dog a small hug and a thorough search of her room for rodents before he would allow her to seek the peace of her bed.

Yet sleep would not come to quiet her thoughts. Rather Emmalie must continue to read and reread the letter and then take up his previous letters and try to understand how one gentleman could have written both! But mainly she could not but agonize over what his confession implied. Had he deliberately broken the last condition, or was it rather done in a moment of weakness? . . . Or was it done because he had found another lady that engaged his feelings more deeply than she ever had, and he used her ''condition'' as a way of ridding himself of a past obligation?

The next morning Spinny would no longer stand on ceremony and intruded. But to all queries Emmalie remained nonresponsive. Yet her appearance had the governess seriously concerned, and she cosseted her with hot chocolate and small iced cakes and lavender water to bathe her temples, and still the young girl remained white and immobile, keeping to her bed. By the afternoon, seeing no amelioration in that condition, Miss Spindle suggested a physician be sent for. Miss Marlowe refused and owned that she was merely fatigued. In concern for her companion, Emmalie made an effort to rise from her collapsed state and make a tolerable evening meal. She further roused herself to go for her evening romp with Gnasher in the garden. But upon returning, although she had some color, there were tears in her eyes which Spinny would no longer overlook. Following her charge to her chambers, the good lady insisted on being told the cause of her distress.

Unable still to speak of it, Emmalie merely handed Miss Spindle the viscount's fateful note and lay back on her bed, covering her eyes with her arm. A scream from Miss Spindle caused the young lady to disarm herself and arise from her bed and allow Spinny to recline there, while she ran for a dose of hartshorn.

''But, how is this?'' the companion demanded,

thrashing about so much her cap totally blocked her vision, and Emmalie had to disengage it while Spinny, oblivious, continued to insist there was some error! Heavens, she would wager her life's savings the viscount loved her precious girl!

"Loved, is correct. Past tense. I believe he loved me while here and for some time after, but it was a passing fancy, I daresay, and has passed away. For he has clearly found another lady to love. And I am left here properly punished for my assuming I could make a gentleman of his propensities faithful to one . . . of such little value as myself."

And at that last summation, Emmalie's voice broke and could no longer be of use. Henceforth, she was soundless—only a rare sigh or choke audible, while Miss Spindle cried aloud as she took the girl in her arms and rocked her. Thus, the pair lamented. Not since Emmalie was a child and had found Boots's body ridden over by the cart had Miss Spindle seen this plucky little girl so overthrown! Emmalie had never allowed another cat to take Boots's place in her life, and Miss Spindle feared, recollecting that comparison, Emmalie would not find another gentleman to fill her heart. When Emmalie loved, she did so completely. And continuing to console her charge and kissing her lowered head, she whispered, "Oh, my dear, my poppet, he has lost a great deal. A million ladies put together could not equal the sum of your worth! And some day, his lordship shall discover that and regret his loss . . . bitterly."

The thought that someday the viscount would suffer somewhat eased both ladies of the solitary state of their woe.

On the following morning, attempting to end Miss Spindle's distress, Emmalie composed herself, at least outwardly, and even discussed with her steward the castle's affairs. Only to have this new control tested by being handed another letter—this from Lady Leonie. It was awash with indignation at observing Reggie with his former ladybird, the beauteous performer, Miss Kitty Jones.

"Indeed, the *on dit* is that he has even bought her a new carriage upholstered in velvet, the exact color of her fabulous blue eyes that have so bewitched all the bucks in the pit. I watched the play last night, and he sat in the stage box while she played every scene to him. So blatant was he, I had to call him to account. To which he had the effrontery to reply I no longer had any interest in his behavior, as the two of you had already parted. 'Not without my being informed,' I claimed. 'My dear Leonie, you are so well known for being in the know, one need hardly inform you of what is already general knowledge.' Thus, he humiliated me as well as you—so infatuated is he with that flaxen-haired harlot! At last you have attained your wish. You may remain unwed. I wash my hands of all arrangements for your future. My felicitations on having secured a castle from the blighter beforehand. Once I would have said that was a fortunate circumstance, but since knowing you better, I say rather it was well thought out and offer you my congratulations on having achieved all you wished."

That, the finale of all hopes of her mother helping by insisting the viscount and she keep to their engagement. And Emmalie, too, could only bitterly congratulate herself on her unqualified success.

Subsequently Emmalie concluded that his rejection was inevitable. Obviously his lordship's heart had ever been dedicated to this Kitty. It would be one thing if he had met a new love and found he cared for her more, then, at least, she would have the memory that at one time Reggie had truly loved her. But, dear heavens, if all along his affections had been reserved by another—then every word, every gesture to her at Cornwall had been sham. All flummery! Gammoning her to win her heart. To prove to himself mayhap that no lady was unattainable. And having proved that, he could then easily toss her aside.

Oh, she could forgive his injuring her pride to augment his, but what she could not accept was his having taken away her pleasure in all literature. For now she scarce could read a single chapter or poem without hearing Reggie's voice echoing every word in her ears . . . in her heart. He was always there, saying the words with her.

Later, upon walking about the castle grounds, chased by memories of their time together there, Emmalie reached a more easing conclusion. Simply this: if Reggie's love for this Miss Kitty was so enduring, why should she not be noble and loving enough to wish him happiness . . . from the depth of her heart? Or what was left of it. For Miss Marlowe had indeed experienced what the viscount had so glibly described—the sensation of having her heart ripped out of her! In keeping with that, she ripped off the golden heart-shaped locket as well. Opening it, she fastened her eyes on his lock of hair within, wincing at her having been gullible enough to give him one of her own brown locks—now probably tossed into the fire! Or did he keep a collection of them somewhere in his rooms to proudly show with this commentary, "And here is a brown lock. Egad, I could not possibly have entertained a lady of such an insipid coloring—see how it is lost amid all the reds and golds and glossy blacks! Ah, yes, I remember the chit—a small insignificant thing she was; would you believe she was close to becoming my wife?"

Perhaps he would not actually say that to someone—rather they would be his private reflections. Unless sometime in the future he shared them with one who would share his name. Which could have been herself! It had been in her power to have been, if not dearest to him, at least nearest to him as his viscountess!

What a widgeon! What a perfect ninnyhammer! To have worked so diligently to lose something of such prime value. All this time pretending she had not had the smallest interest in him and having daily more and more interest in him.

Yet shortly, upon further reflection, Emmalie found sufficient starch in her wilted self-confidence to conclude herself well rid of the gentleman! Certainly he was a lord of grossly libertine proportions to so audaciously display a collection of his present and previous ladies' locks.

Closing her eyes to that image, when she opened them, she had sufficiently come to grips with herself to recollect that the tormenting collection existed solely in her own supposing! But if the collection of ladies' locks was imagined, the collection of ladies was not! And further he was not only a loose fish, but a poor sport. For Good God, ought he not have had the gumption to personally face her with the admission of losing the contest?

In her palm, the removed locket seemed to be pulsing. And as she stared, it called to mind a disturbing counterthought: If after his return to London his affections were otherwise engaged by a renewed contact with his Miss Kitty, why had he sent her the locket containing his lock of hair? She had no answer to this query. Some hope remained that the gesture had been meant in love. But the jilting letter, following hard upon, suggested rather that he had been making a May game of her all along, and the locket was actually an ironic memento mori. Possibly such parting gestures were typical among his set of bucks; for she'd heard Lord Byron was want to give personal remembrances. And Lord Byron and the viscount had much in common, particularly the common actresses from Drury Lane. Indeed, it was known to be Lord Byron's custom to have his current actress's portrait painted by Mr. Holmes. In all likelihood the viscount had already commissioned one of Miss Kitty Jones. Certainly, he'd made no such request for Miss Marlowe's portrait. And if he did, doubtless, he would have been gauche enough to request a miniature!

"Ah, Reggie," she whispered, laughing at herself. He had won all. Not only had he bested her in their contest and was now freed of both herself and the princess but could henceforth freely indulge himself with his actresses and noble ladies to his heart's content. While she had lost indeed. For she was not a lady who played nipcheese with her emotions. Whatever she did, she did wholeheartedly.

In the weeks that followed, Emmalie fought a valiant battle with grief and conquered it. She was back riding about the country, back playing with Gnasher, and even back to reading, although her choice of matter was now more philosophic than romantic. But then, slowly, a new battle began, as Emmalie was visited by an emotion totally strange to her. That shameful companion of lost love one least likes to admit as more than a nodding acquaintance—jealousy.

Images of Reginald and this Miss Kitty Jones would reoccur at every inopportunity. To rid herself of their specters, she resolved to view the viscount and his new lady together. But how could this be contrived? She could hardly go to the theater in London and be, as her mother had, an observer of the viscount's adoration of his lady love onstage! Not with the entire ton watching her watching them and smiling at her suffering. Yet she *must* see them. And both together! That might be the only way to scotch their power over her dreams at night, which left her restless—through all the hours of the day as well. She must uncover why Miss Kitty had made the viscount so faithful even after Cornwall, must measure the depth of their mutual affections to measure the value of her own memories.

Jealousy was a ravenous master, admitting of no delay in its need to be fed with a viewing of the lady who had triumphed over her. For in truth, Emmalie could not readily recollect which actress Miss Jones was. She recalled a blonde who appeared with Kean in several plays. But not enough of an impression had been made to note her name. That could easily be discovered by consulting the playbill, but it had not been kept. One could of course attend a performance, for on second thought without her mother, none would recognize her. Or rather, she could even climb up, where none of her set ever deigned to ascend, to the twelve-penny gallery and observe all from there. But no, she wanted a closer sighting. Much closer. Indeed, only a direct meeting with this Miss Jones would suffice, mayhap a confrontation!

And then, of a sudden, the golden lights in Emmalie's eyes began to expand. Thankfully Miss Spinny was not in the room to see them and quake at the wild deed portended. At the end of her tether Emmalie oft relied on pure pluck. As during a game of chess played with the viscount, when Emmalie had paused, and he'd asked, "What, lurched, Malie?" in the softer tone used during their Cornwall time. And she, seeing a daring move, had laughed and neatly checkmated him. And he, rather than chagrined, had laughed with her, affectionately calling her his "madcap" and admitting she'd landed him a facer!—exceedingly admiring the boldness of the move.

Well, his madcap had another rather daring move. One that had simply flashed full blown into her mind, which hopefully would lead to another checkmating! "Not lurched this time either, my lord," she whispered. A small smile was permitted to make an appearance on her face, after so long being denied. She welcomed it. Broadened it. The prospect ahead had such possibilities and prodded so incessantly, Emmalie could not but promptly obey. Thereupon, she sought Spinny and made an announcement to the startled and then delighted lady of their immediate departure for London.

CHAPTER TEN

DRURY LANE THEATER DID NOT PRESENT A DIFFICULTY for a lady of Miss Marlowe's obvious gentility to enter. Although a guard to the backstage door opened his eyes to object and then closed them at the weight of a shilling in his palm. Walking farther into that area, she noted it was rather shadowed. Which was fitting, as her plans were similarly in the dark. Initially her purpose was simply a few moment's converse with this Miss Kitty. The possibility of making herself known to the lady created the difficulty. Every form of reference to herself made her sink. "I am Miss Marlowe" was unhelpful, for the actress might destroy her by a simple: "Who?" Nor could she continue with an explanatory, "I am the lady abandoned by your current beau." Further, what could she ask Miss Kitty? Observing her from afar might suffice, after all. On the other hand, what point to observe the beauty of her rival? Would that not merely lead to torment?

Her heart acknowledged the sense of her head's objections and yet answered: She *must* see! See what? her head persisted. And the answer was twofold: whom he preferred to her. And how far she should have to change to intrigue him again. Or admit she could never do so, which would at least wrest Reggie from her heart where he still abode. "It is an exorcism," she said aloud and earned a glance from a passing man, but he walked on, accustomed in that place to people talking to themselves. Here, actors dwelled, after all.

Relieved, Miss Marlowe hid deeper into the shadows. Raising her skirt, she stepped over some boxes and planks. Around the bend were several doors. Having once followed her mother to congratulate an actress on her performance, she knew these as the rooms where the actors changed and rested. There was the danger one might commit a serious faux pas by entering a gentleman's room and find him in a state of dishabille! They were oft thus, she'd heard; and she simply could not bring herself to even knock without some assurance on that point. Rather, she stepped back against a conveniently placed chair and accepting its function, sat.

One had to own oneself prodigiously fatigued. Not only had she just concluded a hurried trip to London, but she had been obliged to find lodgings for herself and her maid. At the last minute Spinny was indisposed and remained at the castle. It, therefore, was the first time Emmalie was so totally on her own. An inn nearby the theater had somewhat of a respectable air and yet not likely to be frequented by any of her mother's friends. There Emmalie recouped her energy after the several days' travel to London. And this morning, dressed neatly but not in the height of fashion, she arrived by hack at Drury Lane. Somehow she expected Miss Jones to be waiting for her, perhaps just exiting as she approached, and it would have been helpful as well if the viscount were on her arm for identification purposes. Further, it would also be vastly accommodating if the couple exuded a sense of complete union, so that her hopes should instantly be stilled. And then properly chastened, she could return to Cornwall.

But no such opportune sighting occurred. And so she proceeded within. Admittedly, she had been acting at variance to the commandments for jumping fences. The principle one was not to rush one's fences and secondly, when heading for a jump, never, last moment, pull back, unless one wished to assure a fall. Having broken the former by arriving unprepared at Drury Lane, she would at least honor the latter and carry on. She walked about. At one point, Emmalie had considered gaining introduction to the entire Drury Lane company through several people she had met through her mother. Indeed, Mr. Edmund Kean himself and his actress wife had been to one of Lady Leonie's soirees. Eventually hearing her ladyship preferred the Kemble style of performing, all subsequent invitations were refused. The *on dit* was that Mr. Kean, resenting all the nobles' patronizing ways, had refused even a party for a royal duke, claiming he had been invited not for himself but "as a wild beast to be stared at!"

While thinking of this Kean bestial remark, it was rather apropos that Emmalie should imagine she was actually seeing an animal. Several times she attempted to blink away the mirage. But it remained, coming closer on softly padded, clawed feet. A genuine, golden, growling lion.

In a moment the lion turned its great head and spotted the small young lady quivering in her chair.

Curious, the king of beasts slowly approached for an introduction.

Urging herself to hold her ground as the animal neared, Emmalie once again proved, as she had often done, that she was game as a pebble. She did not bolt, although her eyes roamed the area for assistance. Other people were within call, and that assured her. She made some small attempts to attract their attention, but as had been the case all her life, they passed her by. Her own mind must then rescue her. And it was obliging enough to do so. It realized that none of the people about were showing signs of alarm, which must mean the lion was tame. Mayhap even part of the troupe. Then her memory helpfully recalled some whispers about Edmund Kean's singularities: he owned a large animal of some size. . . . Except she was certain it was a large black horse called Shylock, which he used to ride up the stairs of the theater. That triggered the memory of the *on dit* about the actor's being spotted with a lion on a wherry boat on the Thames! Not believed at the time, but here was the reality before her. Emmalie stood up to her full height and sternly reminded herself the lion approaching was merely a rather large backstage cat.

Now the lion and Emmalie were almost within waltzing distance apart. Sniffing no fear, the lion gracefully circled the diminutive lady. Even when he brushed against her, Emmalie would not budge, facing him steadfastly. With a low rumble and almost a bow, the cat was ready to step away, not sensing either a threat or a treat. But Emmalie did not wish him to leave her. Not since Boots did Emmalie have a cat of her own, and she attempted to establish a relationship with this one by extending her hand for him to sniff. Understanding she was making advances, he regally considered the matter. And when she slowly, slowly, not making any sudden moves, reached his mane and rested her hand there, he did not shake her off. Instead he condescended to rub against her, marking her with his scent as his property. His rubbing almost unbalanced the delicate lady, but she refused to break their connection, feeling a wave of love for the golden beast, and she exclaimed with fervor, "You are quite a dear, are you not?"

Obligingly the lion bobbed his entire body, as if in assent, but more, indicating by this shaking of his mane that he deemed himself rather more than that. Something of Mr. Kean's ego apparently had been transmitted to the pet. "You are magnificent," Emmalie quickly amended, stroking him in such a way that he found pleasurable, accepting her presence. A few moments more and they had fast sealed their friendship. Giving it her official stamp, Emmalie concluded with loving affection, "I shall call you Boots, shall I?"

"You bloody well shall not!" a strong voice came across the entire backstage area like a rippling thunderbolt. Emmalie jumped back. The lion was off in a whirl, rising up and resting his front paws on the small man's shoulders. Casually and with no respect for the lion's reputation, the man pushed him down with a light blow. "Down, Caesar, down boy! Are you in the mood for a boat ride, old thing? Shall you support me in my role of captain of my rowboat across the Thames?"

"When comes such another!" Emmalie gasped.

At that, the dark, unusually brilliant eyes of the man turned their full attention on the girl. And with a small bow, he continued, "Indeed, although Antony is not one of my roles, I admit that line appropriate to Caesar here. But the phrase should have been said, so it rolled over the pit like thunder." And taking a deep breath, he demonstrated, beginning softly and with each succeeding word increasing the timbre and tempo, till the last word was an entire symphony of syllables. "When . . . comes . . . such . . . an . . . o . . . *therrrrrr!*"

"Indeed," Emmalie said, sighing. "When comes such another as you, Mr. Kean."

Pleased by both her statement and her recognition and somewhat affected by the way Caesar was still rubbing against the young girl, Mr. Kean was prepared to be tolerant. "Did you come back here with the objective of meeting me?" he asked.

Emmalie was sufficiently awake upon every suit to agree that was her only objective. He accepted that as natural and allowed her to shake his hand. He would have then turned his heel and gone off on his jaunt with Caesar, but Emmalie, cognizant of an opportunity, seized it. "Is that all? Must I spend my entire life regretting I was in the great Mr. Kean's presence for but an instant?" Having lived all her life with a lady of prodigious self-consequence, she naturally knew the correct approach.

Fairly caught by that appeal, he allowed a few further moments of her basking in the sun of himself. But more he could not give her: first because she did not appeal to him, but mostly because her voice and comportment were suspiciously that of a lady! And the actor had had sufficient noblesse oblige for a lifetime. Especially of ladies who wished to wear him on their arm like a reticule. So he bowed and attempted once more to depart, but Emmalie raised her voice. Had he ever had a dream out of reach? If so, he would empathize with hers, which was to appear on the boards with the greatest actor of all time, Edmund Kean.

This time possibly her Spanish coin rang too false, for he was frowning and fiercely fixing her with his magnetic glance. He himself had languished in the outlands for years of poverty and lack of recognition, despite his great talent. And this little snip presumed she could so gammon him to use his offices for her to skip the training in the provinces and immediately appear at Drury Lane, London's premier stage, and with *Kean*! Never! And he told her as much.

Having made a mull, Emmalie with alacrity altered her request; she had not the smallest wish to be on the stage, rather she could read scripts or prompt, just for a day or two to be part of the Drury Lane family.

"Madam, you forget yourself. One is born into the family of acting, it is not a pastime for ladies with no interest in our art!"

"I! No interest? The moments you have given us onstage, Mr. Kean, are seared into my consciousness—as if you had branded your initials there with the fire of your voice! I refer particularly to that moment when you, as Hamlet, addressed your father, the ghost. All other performers have been content to shout after him: 'I'll call thee Hamlet, King, father, Royal Dane.' But you paused and put the pain of all loss in your voice when softy *whispering*, 'father.' Heavens, I am still in a twitter. Having myself freshly lost my father, Hamlet spoke for me. Indeed, you personally plucked Hamlet out of the stiff declamatory Kemble style and made him a *person*."

Mr. Kean was pleased to expand upon how he had performed this marvel, and they would have been set for an hour's discussion but for Caesar's distracting them with a small roar. Feeling she had not quite secured her position, Emmalie merely leaned against Caesar, using Negus's favorite continuous stroking style to silence him, and attracted Mr. Kean by recollecting another favorite Kean moment: when Hamlet was parting from Ophelia, after ordering her to the nunnery. "You'd halfway left and then turned quickly and took the sobbing Ophelia's hand and kissed it. And *then* rushed off. I was near to swooning!"

Never had the actor found a lady so enamored with the little details of his craft. And he was perfectly willing to allow her panegyrics to continue unchecked. At that point Caesar, serving his master's interest, reacted as trained and inserted his paw under the lady's long skirt and lifted it up to a shocking height. Mr. Kean smiled expectantly. Caesar's trick always livened up their tavern jaunts, resulting in screams of laughter or sometimes anger. But this demure victim, although a lady and proving it by blushing fully, otherwise showed no alarm. Rather she rearranged her dress and calmly explained the proprieties to the beast. "For shame, sir. Would you have me losing every vestige of decency? In our Society ladies must be clothed or be quite cast down. Ah, but you're such a darling, you just did not understand."

Caesar nudged her in apology and was rewarded by a hug.

Actually Caesar's dress-lift was Mr. Kean's test of a lady's willingness to serve him during his intermissions. It saved him from overstepping and yet allowed his not missing an opportunity. But this girl, lady, child— seemed above his testing. And her looking at him with the same affection and fellow good feeling she directed toward Caesar had Mr. Kean uncertain about her altogether.

Of a sudden he did a backward flip that had her gasping. She clapped her hands as a youngster would.

149

"I was once an unsurpassed Harlequin," he confided, straightening his hair and basking in her admiration. A few more jumps had her and Caesar in a heaven of a state. Modestly, he bowed and sat down on the floor next to Caesar—the lady on her chair and they before her. All were set for a cozy chat, beginning with his favorite tale of how he spent a lifetime in the provinces, never being appreciated—in poverty and starvation—and then in one year, two offers for London arrived. The first was to play Harlequin in a lesser theater. He took it, since his son was ill and he'd lost faith in his future, and then, then, just after writing his acceptance, came the offer to star at Drury Lane in Shakespeare! What could one do but take his dream come true, ignoring the other agreement. His fate cried out, he must harken to it and to the devil with the legal hassle that nearly prevented him from ever appearing on any stage.

Miss Marlowe made the expected outcry at that dread possibility, and he was able to assure her he had resolved all—but only by more humiliations, all of which she wished to hear. And so it was understood that since she was such an expert in the theater and especially on his performances, she might be of use in carrying his script and reading lines with the other actors. But the pay would be nominal. It could be nonexistent, she responded, her only wish was to be close to the company for at least a sennight. And so, it was accomplished.

Mr. Kean had power enough to make the Drury Lane committee acquiesce to him, and since he was resentful at being forced to appear in a play not of his choosing, he was not adverse to making some small demands on his own such as her engagement.

In not above a half hour's discussion with the manager, Miss Marlowe officially became a part of the Drury Lane Company until the end of the season, which was more than she needed, indeed more than she wished. On the following day Emmalie arrived to begin her duties. Mr. Kean was introducing her to the full company when he found himself in the embarrassing position of not knowing the lady's name. Skipping over that with an actor's ease, he advanced to the lady's recommendations. They were of the highest, indeed, of lionesque proportions. Attempting not to laugh, Emmalie remembered to give her thanks to Caesar. And later, when she was running lines with Mr. Kean from his new play *Bertram*, she let fall that her own predicament was not unlike that of Imogene, the heroine. For she, too, was in a similar predicament of being forced to wed by her . . . eh, family. Indeed, that was the reason, she confided, for her leaving home and not divulging her real name. Her hope was for some time of freedom here before she was uncovered and taken back to her fate. An emotional man, Mr Kean's sympathies were aroused, and he instantly became her fervent champion. As for a new name, nothing could be simpler, he would call her Ophelia, he claimed, with a wink, and repeated the gesture she had so much admired, kissing her hand with a flourish. When her eyes teared at that gesture, he was even more fired up to protect her. And henceforth, if any of the cast even hinted at her not being up to snuff, he quickly put them in their place.

So much of a defender was Mr. Kean, she was scarcely allowed to be spoken to by anyone, especially not of the male gender. A young man attempting to outstratagem Mr. Kean's protection was Mr. James Lovell, who according to Mr. Kean did not have a future in the business, being of the passé declamation school of acting.

Nevertheless for Emmalie the young Mr. Lovell's determined pursuit was rather pleasing. It was the first time a gentleman had shown interest in her for herself! So occupied was Emmalie in fending off Mr. Lovell's attentions and appeasing Mr. Kean's irritation, she almost missed the entrance of the leading actress of the company, the Imogene of the play, or Miss Kitty Jones herself!

Greeted by the obligatory "meowing," Kitty arched her back and smiled all round. She had jewels to show and compliments to tell. All of the gentlemen and some of the ladies clustered round to hear the particulars. Hurriedly edging closer, Emmalie looked her fill. The lady was imposingly tall and blazingly blond. There was a silhouette precision to her profile, explaining the reason for Miss Jones's oft playing her performances sideways. One expected the lady to be fair of face, Emmalie told herself, but not so perfectly featured. And so *perfectly* proportioned. A beauty indeed! Gone were all Emmalie's hopes of a blemish. Perhaps a tooth out of line? Not one. Nor could she detect even a mere squint in the actress's eye! Rather both orbs were round and deeply blue. And then Miss Kitty began to speak, and Emmalie breathed a relieved sigh. There *was* an imperfection. It was the actress herself.

Miss Jones's first act was to order an elderly actress out of her dressing room, refusing to share. Next was her comment upon Miss Ophelia Browne being brought to her notice. "Rather short for the boards, ain't she?" Which proved Miss Kitty did not think before she spoke, for she said it to Edmund Kean, who, similarly statured, did not find it either apt or endearing.

After this beginning, Emmalie, not having the smallest desire for another meeting, had to force herself to attempt further contact. Actually, Miss Kitty was accustomed to setting up others' backs, generally by her begrudging attendance at rehearsals, during which she clearly gave indication that she was saving her energy. Mr. Kean, with some tolerance, allowed that she was more animated onstage. "Watch her come to life when the young bucks rise up," he advised Emmalie. Which meant, Emmalie explained to herself, that the lady probably was totally different in a gentleman's presence, such as the viscount's—excusing his choice. Otherwise, she was near to assuming he had windmills in his head.

The most admirable member of the company, Emmalie deemed, always excepting Mr. Kean, was an elderly actress, Mrs. Windsor, on the boards for nigh on twenty years. She had clippings of herself in plays with Mrs. Siddons herself. Emmalie delighted in reading those and other reviews of Mrs. Windsor's performances as Lady Macbeth and Queen Gertrude. Apparently not a single actor was ever very far from his book of reviews. Every dressing room had one. Not to mention playbills and mounted posters. Mrs. Windsor was quite willing to share her expertise with the newest company member. And thus Emmalie found herself with a substitute for Miss Spindle, whom she'd sorely missed. Daily, she received instruction on everything from the natural way to speak in iambic pentameter to the correct procedure for applying color to the face. Although she knew her mother was not above the addition of some rouge, the amount of painting required for the stage had the girl in a continual blush. Indeed, with a laugh, Mrs. Windsor informed Mr. Lovell, who was always hovering close by, that there was not the smallest necessity for adding color to the young face, for the lady blushed through each session. And even at that story, Emmalie-Ophelia turned pink.

Yet that stage makeup uncovered a new, more attractive face for Emmalie. First she learned to study the shape of her eyes to best alter them to fit different characters. One lengthened one's eyes to depict women of easy virtue or sophistication and made a circular shape for young ladies who must observe life with wide open eyes, permanently painted on. One's voice and gestures were the main performing tools, but eyes were not far behind. Fluttering of lashes, downcast glances, direct stares—all had their place. Indirectly, she became aware that her eyes were her best feature which she could emphasize even for daily view. As well, a new arrangement of her hair was devised with front sections cut shorter and curled with a heated iron to form a fringe around her eyes which emphasized them. The new curls gave her height as well. The full style was given classic authenticity by being entitled: *à la Medusa*.

"Adorable," Mrs. Windsor exclaimed, pleased with her efforts. Mr. Lovell had so many compliments Emmalie's cheeks were continually afire. Never had Emmalie felt such a sense of family as she did among the troupe of Drury Lane. Of them all, the one person continually treating her with distance was Miss Kitty Jones. Yet Emmalie hovered quite close to the actress. For she had several objectives. First, to find a finer nature hidden under that peevish temper (not yet uncovered). Second, to steal an enhancing trick from the enchantress (no tricks, Miss Kitty was just plain exquisite by nature). Lastly and primarily, to view the actress with the viscount as originally planned (he had not yet presented himself at the theater—one had hopes, however, after the opening). Barring that, Emmalie attempted to subtly bring up Reggie's name in conversations with the star—which were rare, as the actress hardly condescended to familiarity with a lowly newcomer. She even refused to address Emmalie as Ophelia, deeming that an affectation. And addressing a younger lady as Miss Browne was too respectful, possibly suggesting Kitty herself was of a lower class. Therefore, she used the appellative of "Miss."

Most offensive to the leading lady was the differential way the rest of the troupe treated Miss Browne. Mr. Lovell bowed when bringing Emmalie her tea, and even Mr. Kean would wait for her to sit first. It was beyond bearing. Kitty could not resist correcting the novice. "Miss is not accustomed to our ways. Backstage, we is not standing on ceremony, Miss. Gentlemen sits as a lady stands. Nor does gentlemen bring ladies their refreshments. We is all on our own here. Except Mr. Kean. He has his man, Phillips."

Emmalie apologized with pretty confusion to all, but the gentlemen merely cast dark looks at Miss Kitty and insisted on treating Miss Browne with the gentility she deserved. So Miss Jones was in a deeper huff. Her only revenge was to flaunt her success with gentlemen of the ton, hoping this mousy lady would turn pea green. The first reference to her titled suitor produced more of a reaction than even Miss Kitty had hoped. She had the lady's total attention. And even more so when she continued, "I got me a sweetie who is good to me and treats me like a lady, for all he is a *lord* and all. And if I is planning to be one with his lordship, I says only— stranger things have happened."

"Are you referring to the Viscount Wynnclife?" Emmalie asked bluntly.

Toying with her a bit, Miss Kitty hid a smile behind her hand. With some agony Emmalie waited for the reply. But seeing her audience fully absorbed, Kitty, with her actress's training, bided her time before stage-whispering, "I calls him 'Wynnie' . . . cause he whinnies on my entrances, and cause he calls me a 'prime piece of flesh' . . . *and* cause he whinnies when . . ." She stopped abruptly and "he-heed" behind her hand, asking that she not be pressed for further revelations. Miss Marlowe stiffly agreed. Upon which compliance Miss Kitty frowned and added, "Cause if you was to ask for more, I is so open, I would tell all and very like might shock such a delicate little miss."

And she winked so broadly at her listener, Emmalie could only flush and hurriedly depart.

Broadly was the most apt term for the actress, Mrs. Windsor claimed upon realizing Ophelia Browne was in a rare tweak because of that performer's airs. "On-stage I should say she breaks every one of Hamlet's injunctions to the players. She 'out-Herods,' she struts and bellows and always sets on the barren spectators to laugh, showing the most pitiful ambition of a fool."

But it was Miss Kitty's fan that put most of the cast

in some dudgeon. She made prodigious and scandalous use of it, detracting from their lines. Even offstage the fan was kept in motion, Emmalie observed. Closed, it was stuck into the low décolletage of Miss Kitty's gowns and fished for before all with many a wink. Whereupon, she would open it and fan that part of her anatomy which had housed the fan previously. Oft, she would simply walk about with the closed fan sticking out of her cleavage. This was also done onstage, Emmalie was informed, much to the delight of her admirers. But the main use of her fan during a performance was to call to mind her lines.

"Whenever Miss Jones goes dry," Mr. Kean exclaimed in disgust, while teaching Miss Ophelia Browne the importance of a thorough knowledge of one's lines, "she brings out her trusty fan to fan her memory into operation. Shoddy practice, that! Although I've heard of writing key words on one's hand as well. But neither is a practice a professional would employ!"

"A professional she might be," Mrs. Windsor inserted, "but certainly not a professional actress."

General laughter. Not that Miss Jones cared a whit for her fellow actors' estimation of her talent. For without engaging in scarce half the training or effort of the others, she had already achieved top billing and benefits. And to keep both she had her own claque. And she had her own viscount as well. She scarce needed more. And gave her own kind of advice to Emmalie.

"Well, Miss, I am a-thinking if you is set to be an actress, you best not waste your time reading all them plays. An actress need only read her part. La! I never bother with the rest."

"Heavens! Then you don't know the outcome, or why Imogene says what she does, or even what happens to Bertram after Imogene's death!" Emmalie exclaimed in wonder.

"Why should I? All I do is count the speeches and how often I is speaking alone. And not enough in this one, which first made me monstrous angry. And I said to Mr. Kean, 'La, me followers will make quite a brouhaha if I isn't given enough to say and time to strut.' And he said something in Latin, and I says, 'You knows, Mr. Kean, how I don't speak naught but English.' And he says, 'If that.' So I was monstrous peeved, Miss. But things always is for the best. My not speaking gives me time to spot the bucks and ogle my sweetie.'' And she broadly winked and dove into her décolletage for her fan and with it gave the shocked lady a humorous poke in the ribs. All of which Emmalie bore with a set smile, realizing this was her opportunity to introduce the topic necessary for her peace of mind—or the viscount's current whereabouts.

Flushing at her lack of delicacy, nevertheless, Emmalie forced herself to say, ''And your sweetie, eh, the Viscount Wynncliffe . . . is that who is going to be watching you?''

Miss Kitty merely winked.

Disappointed and determined, Emmalie pressed. ''He has not been to visit of late?''

The beautiful actress wrinkled up her nose and whispered mysteriously, ''He comes when he comes.'' And then he-heed herself off, leaving Emmalie at liberty to think what she would.

Berating herself for not directly asking when the viscount would be making his appearance, Emmalie hoped for another opportunity. But it did not present itself. Every moment of Emmalie's private time was taken up by the antics of Mr. Lovell and Caesar. She ran away from the former and ran about with the latter. Caesar had begun to feel that Emmalie was his own private plaything and oft would not permit even Mr. Kean to approach her too closely.

In that regard Emmalie felt him more of a chaperone than Spinny. Whenever Mr. Lovell dared come too near to her person, Emmalie had merely to raise her voice and that actor, loudly complaining, was sent running to the protection of his dressing room, while Caesar was rewarded with a hug and a kiss.

Having too much confidence to assume Ophelia Browne really did not wish for his attentions, Mr. Lovell protested, "By Jove, why are you holding me off? I am heroically cast by nature. And thus must always be the hero to every young lady. Come to my dressing room to see the letters displayed—most from ladies of the highest ton. They invite me for tea and hope I shall remain for a private tête-à-tête. You've heard of Lady Bessborough's daughter, Lady Caroline Lamb, who disgraced herself over Lord Byron? By Jove, she has sent me a letter that says, 'That pale face shall be my death.' "

"Then she is remarkably repetitive, by Jove," Emmalie replied, mimicking his aping his betters by his constant use of ton slang.

"What do you mean, by Jove?"

"Merely that Lady Caroline said exactly the same words to my mo . . . eh, to another, concerning *Lord Byron*."

"If, by Jove, you doubt, I ask merely that you come to my dressing room for the proof! And I shall dashed well show you moreover the scope of my feelings for you. Just step into it, you shall not regret what awaits you there, by Jove!"

"I believe I shall . . ." she said softly, and then with a smile added, "regret it, I mean." And left him chagrined. There was no possibility that Emmalie, even as Ophelia Browne, would enter a gentleman's dressing room. It was well known what a lady could expect visiting there. That was especially the case, Emmalie heard with regret, in regard to Mr. Kean's rooms. No one dared interrupt when the door was closed, for he was inevitably occupied with ladies from the taverns. Mr. Lovell had attempted to follow the leading actor's lead but found performing between acts lessened the quality of his performance onstage. This carousing and wenching, Mrs. Windsor felt, gave a disgust of all actors when it was not the general theatrical mode of behavior. Certainly Mr. Kemble, an actor she had often appeared with at Covent Garden, would not be guilty of such excess. She faulted Mr. Kean for setting this repugnant example, which was gradually tainting the entire moral climate of Drury Lane. And she protected her new young friend fiercely, almost as devotedly as Caesar, keeping a watchful eye out for her.

Not that Emmalie ever was in danger of a dalliance, since she rarely was free of her duties running lines from the moment sufficient actors discovered she possessed a remarkable memory for all the parts. She could quite outprompt the prompter. That ability was the reason, along with Mrs. Windsor's urging, that Ophelia Browne was given the added responsibility of understudying the female roles. As yet, there had been no need of her services, nor likely would there ever be, the frightened young lady was assured. For only at the point of cocking up one's toes would an actress surrender her moment of glory. In the interim, however, and as per custom, she was called upon to appear in one afternoon's rehearsal with the full company for the leading lady's part. Since Emmalie was among friends, she took all with tolerable composure, similar to reading novels aloud with a certain lord. Any suggestion given was taken with gratitude. Hence, so many were of so conflicting a nature, she soon found herself unable to perform at all. At that, Mr. Kean took her aside, and speaking as he rarely did, with disinterest, he urged her, "Think of the character only. Forget all these tricks of drawing out one's voice and walking to stage right or left. That is for bored actors who need to make one's performance into a simple technique one can follow night after night. I say two words: Be Imogene. And she shall tell you how to speak and move for her. Be her."

And Emmalie realized that actually was the only way

at that late date she could perform. She had to turn to the one gift she'd always possessed in surplus: imagination. And with a bow to Mr. Kean, she gave him her hand and became Imogene. Knowing the character's situation so well and sympathizing so deeply, she was soon living Imogene's life.

The rehearsal was concluded with a round of applause from all the actors and another kissing of her hand by Mr. Kean. "You have done it! You walked into her skin."

That baptismal over, Emmalie relaxed. But everybody warned this was the end of all ease, for coming hard upon was opening night—that dread yet desired moment above all. It was nigh. It was the night!

Bertram began with a wild storm and continued with shrieks of madness. It concluded in another storm of applause. This Gothic drama appealed to the audience's love of excess, for it had everything from haunted castles to murder and madness. Imogene's scene that should have been memorable, Miss Jones turned into a betting session on how far she would bend over when curtsying. Thus she showed her full talents. Her acting had Emmalie wondering why she was given any roles, until her powerful following made itself known. Indeed, groups of bucks attended in the pit just for the pleasure of seeing her in her very act of bending over, and then the crème de la crème of Society's gentlemen purred aloud in pleasure. It was small wonder the Drury Lane Committee continually renewed her contract. Then, too, Mr. Kean always preferred lesser actresses and actors around him, for fear the spotlight would for a moment veer from him. Miss Kitty's applause was tolerable, since it was simply for her physical appearance and not her performance. Indeed, there had been a moment after Emmalie's demonstrating some talent in the rehearsal that he had withdrawn himself, treating her with a degree of aloofness that only melted when he realized she would not be repeating her mistake.

Never having had a family, being part of this group had been a happy time for Emmalie, and she had almost forgotten the existence of the viscount. Certainly he was not making himself visible around Miss Jones. Wild hopes that he had repented of his momentary lapse and might even have returned to Cornwall sprung up to be replaced by the more likely scenario that he had gone on to another lady. A hurried note to Miss Spindle earned a reply of a full sheet in which she had crossed her lines closely with many a fear for her safety, but with the information that she had not heard a word from the viscount. It was the second possibility then, and here Emmalie was wasting her time living in this private world behind stage. Yet she felt obligated to stay until the season was over.

The memory of the viscount often most painfully occurred upon hearing two of the most moving lines of the play. Indeed, they continued to sound in her ears and echo in her soul. "Have we not loved as none have ever loved. And must we part as none have ever parted?" She had loved, at least, as none had ever loved, and they had parted as none had ever parted. And now, after having followed the viscount, she found him still parting from her.

Miss Jones made another reference to her "Wynnie," which had Emmalie questioning her about how faithful his lordship was, since it was a sennight after the opening and he'd not yet been to a performance. Thoroughly squelching Emmalie, the golden lady responded he had been to *several* showings. Possibly Miss, having never had the honor of personally meeting the viscount, did not recognize him as he was not occupying his usual box, rather had joined his friends in the pit for closer viewing of herself—although he had *privately* many a much closer viewing of her person, Miss Kitty he-heed, leaving "Miss" flummoxed.

During that evening's performance, Emmalie positioned herself in the wings and peeked out. Despite initial varied reviews, word of mouth had turned the play into a prodigious success. Not only the pit and boxes but the gallery was packed and groaning, echoing the actors' torment. She concentrated on the pit as advised by Miss Kitty. Yes, he was there! She was riveted. It was his old social self, dressed complete to a shade: starched neckcloth, quizzing glass, signet ring, hair fashionably cropped. And then she gasped. Intolerable, he was laughing through every speech. All this time Miss Marlowe had not been part of this company's heartbreaking effort for perfection without becoming one with them. And his lordship's finding the tragedy so humorous was a direct insult to herself as well. He was apparently vastly entertained by people opening their whole hearts before him, she concluded grimly. Yet she was unable to stop gazing at his every ironic expression. Not until the stagehands pushed her aside in their efforts to move the sets did Emmalie finally abandon her position and retreat to her dressing room where she could more properly conceal her emotions.

She had more feelings to contain on the next night as well, when it was whispered that Miss Kitty would, in the intermission, be receiving in her dressing room none other than her current "sweetie," the Viscount of Wynnclife.

It was exactly what Emmalie had come to Drury Lane to observe: Reggie and Miss Kitty in an intimate situation. Somehow she could not believe the two were a pair. Obviously she had to have it shown to her, and only then could she break out of the spell Reggie had cast on her. And with this resolve Emmalie stepped out of her room into the hall.

As was required for an understudy, Emmalie was dressed as Imogene, which minimized the likelihood of the viscount's recognizing her. Further, he would scarcely be expecting to see Miss Emmalie Marlowe in such a surrounding. One usually saw people only in relation to their position. Indeed, Imogene's long blond wig which, having been made for Miss Jones, was of such size (the hair ending almost at her ankles and hiding almost Emmalie's entire person) it gave her confidence to walk directly to the entrance of Miss Kitty's dressing room. Not that she intended to do more than glimpse in. Already there was a want of delicacy about her behavior that persuaded Emmalie not to linger more than was natural—en passant. Hopefully she should at least observe the viscount's first greeting of his lady-love. Maybe even their embrace. But just then, Mrs. Windsor entered their dressing room with the word that the Viscount of Wynnclife, no less, was already in Miss Jones's dressing room. "He arrived before the act was over and waited. A clear indication of his eagerness, one would say," the elderly actress said with a laugh. Thus Emmalie had verified by a reliable source what she knew was so but just hoped, wildly, madly, was not. For since having come to know Miss Kitty Jones, Miss Marlowe had concluded that if Reggie was truly besotted by that goosish, totty-headed twit, Emmalie had seriously misjudged him. In effect, built him up to a grandeur that his very acquaintance with Miss Kitty deflated. Still, after all this effort, she would not trust to hearsay. She would see the two. Snoop, if she must! This emotion for the viscount, that flared at just viewing him in the pit, had to be put out!

Accommodating fate made all easy for Miss Marlowe. The dressing room door was ajar, so within was clearly observable from a distance. Indeed, it appeared like a stage set, with a lamp arranged in such a way that the viscount's blond head was visible to all. Obviously Miss Kitty preferred an audience for every performance. Knowing she was following the actress's cue, still Emmalie could not resist approaching closer. There was the viscount with quizzing glass raised for full observation of Miss Jones in her costume, and then, languidly he let it fall, as he remarked, "My dear Kitty. No matter the long wig nor the wide-eyed circling of your eyes, you simply cannot personify a pathetic, imposed-upon *maiden*. In faith, you are too much of a woman!''

Pleased by that observation, Kitty he-heed and resorted to her closed fan which she used as a dagger, pointing its tip menacingly at his lordship and then slowly touching him with it on various parts of his anatomy. "You oughta know how much of a woman I is, Wynnie. But I is more of a woman today, since you give me this sparkler of a ring.''

Kissing her hand, Reggie captured the fan now being dragged up and down his thighs, and then he deposited it boldly within the lady's bodice. "Keep your fan where it belongs, my girl, until I request demonstration of its wanton ways.''

Curtain time being called, he wished her well for her performance. He should be viewing her every move and purring along with the rest of them, he said, then jauntily exited. Instantly Emmalie stepped back and would have tripped if Mr. Kean had not appeared behind her and caught her in his arms. Thus when the viscount passed them by, he saw merely another one of Kean's ladies being embraced by the actor.

"You are at it rather early, Edmund," he said with a grin. "Does this bode ill or well for the performance?''

"I have never *not* performed well,'' Mr. Kean replied and cursed the lord under his breath. "These starched-up lords and their assumptions that life is a play with them eternally playing lead!'' he said bitingly as the viscount nimbly raced down the stage stairs.

"I wish he would trip,'' was all Emmalie said, but it delighted Mr. Kean.

This mention of someone's tripping was actually quite prophetic, for Miss Jones tripped on her entrance, too distracted by her eyeing the viscount in the pit. She performed valiantly throughout the first act, only ruining the entire play by having the audience more concerned by her obvious limping and her groans of pain than the plot being unfolded! Every second sentence she grabbed her ankle or lifted her skirt to be applauded for the shape of the injured limb.

During intermission, the viscount came running to inquire after her welfare. But his commiseration was cut off by the entrance of an enraged Kean, demanding she stop upstaging him with her groans.

"But I is in pain!" she complained.

"Suppress it! Damn it! Your only groans should be those that must come from Imogene's lips! Husband them, if you please, until the mad scene. And then let loose! You might finally bring some pathos to a scene you have been performing as if you were a stock! Otherwise speak and sigh only what is set down. Balls o' fire, you are driving me mad!"

In cold hauteur the viscount interfered to inform Mr. Kean that Miss Jones was never to be addressed in such a fashion in his presence.

"You go to the devil as well!" the outraged Kean continued and then threw some Latin phrases that usually totally intimidated all other opponents. But the viscount was not only not flustered but rather responded in kind, which elevated Kean's fury, for he could never bear being bested. The duel then turned to lines from plays. As long as Kean kept to Shakespeare, Reggie could give a good account of himself, but when he began on the light comedies, Reggie merely grinned. His self-consequence not involved in this joust, he allowed that he could scarcely outdo an actor in knowledge of his lines, which had Mr. Kean exclaiming, "I am not *an* actor, my lord, I am *the actor*!"

At that point Kitty, to get their attention, stamped her injured foot so forcibly, she let out a howl that was heard beyond the footlights. And after that, her groans were so prodigious, one had to listen between them to understand her refusal to carry on with her performance. Which had Kean even wilder. Never had he heard such lack of professionalism! Kitty continued crying and then sought the comfort of her lover, leaning against the amused viscount, who perfunctorily patted her shoulder.

"This is a better performance than you ever gave on-stage!" Mr. Kean cried out. "But then, I expect, this is the place where you do your best acting! Stay in your lover-lord's arms; we are fortunate to have a genuine actress in the wings. Ophelia shall take your place!" And on that line Edmund Kean turned on his heel and exited.

Thereto Miss Kitty Jones was up on her feet—both of them—crying, "Miss shall not take me place, not while I can hobble on!" And hobble on she did.

An amused viscount followed in her hopping wake. Hidden by a crowd of laughing onlookers, Emmalie hung back, somberly staring at her once great love passing inches from her face, and once again, as in the beginning of their relationship, not seeing her.

CHAPTER ELEVEN

THE NEXT DAY THE ENTIRE PLAY WAS IN A HOBBLE, for Miss Kitty once again announced she would not perform the play as it was. She made them reblock the performance and assign various actors to carry her around the stage.

That was not liked above half—neither by Mr. Kean, who resented further distraction, nor by any of the actors chosen for the privilege of bearing the leading lady about. Once again Miss Browne was suggested. Once again Miss Kitty valiantly agreed to attempt another appearance, and Miss Browne was informed by Mr. Kean that she would not be needed. "Our Kitty is going to make an ass of herself tonight, so that rather than purring for her, the pit shall be braying—at us all!"

The relief on Emmalie's face had him laughing aloud—but he said truthfully and in an attempt to give her courage, in case she might be called upon to appear sometime, "Even at your worst you would perform better than that viscount's plaything!"

That last description wiped out Miss Marlowe's joy at her compliment. And yet Mr. Kean's sarcastic view of the two lovers forced Emmalie to stop gammoning herself. His lordship and the actress were hardly a devoted couple. Rather than evidencing a sincere regard for each other's presence, they seemed to regard the other only as the source for mutual presents—of the monetary or physical nature.

What felt Emmalie after this humiliating admission!

The lesser the new love, the lesser must have been the one abandoned as well. If one could exchange a guinea for a shilling, how devalued now the guinea? Herself, of course, being the guinea, she concluded with a grin at her assessment. Keeping it in the numismatic vein, not only had Reggie originally been giving her Spanish coin in his declaration of love, but now he himself seemed to have lost much of his own metal by this twopenny theatrical involvement. It should be quite easy to forget a gentleman of such *little* value. Except it was not. Rather her hopes were once more raised. Could it be that since his feelings for Miss Kitty were diminishing, Reggie might be considering returning to her? And if he did, could she possibly want him? she asked her heart. It remained silent. Not so composed was her heart, however, the following evening, upon her walking into the theater and viewing a handbill being distributed. Indeed, her heart was almost in full arrest as she read that Ophelia Browne was scheduled for tonight's performance.

"Your moment has come!" cried Mr. Kean, in much the manner that a hangman would address a prisoner.

Shrinking, eyes widening in terror, larger than any paint had been able to create, Emmalie responded, "No, indeed! You all assured me this should never come to pass. No! Dear heavens, *no*!"

"Yes, by Jove," Mr. Lovell cried out. "And I am dashed delighted! Finally the action of the play shall have first consideration, rather than whether a certain Miss Kitty can navigate from door to chair!"

Mrs. Windsor, not allowing her protégé to protest any further, put her arms about her, smothering her with effusive felicitations and her usual flowing, scene-stealing silk scarf. "Good God, child, are you aware of what awaits you? Do not refine too much on the problems, but rather that you are about to experience one of the glories of life! To be onstage before a houseful of people, all waiting only for your next word—all sitting patiently and observing your every gesture, eager to laugh or cry with you, is a delight of such proportions that can never be forgotten. It is a draught of delight. A heady brew that shall go to your head, and you shall never again see yourself the same—as of no importance or of lesser than others. For once you have led an audience, had them in the palm of your hand, you can lead and control any *one* person.''

Mr. Kean keenly appreciated the comparison to acting as a heady brew and suggested that such a draught be prepared for Miss Browne to give her white cheeks some color and a little lively buzz to her veins. Mrs. Windsor disdainfully assured Mr. Kean there was sufficient color in the young lady's cheeks, and she needed no further stimulant, that, indeed, *no actor* needed any stimulant beyond the applause of the crowd. She said that pointedly to both Mr. Kean and Mr. Lovell, who apparently already had had a pint.

Once more Emmalie attempted to interrupt their discussions to assure them that she was not up to the occasion, that the thought of so many people's eyes on her was sufficient to put her into a swoon, and since they then should have to carry her about—just as well as they had refused to do Miss Kitty—it was much better if Miss Kitty could be persuaded . . .

''But the lady has not even had the courtesy to attempt to perform,'' Mr. Lovell exclaimed in a huff. ''A note sent round,'' he continued, ''informed us of her inability.''

''Every performance informs us of her inability,'' declared Mr. Kean, making his aside broader, as if talking to the audience at the footlights.

''By Jove,'' Mr. Lovell carried on, still sunk in his grievance. ''Tonight her complaint is not a sprained ankle but a strained relationship with her noble lord. We should announce to the audience Miss Jones is unable to appear due to a previous amorous commitment in reality.''

"*Realty* commitment say rather, dear boy. It is our dear Kitty's last (wobbly) stand to wheedle an estate from her recalcitrant lord."

With an immediacy she could hardly credit, Emmalie forgot about that night's performance and questioned Mr. Lovell and Mr. Kean as to their source of knowledge.

"By Jove," Mr. Lovell exclaimed, "the source is herself."

"As always," Mr. Kean inserted. But the great actor was rather restless, tending to find discussions in which he was not the topic limited in interest.

Au contraire Mr. Lovell delighted in backstage bumblebroth, and to prove his inner knowledge, he gave Miss Ophelia Browne the particulars. "Ever since hearing her viscount had given a castle to his fiancée, a prim young daughter of nobility, our Kitty was as vocal as a town crier." Using a high falsetto voice, he mimicked Kitty's exact words: " 'I ain't swallowin' it! Everything to her who am nothing to him and me who am everything to him gets naught!' And then when his lordship stopped coming round, she was yowling like a cat about to be drowned. Gad, who knows what happened, but one weekend she came back purring like a cat that had gotten into the cream, claiming she had an estate practically in her pocket."

"What the devil do you mean, Lovell, discussing these *on dits*?" Mr. Kean demanded sharply, losing his last bit of patience. "Are we giving a performance tonight, or shall I order tea and we can all sit around back here chatting, while the audience wonders why they've paid their blasted shillings!"

Mr. Kean had worked himself into one of his usual rages, causing Mr. Lovell, accustomed to them, to hardly flinch. Although he did move on, throwing back a reassurance to Miss Browne that acting was merely like expressing one's love for a lady (or in her case, gentleman) with this difference: that one did it to a whole audience rather than to just one. And with that, he winked intimately at her and took himself off to dress.

Bristling at an underling giving directions while he was present, Mr. Kean turned to Emmalie and ordered her to listen only to himself, he was the expert, and she had already done well by following him, had she not? Her dress rehearsal performance of Imogene had been, if not professional, at least tolerable enough to be on the boards with him, and *that* he could not often say about any of this company. She must just again concentrate on her character. "Imogene is waiting. Do not allow yourself—neither your fears nor bodily ills—to deprive her of that one moment of existence."

So moved was Emmalie by that, and recollecting she had been Imogene before, and being swayed by Mr. Kean's fervor and presence, she assured him solemnly she should not let either him or Imogene down.

"But you are not to have a word to say about it! You are not to be thinking of me as Edmund Kean. I am Bertram! I am wildly devoted to you. We are in a castle, you and I, exchanging our love, and I shall wither the hearts of anyone who tries to take you from me, and you shall go mad for having lost me! Do you not feel all that? Do you not hear Imogene—her feelings kept suppressed in her bosom so long—crying out to all: 'I am alive! And *I love*!' ''

There were tears in Emmalie's eyes at that. She could only nod and allow herself to be whisked off by Mrs. Windsor to be dressed in Imogene's clothes. From then, up to the moment when she was set to walk onstage for the first time, she kept Mr. Kean's words in her mind and before stepping out, whispered to herself, "I know what it is to love, and I shall speak my love tonight to all and my grief at my loss. . . . For Imogene and I are one tonight and perhaps always!"

Once again tonight Reginald sat in the pit awaiting the appearance of his favorite, Miss Kitty Jones. This time he was accompanied by his friend, Lord Lanadale. The play was filled with so many screams and so much hyperbole, it was positively Gothic, he warned Basil. He must prepare himself for not only all the clichés and unrestrained emotion, but for a jolly good dose of humor when Kitty entered with her one expression of fixed alarm throughout. Indeed, the viscount had concluded privately that Kitty tilted one's life totally to satire as she equally did the play. Not that she was a comedienne, Kitty was unconsciously droll, which actually made her even more amusing. And after her injury, she surpassed even herself and turned *Bertram* into complete comedy. For the entire story line was then subordinated to how Kitty braved the pain and how and where she rested her injured limb. Settee, stool, even a handy doorknob was used for that purpose, causing her skirt to rise to such a point, the pit could only howl in appreciation at all the exposure of skin.

Her pretending to be surprised at the elevation in her clothes and primly putting them in order, only to have the same inadvertence overcome her a scene later, was prime watching. Quizzing glasses were being shined and held at a ready for these "inadvertencies" and the resulting displays.

The young bloods who had come purposely for Miss Kitty's displays were up on their feet at the announcement that Miss Kitty Jones would not be appearing tonight, as she had sustained some injury during the heat of a performance and was recuperating.

"During her performance of what?" was shouted out and received some laughter. But most were grumbling, and Miss Kitty's claque was roaring in disapprobation, until Mr. Kean was forced to appear to request their patience. He shamelessly pandered to their knowledge of the theater, to their love of the English language, and even to their fairness as Englishmen, which stopped their "meowing" as they began to preen at their uniqueness, content to allow the greatest actor of their time to perform for them. Even the viscount applauded and prepared to accept the play's being acted without its comic heart.

"Egad, Reggie old boy, ain't you concerned about your ladylove?" Basil queried. "Not going to run around and see how she does?"

"More likely with whom she does," the viscount said calmly.

"I say . . . what are you saying?"

"Simply that Kitty strays. . . . And when I refused her request for my Richmond holdings, she as much as told me it was not financially feasible for her to confine herself to one lover who was such a clutch-fist."

"This, after all the jewelry! Not to mention the carriages and town house!"

"Alack, my friend, when a relationship is based on monetary reasons, a lady, as an investor, is likely to demand a doubling of her dividends for her undivided attentions or she needs must multiply her sources. Perfectly understandable, I daresay. Would that all of one's affairs could be summed up so tidily." He spoke with indifference, dedicating so much attention to the precise polishing of his quizzing glass that Basil no longer felt concern for his companion. Indeed, Miss Kitty Jones had lasted longer than most.

The viscount was experiencing the relief he usually felt when an affair was over, and Miss Kitty had long since served her purpose of winning his release from Miss Marlowe. Actually Miss Kitty had only been tolerable for her blatancy. But she had been wearing out her amusement value. Being justly named, Miss Kitty not only had feline grace but a natural limitation in seeing another human's face. Oh, she was able to recognize the various gentlemen, especially those she'd marked as her possessions by rubbing them with her scent. Thus, it was always herself she recognized on them. Not to carry the simile to absurdity, she similarly remained faithful as long as one fed her.

Basil was quite eager to provide such provisions in order to possess this pet of a lady. To which Reggie gave him not only his permission but his heartfelt encouragement, that is, if he could bribe the actress away from the earl, whom apparently she was seeing tonight.

Elevating his glance, the viscount gave the boxes a minute examination and discerned no lady worth his bow. He nodded to one or two and then left off. Never had he felt himself in such a prodigious state of ennui. Dash it, he found social ladies too impossibly fluttery, thinking him most serious when he was jesting, and when serious, assuming him to be funning. Having recently had the ease of sharing his thoughts with another without having to say a word, this constant explanation of self set up his back. He'd as lief continue with ladies of Kitty's stamp, who needed no explanations. But they wore on one as well and had to be changed for freshness.

The sounds of a mighty storm silenced not only the viscount's self-thoughts but Basil's self-chatting. The play was beginning. While the audience leaned forward, preparing to be entranced, the viscount hung back, challenging them to even hold his attention. Before the end of Act One, both had been accomplished. Basil, having come to laugh, was rather moved. And as for Reggie, he found beyond the melodramatic plot were gleams of power—in the emotions of a man and woman pushed past conventions, past decorum . . . to open feeling! Undoubtedly the change of the heroine had eliminated the principle hilarity, but more, this understudy was altering the very slant of the play, righting it, egad. No more was Imogene groaning and fanning away the verbiage directed at her with indignant indolence. Rather this Imogene was alive with a love that overwhelmed her. And thus, the passion that Edmund Kean's Bertram felt for her was no longer unbelievable, but understandable . . . if not shared. And his forced separation from her became painful to watch, and his subsequent uncontrolled revenge, while not forgivable, at least now could be understood.

The pit buzzed over who this new young actress could be. Ophelia Browne was the answer, but that did no more than denote her. And as the play progressed, and one began to see more than a pathetic child with long blond hair almost to her ankles, she became the fused focus of emotion that elevated the drama to a new pitch. Not only was the monstrous Bertram softened back to his old humanity at his Imogene's madness, but the audience was similarly affected. Miss Ophelia Browne made much use of that long blond hair in her madness, plaiting it and laughing like a little girl dressing up in her mother's fashions. And her sadness was not a sham groan, but, as seen from the pit, the large dark eyes were spilling tears. At her death, there was not a person in the audience, not even exempting the viscount, who did not share the anguish of Bertram's loss.

The applause was well earned that night, the viscount commented. At one moment he had been shockingly close to an unmanly emotion. Not since a boy in short-coats had he found himself so scandalously near to losing his composure. The only explanation was an excessively unshakable conviction that the play that night was speaking directly to him. Possibly it was due to the heroine's being of such a small stature that she unavoidably reminded him of Emmalie. Even the gestures and the timbre of the voice were hers. Not to carry the comparison to absurdity, he would not grant a similarity in the face. Nor in the assurance. Egad, would this be the way of the future? That one lady should appeal because her smile was that of Emmalie? And another because of a similar laugh? Was he doomed, he asked himself with an ironic smile and shake of his head, to a series of short ladies in the hope that through the outer physical similarity, he would find Emmalie's soul?

Along with a crowd of noble bucks the viscount was

off backstage to congratulate the cast and to have a closer viewing of this Ophelia Browne. Already Basil was warning him off the lady, for he had found her so moving he wished to kiss her hand in tribute, as well as the rest of her.

Meanwhile Miss Browne backstage was being prodigiously reassured by Mrs. Windsor and tolerably so by Mr. Kean that she had not disappointed. Most gratifying was the rest of the company's closing rank about her in a congratulatory joint embrace. Just surfacing Emmalie spotted the Viscount Wynnclife, trailed by Lord Lanadale, approaching for introductions. After a few moments of being surrounded by them, the young girl had recourse to her hair again, letting it trail across her face. Then turning to Mr. Kean, she whispered, "Save me from these lords." He, still in his Bertram mood and agreeing completely with her attitude toward nobility, was nothing loath.

"Miss Browne is too overcome to converse with anyone. She accepts all your praises with humility and appreciation, but begs to be allowed to retire to her dressing room without further ado." And almost bearing the weight of her slight person on his arm, he escorted her to the shared dressing room with Mrs. Windsor.

The gentlemen who had come backstage to philander settled for the lesser leads, and eventually, after some desultory conversation, only the cast itself was left.

The viscount stepped into Miss Jones's dressing room to leave a parting note, civilly expressing regret at having missed her and uncivilly adding that the audience had not had similar cause for regret at her absence. In the comfortable chair in which he had so oft rested while waiting for Kitty to change, Reggie was lost in that same inexplicable sensation of being in proximity to Miss Marlowe. Supposedly that derived from Miss Browne's influence; although standing alongside that painted actress had vitiated that resemblance; he'd been seriously disappointed, for the long pale locks were comically stiff and wiglike, while onstage they'd given her some naiad airs.

Yet this farcical Emmalie, so inferior to Miss Marlowe, released his deep need to once more behold the authentic young lady. Hence, Reggie fell into a reverie of imagining himself making a surprise visit to Cornwall, merely as a gesture of friendship and renewing same. But nonsense! If he should return, he should find himself in the same queer stirrups out of which he'd with some difficulty dismounted. Having been valiant to cease his attempts to engage her affections, just when he was certain she would shortly be returning those tricefold, he could not now adjure that nobility. No, by gad, he had left her for her own best interest. And he would not allow this sentimental mood, called up by the pathos, say rather bathos, of the play's end to persuade him to overthrow his valiant act!

Standing up and with a mock bow, the viscount thereupon bid adieu to his Drury Lane enchantress—otherwise engaged—and to all thoughts of Miss Marlowe summoned by that faux Emmalie with her long pale wig.

At precisely that moment, having divested herself of that wig and most of her makeup, Emmalie, in a hooded brown cloak, was slipping out into the hall. There she observed through Miss Jones's open dressing room door, a gentleman's form that rooted her to the spot. The Viscount of Wynnclife. Still waiting.

In the elation at her successful performance, Emmalie for the first time had lost awareness of his lordship as being her objective for being in the Drury Lane Company. Hearing the applause, she understood Mrs. Windsor's comparing the feeling to consuming a heady draught. Indeed, if not drunk as a lord, she was at least a trifle above par. This sensation had been hers once before, upon secretly sipping from the leftover champagne glasses after one of her mother's routs. But this time, besides that, there was a new feeling of actually having found her pride. She was even sensible of a possibility that she could have a theatrical future. That faded as did all her delight at the sight of the viscount coming backstage, and she hid in Mr. Kean's arms until led to safety out of his lordship's sight. Waiting in the dressing room till all visitors had departed, Emmalie was in a quake. Mrs. Windsor had looked out into the hall over a half hour since and returned with full assurance that none of those plaguey bucks were hanging about. The path was clear. Only then did Mrs. Windsor depart. Yet Emmalie, like a rabbit safe in its hole, was loath to leave. And she waited even longer. Now that her apprehension of coming face-to-face with the viscount had sizeably diminished, she allowed the satisfaction of her triumph to return and rather multiply at the thought of Reggie being in the audience. Further, his not recognizing her proved, beyond doubt, she was a new person. Remade!

At length, Emmalie had stood up, donning her brown hooded cloak. She had given even Mr. Kean time to finish his celebrating with his current lightskirt and be gone. Most of the lamps were extinguished when she opened her dressing room door. And only then did Emmalie Marlowe, now Miss Ophelia Browne, step into the shadows. The patter of heavy feet indicated Caesar was still roaming, which meant Mr. Kean had not yet departed. Phillips did not generally allow Caesar loose if any stranger were about—which was further reassurance of no intruders. Thus Emmalie openly walked past several deserted dressing rooms and then past Mr. Kean's closed door and Miss Jones's open one, almost directly into the tall form of the viscount rising before her. The very next step would have had Emmalie beneath the swinging lantern, left burning for safety's sake and bright enough for immediate observation.

Stopping in her tracks, Emmalie's only recourse was to back up. Breath held, she did so. The viscount had now blown out his candle. In one more instant he, too, would step into the hall. Quickly, her hand reached back, touching the doorknob behind her, and, in one rapid motion, she entered into a dressing room, quickly closing the door in relief at her escape. Then she turned.

Mr. Lovell was delighted. After all this time, Miss Browne had come to him, and on the night of her triumph! Providence must have arranged for him not to be occupied as usual, he thought in satisfaction, for her entering signaled only one thing to him. Having had several draughts of ale only added to his fervor.

"Ah, little Ophelia! Nymph in your horizons be all my dreams dismembered!" he greeted, ignoring having, botched the quote, carrying on like a true trouper. "Have you come, by Jove, for some of my remembrances?"

"Mr. Lovell, forgive my intrusion. I entered the wrong dressing room in the dark," Emmalie said quickly and opened the door to retreat. The viscount, blast him, was still standing at the other doorway!

Turning back to Mr. Lovell, she attempted to explain her dilemma, but he weaved toward her and, still stuck in his Hamlet mood, whispered with a lascivious wink, " 'Lady, shall I lie in your lap?' "

" 'No, my lord,' " Emmalie replied in character.

" 'That's a fair thought to lie between a maid's legs. . . . Do you think I meant country matters?' "

" 'I think nothing, my lord.' "

As Emmalie was attempting to distract him by keeping to the role, he was distracting her by pulling off her hooded cape. It fell to the ground. Bending to retrieve it, while he still leaned his weight against her, sent her frail form toppling, and she fell flat down. He took that as an invitation and fell atop her. On the floor, the struggle was now in earnest. Both having sunk beyond reproach.

"Mr. Lovell!" Emmalie cried in despair and growing alarm. "Control yourself. This is not in the play!"

"Blast the play. I'll never play Hamlet anyway. I'll play country games with you, instead, my girl, and by Jove, I never saw such a tasty mite. One gulp and you'll be mine," he whispered, and began disarranging her apparel and then taking a swig of her ear and lips.

She shrieked at the full volume Mrs. Windsor had taught her to achieve by projecting her voice enough to split the ears of the groundlings. Her modesty being offended was naught next to her person being so handled, and she was in terror he would go beyond these liberties to forcing himself on her completely!

Once more she cried out, as she had been taught, taking a deep breath and projecting her voice.

And she was heard by two who instantly came running to her rescue.

The viscount was there first, pulling the drunken sot off the terrified girl. Just at that moment her second rescuer arrived. Caesar.

His growl was sufficient to get all attention as he bounded toward the sobbing girl he loved. Emmalie rose and held onto Caesar's flank. Still the lion was growling at his fiercest, turning from one man to the other, letting them know he could take both on at once, and they were quick to believe him. Mr. Lovell had never seen Caesar so wild, and he instantly sobered and backed away in terror, tripping over his own dressing table stool and then crawling, attempting to hide behind that, whimpering and cowering.

The viscount stood his ground, staring in some dismay at the beast. And then his gaze shifted, and he looked his full at the tear-stained, disarranged lady he had rescued.

It was Emmalie. He was too astonished to say a word, simply fixed his eyes upon her most constantly, expecting her to disappear in a puff of theatrical smoke, along with her lion. Or reveal herself as the sham Emmalie after all. The lady was ignoring his gaze, seeking to restore her decency by holding together her torn bodice.

And then she fleetingly looked at him, taking a breath and saying as calmly as possible, "My lord, it appears I must thank you for my deliverance."

It was Emmalie's own voice. And the viscount, as usual in moments of surprise, instantly hid behind his noted sangfroid, as he dryly replied, "It appears, Miss Marlowe, that Boots has grown appreciably, has he not?"

Emmalie merely nodded, too overwrought to play his social game. After all this time, they came face-to-face, and her presence was apparently a matter of such indifference to him, he offered her only a dampening sally, while she, so flushed, could do naught but turn and run out of the room and out of the theater.

The viscount's following was thwarted by Caesar's once more taking exception to Reggie's motion, necessitating his lordship having to deal with him first. He merely raised his quizzing glass and gave the lion a look, then said calmly and firmly, "Sit."

Caesar, no longer having his friend to defend and hearing the voice of authority, while not actually sitting, at least did not spring. Whereupon the viscount simply walked passed him, closing the door behind him, keeping the hapless Lovell prisoner with the beast.

In a few quick steps his lordship was out of the theater, but not soon enough to catch Emmalie departing in a hack. After some questioning of the jarveys anxious to secure his patronage and not gathering any useful information, the viscount returned to the theater. It seems he had reason to converse with Mr. Kean. While he and everybody in the theater world knew what it meant when Mr. Kean's dressing room door was locked, he calmly banged away on it until the disheveled actor angrily opened the door. "Unless there is a fire, I'll blast you to kingdom come for interrupting me!" he growled, very much like his pet Caesar, whose increasing growls were (parenthetically) now so loud, it was obvious Mr. Lovell must be in some distress.

"I hesitate to interrupt you," the viscount said without the hint of an apologetic tone, "but there *is* a fire . . ." He paused and then continued matter-of-factly, "in my breast. I am in love with your Ophelia Browne and wish to discuss her. And further, I fear it is too inconsequential to mention, but I suspect your lion is eating Mr. Lovell."

"Caesar never eats more than is good for him!" Mr. Kean replied with unconcern. "And Mr. Lovell is no loss to the theater." Obviously, the great actor, too, was half-sprung, as he laughed at that conclusion. Then looking with more serious consideration at the noble before him, he concluded companionably, "As for the fire in your breast—come in and take a drink, and we'll put it out!"

The viscount bowed at the invitation and entered.

CHAPTER TWELVE

IT WAS A FULL SENNIGHT SINCE EMMALIE HAD RE-
turned to Windsrest, having decided that she did not
really wish to be an actress, after all. Nor was she interested in discovering any further details of the viscount's relationship with Miss Kitty.

That entire episode in her life was over; she had only
to await the repercussions. Since the viscount had discovered her identity, he would most likely reveal all not
only to Miss Kitty Jones but to her mother.

While in error concerning the former supposition,
Emmalie was not in the latter case. The result was that
Lady Leonie arrived the very next day without the comfort of Pug or Negus or even her favorite dresser, which
indicated her haste if not her alarm.

Lady Leonie's entire experience with her daughter of
late had her so accustomed to surprise that she would
have been surprised only at the unsurprising occurring.
That indeed was her first comment upon Emmalie's
welcoming her, and then, distracted by the castle that
might have come straight out of *Monk* Lewis's most
vivid imaginings, she added as an aside, "But how positively Gothic! One could not possibly live here and not
be imagining headless visitors at all hours of the evening."

"That would not incommode me in the slightest. All
my life I have lived in Society with your friends—not
one of whom has ever shown the slightest need for his

head. Especially upon visiting you at all hours of the evening!"

At that Lady Leonie relaxed and even smiled. "Rather pithy, that. Indeed, it sounds very much as if you were quoting me. Actually, I have thought that very thing about all my friends, *especially* those visiting at all hours of the evening!"

Emmalie smiled begrudgingly, realizing one could not outjockey her mother, and Lady Leonie was continuing, as usual, with the final word. "You are progressing, my dear. I am delighted at the difference leaving home has done for you. All these years worrying about you and how to bring you out. And all I had to do was throw you out."

"You did not, Mother, I left. I really wish you would not alter the facts just to make a more effective remark."

"Effective remarks are more important than facts. One can always change the facts, but remarks remain forever, especially if effective."

Emmalie grinned. "You are incorrigible. Why did I not realize all my life that you were merely playing at life, while I was being in earnest? That is why we were never able to live in the same world. I was living an earnest tragedy and you a sparkling comedy."

Her mother patted her daughter's arm in pleasure at the level of their conversation. "One's early life is always a tragedy particularly because one is so earnest about every little occurrence. After one has gone through enough tragedies, such as the loss of hopes and love, one begins to see the importance of comedy— particularly if sparkling. You have definitely matured enough to advance to the comedy in your life—what else would one call this escapade of yours on the stage? Miss Ophelia Browne of the Drury Lane, appearing with that drunkard Edmund Kean and defended by a lion! That I fear has surpassed light comedy and sunken into outright farce."

With that, Lady Leonie expected she should have, as she usually did, overpowered her daughter by her pronouncement. But the new Emmalie, the Emmalie that had lived in a castle of her own, who had learned from Mr. Kean and Mrs. Windsor that one's feelings must always be held in check while one performed, and who had seen herself applauded and felt not only one man's approval but having that rare occurrence of the pit rising for her and showering her with huzzahs—this was an altered Emmalie, indeed.

Yet Emmalie's silence encouraged Lady Leonie to continue unchecked, "One might even say your recent actions are shockingly close to vulgar."

"Oft what is shockingly vulgar in others is merely high spirits in oneself."

"You perhaps should know best about *spirits*—living in this place, not to mention having been for some time in close proximity with the perennially half-sprung Mr. Kean."

"And you, too, are not unfamiliar with spirited people. For His Royal Highness, I have heard you say, has often been in his cups, especially when making proposals to you."

The family match continued, the weapons chosen: rapier wit and attempting to foil the other with a single reposte. Both ladies were invigorated by the contest. But Lady Leonie, long the champion, smoothly parried, "Indeed, you are correct about the prince. However, I own His Highness is vastly uplifted when slightly foxed. Otherwise he suffers sadly from remorse. For which he has just cause, and that makes him insist all else act with a morality he never attempts. But I must object to one of your allusions. His proposals to me have always been made when he is at his most clear-headed. As have been my refusals. Speaking of which, are you never going to accept the poor viscount?"

"I collect it is from him that you heard of my adventures onstage?"

"He came to me directly, assuming that I would have some influence over you, not realizing that whatever my influence, it promptly vanished upon your discovery that mothers are personalities in their own right. And I, I allow, am more of a personality than most."

Emmalie acknowledged that and, having seated Lady Leonie in the saloon, now waved away the butler bringing tea. "I shall be mother, shall I?"

"I should so much prefer that arrangement," her ladyship said.

"Haven't you always?" came from Emmalie.

"Haven't I always?" from Lady Leonie.

At which concert of speech and understanding and at Lady Leonie's frank admission which explained much to each other, they both smiled in unison as well.

"I so much prefer you now," Lady Leonie said, finishing her tea and then looking at her daughter with sincerity. "But I have always loved you, Emmalie . . . and wished the best for you. And that is why I wished you the viscount. Upon my word, if I had had the opportunity in my life to have been married to someone like Reggie, my life might not have had to have been restricted to comedy, after all."

"Reggie makes my life veer between farce and tragedy. There is no gentle comedy between us anymore. I thought there was, and even love, when he was here at Windsrest, but then he left me for Miss Kitty Jones, and I was devastated. And I was determined to discover what she had that so attracted him or at least see them together. I expected that once observing that union, I should have to accept it, as one does after seeing the body of a deceased. I told myself that once ascertaining that he was truly happier with her, I could at last release him."

"Then you love him?"

"I've always loved him," Emmalie admitted simply.

"Heavens! Why then this idiocy? Subjecting his lordship to test after test, as if he were back at school! Only what a schoolgirl herself would devise, not a lady whose affections were genuinely engaged! Why not accept him when you had him?''

"Quite elementary. From an elementary schoolgirl. Because . . . I wished him to love me. Ridiculous, was it not? Because I was under the gross misapprehension that if one were to pledge one's entire life to another and consequently live in close harmony with him, one should expect a certain reciprocity of feeling. I collect you think I was inclined to refine too much on such a prospect?''

Lady Leonie smiled and nodded. ''One must accept what is handed to one in life.'' And to illustrate, she took her daughter's hand and said, ''I put him in your hand. All you had to do was close your fingers over him.''

Emmalie shook her hand loose. ''That indeed was reason enough not to accept him. As I would no longer accept dresses that were wrong for me nor Society that was wrong for me and pretend my life through—that all was correct.''

"There is an inconsistency there. You would not accept him because I gave him to you, and yet you wish him above all others?''

"That is why I had to test him, to make him aware of me. To make him love me and want me above all other ladies in his life . . . forever.''

Lady Leonie finished her second cup of tea and looked at her daughter. ''I do not know what to say to you. My usual remark would be something on the like that if one wants to live a romance, one must suffer the pangs of it. You turned your relationship with Reggie into a romance of Gothic proportions—only *Bertram* could exceed it. But what do you wish? Life is not a stage play. We are in this castle, but there are no storms occurring that shall prepare the audience for Reggie's coming here and storming down your castle and swimming the moat and capturing you. You insisted he play

187

the hero for you; you gave him test after test. But in reality gentlemen always fail the tests we give them. Precisely for this reason: women are intelligent enough to always assign them only those tasks that they can easily accomplish. Never impossible ones.''

''And merely being faithful was so impossible a task?''

Her ladyship almost choked on her last swallow. ''Do not tell me! Good heavens, was *that* the last condition, not to be mentioned to me? And you had the indelicacy to even pronounce it, let alone expect a gentleman of Society to fulfill it! I wash my hands of you, Emmalie child. All my newfound respect has vanished. Heavens. Heavens above!''

''I repeat,'' Emmalie doggedly insisted, ''why is merely being faithful so impossible a task?''

''Merely being faithful, I have discovered among all my friends, is the *most impossible* of all tasks. And, if you'll recollect, Reggie was one of my friends. You knew his ways. One must accept a man as he is and laugh with him about it.''

''I shall not!'' Emmalie allowed her storm of emotions, always kept so primly repressed, to surface. Rising, she walked toward the portrait of a previous Viscount Wynnclife, who looked uncannily like the present lord, except for the armor. ''I feel too much to accept your way of gliding through life and playing games.'' She said this facing the portrait, so it was uncertain to whom she was making this pronouncement, although in a slight turn she was facing her mother and continued calmly. ''Although I have discovered I possess some talent for playacting. Actually being an accomplished actress offered not the smallest problem, for I had been taught by one of the most brilliant and accomplished actresses of our time who had a stage of her own in her home.''

Lady Leonie rose and curtsied to that. And walked a bit about the room that was hung with velvet hangings and armaments. "Are there secret passages?" she asked with a little girl's delight.

"No, Mother. The secret passages are only in one's heart."

"Ah, Emmalie, make up your mind. You veer from comedy to bathos, even in your remarks. Are you a heroine in a Gothic play or a social comedy? Determine at least your milieu, or you shall find yourself fitting in nowhere."

"That has always been the case. And why cannot I play all kinds of roles? Why cannot I have a gentleman who can equal me in my scope? Why must Reggie have so disgraced me by loving one so beneath both of us as Kitty Jones! I lost all respect for him the more I knew her. Truthfully, there are actresses, and I have met some in your own saloon—Mrs. Siddons, for one—for whom it should not have been such a humiliation to be passed over! But *Kitty*! I am confident I did her role better without the slightest experience. Indeed, anyone, even the town crier calling out the lines, would have improved on her performance!"

"Reggie told me you were superb. That you reduced him to tears."

Emmalie's face was a mixture of hope and suspicion. Very like when she was a little girl on the sidelines, asking to be allowed to join the group and suspecting she was only asked for a yet to be revealed joke. Defensively, therefore, she responded, "Yes, I had observed the viscount being reduced to tears of mirth during several of the play's performances!"

"But not the one with you in the lead, which I regret missing most sincerely. From him and from several others, I have been informed that the play suddenly rose to 'new heights.' Mr. Hazlitt was the one who used that phrase. Reggie merely corrected him and said 'divine heights.' "

"You are jesting . . . surely?"

"Again, you never know when I am being serious,

do you? I am always serious about you, perhaps that has been my mistake. I should have played you as I played all Society, for the humor, but I could not, you always meant too much to me. You were . . . you *are* the only thing that does.''

"Mother! Are you veering into melodrama?" Emmalie demanded, uncertain, and yet wishing with all her heart she could believe her mother in earnest.

"I deserved that response, I expect. But it is true."

And Emmalie, dropping all her attempted and defensive lightness of touch, took a breath and looking at her mother said softly, ''Then I shall risk telling you that I have always wanted you to tell me that.''

And Lady Leonie risked, too, by not saying another word and simply approaching her daughter and taking her into her arms.

Twenty-one years of separation had been bridged in that one quick gesture, and it left both ladies astounded, delighted, frightened, insecure, hopeful, awkward, satisfied, and laughing—all at once.

"And now?" Emmalie asked, after they separated, demonstrating she was still a little girl expecting her mother to tell her what should happen next.

Lady Leonie, given that cue and always ready to tell everybody what they should do next, said matter-of-factly, ''And now, I shall do whatever you wish to help you achieve whatever you wish. . . . Even if it is accepting you as Ophelia Browne or getting you to accept Reggie.''

"Oh Mother, I care for you, but you are too simplistic. I have already found that I could be an actress if I wished, and I no longer wish it. And I no longer wish for Reggie either, not if he prefers ladies of Kitty's stamp.''

Lady Leonie sighed and sat down and fortified herself with another cup of tea, which was cold, so she put it down with a clink. Then fixing her daughter with her serious, evaluating mother's glance, said, in her familiar, all-suffering tone, "I am not the simplistic one, it seems. I love you, Emmalie, but you continue to show signs of being a child, which irritates me. Gentlemen, I told you, always resort to occasional passing flings with ladies of that stamp, especially if they have been rejected by more worthy ladies, such as ourselves."

"What do you mean *passing* flings?" Emmalie responded in her pupil-at-her-mother's-feet tone, as of old. Unfortunately, these two ladies had too many years of having played set roles for them not to be able to quite avoid slipping into them whenever together, regardless if the roles no longer fit. Indeed, the roles even pricked at the attempt to force them back on. "Are you saying . . . the viscount and Miss Kitty are no longer . . . together?"

"Oh heavens, that is quite a thing of the past! She has left the stage. Imogene is now being played by a newcomer—somewhat in your style. But Miss Kitty has achieved all she wished by being granted her estate and grounds and becoming the current delight of the Earl of Carnivore. Quite the proper dish for that lord, I should say. His other passion is hunting. And as he never advances in his speech beyond 'Tally ho,' they should deal extremely well together, for from what Reggie told me, she has very little conversation."

"She did not need 'conversation'—my observing them together showed that she uses her fan to get a gentleman's attention, the way you and I use words."

"Really! How extraordinary!" And removing her fan from her reticule, she looked at it with wonder. "Of course a lady ought never demean herself to observe a gentleman with his light-of-love. However," and her eyes lit up with anticipation, "since you have, I'd as lief hear the full particulars. Especially the use of the fan." Then, shaking herself out of those extraneous erogenous thoughts, she hurriedly returned to her point, "If you love Reggie, you must forgive him his lapse, since it was your request the two of you remain mere 'friends.' I can attest to his being a delightful friend. But I had hoped that you and he would be more. I have always suspected him of being a secret romantic at the core, and having observed this castle, decorated by him, I gather, I am assured of it. And since you have a shockingly wide romantic streak, yourself, which must come from your father's side, you are without question meant for each other. I am so pleased to have been proven correct in my match. One often believes one's own opinions are infallible, but life has a way of constantly attempting to make one lose faith in that infallibility. You have restored my faith in myself. I shall restore you Reggie.''

"No, Mother. You need not do anything. If he is a romantic and he loves me, he shall find me here. He knows where I am.''

"There you go again making conditions. A gentleman may love and not do anything about it, until a lady helps him along. You cannot hide here in your castle. You must meet Reggie and conquer him in his own milieu. In my saloon, if needs be. And I, aware of all your talents, can only believe that Society needs you as well. You shall vastly improve us. Indubitably that is the solution. *Your* test, if you'll accept one from me. It is Reggie's world, he shall never accept anyone who cannot manage that. Emmalie, child, it is your destiny to enter Society and play by its rules, and yet conquer all, and thence conquer Reggie . . . and, I predict, your poor mother as well.''

Emmalie laughed. While her mother's confidence could not help but please, she still hesitated, having, in the interim, fallen back to her previous habit of retiring from people, and then, too, going into Society with her mother was too akin to the position she had been in all her life, which had so effectively diminished her.

Yet her mother was urging her to accept the challenge, and Emmalie, having made it the mode to put others to the test, could hardly refuse one for herself.

Throughout, Emmalie's instincts warned her, but she was back to listening to her mother. And Lady Leonie, sensing a weakness in her daughter, was quick to capitalize on it.

The weakness was one most people had—wishing to be told all would happen just as one wished it would. And her ladyship, wishing for that herself, was quick to do so: asking Emmalie to think what she, who had defeated Miss Kitty on her turf, could accomplish on her own battlefield! "Indeed, I predict that in a very short time you shall have Reggie feeling you are the best of all the ladies in Society . . . one he would wish to offer for *on his own*."

That last phrase was the very key to all Emmalie's hopes. And thus, against her instincts and swayed by her dreams, Emmalie nodded.

She was back to not speaking.

CHAPTER THIRTEEN

HAVING RETURNED WITH LADY LEONIE TO HER TOWN house at Regent's Park, Emmalie was preparing for her reappearance in Society. It was, both mother and daughter agreed, rather difficult to make an occasion of Emmalie's reentrance, since this was not exactly her first Season. Indeed, Season after Season, she had been like an afterthought to all.

"That was the old Emmalie," Lady Leonie pronounced. "The new Emmalie persuaded an entire audience that she was another person. I daresay it shall scarcely be beyond that lady's power to impress a few guests at her own home. One must start small, of course, and invite only those hardly likely to present more than a tolerable challenge. . . ."

"Pray cease, Mother. I shall no longer accept anything small about me. There is only one way an insignificant person like myself can make a significant coup, and that is to start a rumor, and then, when all of Society is agog to see me, invite them to do so. Ergo, all shall arrive prepared to be thinking of me. And only then shall I not fall into that pit of oblivion that has been my burial site all these years."

Rising, Lady Leonie approached her daughter, and to the girl's surprise, she kissed her on the forehead. And then keeping her hand on the girl's soft brown curls, she whispered, "There is a world of good sense in that idea pot, is there not? You are undoubtedly correct. My scheme would have failed. Indeed, I did not have much hope for it myself, even while saying it. Your way is the only way. Although I cannot for the life of me conclude what rumor we shall spread. But then, I no longer have to fatigue myself to devise anything—I need only turn to you.''

Emmalie, blushing in pleasure at her mother's assessment, replied, ''I fear the only effective *on dit* would be one of a scandalous nature, and I cannot for the life of me think of anything I've done in that department.'' Emmalie's spirits threatened to sink, so she quickly rose to prevent that possibility and said directly, ''Would you be willing to lend me one of your cicisbeos and allow us to spread the tale that I have cut you out?''

Expecting her mother to be affronted or at least reluctant, Emmalie was astonished by her ladyship's laugh of delight. ''By all means, pick whichever one you wish. Although Pug, who is my most dedicated, might not have enough importance to interest.''

''Yes, it cannot possibly be Pug. Besides,'' she murmured, half-thinking aloud, ''he could never transfer his feelings. His love for you is of too genuine and lasting a nature.''

''Pug's! Poor dear Pug who writes me stanzas to my eyebrows and cries if I cut off a lock of my hair.''

A sense of fellow-feeling with Pug overwhelmed her for a moment, recollecting how often the two had followed in her ladyship's wake, both equally ignored, and she cried out with some asperity, ''Who else would care about your hair but one devoted to your person?'' And then recollecting that her mother and she had ended their differences, Emmalie said with a more gentle tone, seeking to explain Pug's feelings, ''Reggie gave me a locket containing a lock of his hair, and I have looked at it untold times. One must have deep feelings for a person, indeed, to develop an affection for his hirsute leavings.''

Lady Leonie restrained her amusement, but she could not but recollect that she and Reggie had always thought alike about hair mementos. He'd claimed, indeed, that giving such was a gross affectation and invasion of one's person. Yet he'd given one to Emmalie, which must mean she'd already tailored him to her specifications; and hence fitting him to their full pattern should be a thing of tolerable ease, after all. And she smiled.

Meanwhile Emmalie was still considering candidates for the scandalous *on dit*. "Your most devoted admirer is the Prince Regent. But he never deigns to incline his head to my level, preferring his ladies of a more heroic cast. Nor do even you have enough influence to persuade him to sham it."

"Are you manipulating your own mama?" Lady Leonie said with a laugh. Her famous graceful walk was demonstrated, as she considered. "One could approach him, I expect, but dealing with His Highness, one must recollect that he has never had to please anybody but himself. Nor does he care to be made use of. And if so, he expects payment of the most dear."

Instantly understanding her mother's hint, Emmalie discarded the prince. "I do not believe this game we are playing is worth *that* sacrifice from you, Mama. Nor would I accept it. There must be someone. . . . It is a pity Lord Byron left London in disgrace. The other most famous scapegrace is, of course, the viscount himself. And somewhat to a lesser degree, his friend, Lord Lanadale. Hmm?"

"We cannot ask *his* complicity. He is devoted to Reggie and shall immediately reveal all to him, and then where are we?"

"Indeed. Where are we? We wish Reggie to know about my new desirability, but we wish him to believe it is in earnest. Hence, I must make Lord Lanadale form a *tendre* for me and then confess that dastardly betrayal to the viscount. Yes! That's it!"

"Hold, Emmalie dear, how can that be *it*? You are overstepping! While I do not say Lord Lanadale would not succumb to your charms, it might take awhile actually. And I hesitate to bring this reality to your attention, but Reggie has the annoying habit of always immediately selecting another lady. It should be preferable, therefore, if we caught him now—between . . . I mean while his memory of you is still fresh.''

Discerning her ladyship still lacked confidence in her daughter's intriguing Lord Lanadale, Emmalie laughed and put that to her, while Lady Leonie made half-hearted denials. Not affronted, Emmalie countered, ''You were not there on the night of my performance. Lord Lanadale was one of the first at my feet. Dashed anxious to meet me. Ah ha! That is it! I shall confess to him that I am Ophelia Browne, and he shall be so intrigued, he shall be anxious to help me keep my secret. Or at least he shall give the appearance of a conspiracy of interest with me. And that shall suffice to intrigue the viscount.''

''Possibly. But you are not acquainted with Lord Lanadale's full character. He is known as quite a rattle. Anything confided to him will soon be all over Society.''

''Famous! Let them all know I have appeared onstage. That shall be enough of a reason for wishing a closer viewing of me, would you not say?''

Lady Leonie and her daughter shared a satisfied smile. ''It is particularly gratifying, is it not, to discover that the truth can be as effective as a load of gammon. It restores one's faith in the verities of life.''

''Indeed, Mama, when attempting any stratagem, it is undoubtedly best to keep as close to truth as possible. Then if all blows up in our faces, we can at least have the comfort of having been honest.''

''I have never found comfort in that. But I am learning a great many home truths from you. It is so reassuring to discover one's child has so much to teach one. It makes me feel prodigiously younger.''

Both ladies were of an age when they could not help but feel it a decided pleasure to change places; the older feeling younger, and the younger accepting her new dominance. And when Negus arrived, he was totally in a pet to discover himself put aside while Lady Leonie patted her own daughter!

In her old apartments, Emmalie made haste to inform Spinny of all that was occurring and to take pen in hand for a note to Lord Lanadale. It requested his advice on a subject of grave secrecy, having to do with a lady's honor. Upon being shown the epistle, her ladyship offered one suggestion—that she sign it instead, for his lordship might not immediately respond to a letter from a young lady with whom he was not acquainted nor should such a young lady write to him on so intimate a topic! Acknowledging the correctness of that, Emmalie handed the note to Lady Leonie, who wrote it in her own style and flourishes.

As the days passed, the ladies became inseparable. Always they must be in discussion over some new stratagem. They were similarly together on the visit to Mrs. Reynolds, who had the honor of her mother's custom. Having bought so many gowns from this designer, Lady Leonie had not the smallest doubt that she would betray every word overheard. "She always has," her ladyship said reassuringly. Therefore, while ordering much needed new wardrobes, they would also discuss in Mrs. Reynolds's hearing, the choice tidbits intended for general knowledge.

Here was another occasion when Emmalie newly demonstrated her altered self. For she was the one making the decisions for her apparel. Using all assimilated from her experience onstage, including particularly Mrs. Windsor's advice, Emmalie determined the role she was to play for the ton, and then costumed herself accordingly. First and foremost, the initial gown must be bold to justify the scandalmongers' wildest whispers and yet have an ingenue quality to create concurrent doubts—making her a proper enigma.

Abandoning her predilection for brown, Emmalie as

well discarded her mother's suggested white or pale-colored muslins suitable for young ladies. Without hesitation she chose gold as her color, it being sufficiently outstanding, having its own intrinsic allure and yet, overall, a softness. And it emphasized the gold in her eyes that the viscount had so oft mentioned. Emmalie was in a state of ambivalence whether to make it her style to *always* appear in that one color . . . or to vary.

Lady Leonie had no such conflict, allowing that one color might be effective onstage for an evening, but in reality would seem theatrical. Emmalie must not allow others to realize how orchestrated she was. For while most people desired to be led about by the nose, their noses would be sadly out of joint if they realized that was exactly what was occurring. Subtlety was required. Emmalie agreed to soften her drama by choosing a variety of colors—although she intended to stay close to the ocher family. Coral was selected first, being bold enough to stand out from the usual pinks, yet also containing a touch of gold giving it the needed credentials for Emmalie's wardrobe, as did her outfits of lime, aquamarine, and apricot.

Further transformation resulted after a visit from Mrs. Windsor, who brought her paint box. Emmalie's hair was recut on the top and her maid taught by Mrs. Windsor to curl the ringlets that fell round her ears and the smaller bangs that aimed at her widened eyes. Deft touches of paint added the correct alterations and drama to her features without the exaggerations of the stage. Lady Leonie, intrigued, brought Mrs. Windsor to her own bedroom to attempt what could be done for her.

Discovering Ophelia Browne was Lady Leonie's daughter and the fiancée of Viscount Wynnclife was to Mrs. Windsor too dramatic not to fully enjoy! She would keep the secret, she assured the ladies, but from her knowledge of the world, it was best not to assume others were not spreading the word. Also she recommended that an ordinary assembly would not be sufficient to introduce the new Emmalie. Not even a ball would do. "Think *drama*!" Mrs. Windsor urged, in her famous echoing tones that awed both ladies. All three obediently thought drama. Mrs. Windsor supplied some, by lifting her hand and silencing all suggestions, pausing deliberately for total audience attention, then announcing: "At the ball—let there be a play! With Emmalie in the lead. She's at her best treating others as an audience."

Emmalie was quick to agree and Lady Leonie to disagree. One could hardly turn one's house into a theater! It wasn't done. The most that could be tolerated would be a tableau.

No sooner was that word out, then all three, in unison, agreed that was the very thing! So to begin the ball, a tableau was scheduled, featuring Emmalie. And after more discussion, the ball became a costume ball with a theatrical theme.

In the days following, Emmalie continued to alter herself. Principally she decreed she should no longer accept anything diminutive, which meant a change even in her name. Ophelia, of course, could not be considered, but "Emma" met with both her mother's and Mrs. Windsor's approval. Emma she was, and Emma, in her mother's stead, met Lord Lanadale with Mrs. Windsor at her side. Her objective was to implore him to keep her performance at Drury Lane in the strictest confidence—especially from the viscount.

"You, I instantly discerned had recognized me. Otherwise I should not now have taken you into my confidence. I said, did I not, Mrs. Windsor, at that moment, that Lord Lanadale is too awake upon every suit to be gammoned. And yet, all this time, you have not disclosed my secret—necessitating my extending to you my profoundest gratitude. And, of course, I wished to see you again. There was something between us that night. It was you who took my hand and said, 'I cannot bear to part with you,' or did I confuse you with another gentleman?''

"Odd's blood, it were me, alright. I always know what to say to a lady. Known for it, don't you know? Ain't ever left a lady without giving her something to think about. Righto. Miss Marlowe. Knew you in a shot. Told Reggie . . . well, no, I ain't told him. Have I?''

"On no," Emmalie cried. "We must allow him to come to his own conclusions. Naturally, I could not expect you not to hint of your greater perception.''

"Emma, dear heart," Mrs. Windsor interrupted with her natural queenly dignity, which gave every word she said the quality of an official pronouncement. "You must remind his lordship not to spread the story to the ton. Your appearance at the costume ball in a sennight, as Ophelia, shall not have the proper drama, else. I myself shall come dressed as Queen Gertrude.''

"Oh yes, the theme of the ball is to be 'Favorite Literary or Theatrical Characters,' and since mother and I are most anxious for the most attractive men in all London to appear, she has given me leave to hand you the first invitation.'' And she did so with much flourish.

His lordship was brimming with glee at not only having been selected for so much special attention but for being in the know ahead of Reggie. Actually ahead of all Society! And this Emma, with her magnetic, golden-lit eyes and her profusion of curls worn all about her head, was entrancing. Even more of an angel than she had appeared onstage. And how dashed splendid of her to have taken him into her confidence before all. He'd be dashed if he told a sole soul!

And Lord Lanadale kept his word a full day. But at his club, when all were sitting around the bow window staring at the various people walking by and making their usual comments, Lord Lanadale let some of his knowledge slip. He would have burst with it, else.

"Anyone got Lady Leonie's invitation to her costume ball?"

No one had. And the viscount was astonished to see one in his friend's hands when he, her ladyship's favorite, had not been favored with such. Further, it was obvious from Basil's nonchalant airs that he had a great deal more to say. Usually Reggie would have attempted to suppress the man's love of tattling. Nothing more fatiguing then the latest crim. con. stories about people he had long lost interest in. But if it concerned Lady Leonie, it was close to Miss Marlowe, and that must always have first attention.

Therefore, Reggie invited Basil to go on the strut with him on St. James's Street. They did so. And before they had ogled two ladies, the viscount had the whole of the story. Emmalie was Emma and was to be at the ball and dressed as Ophelia. Impossible to believe!

He had been overcome by Emmalie's appearance on-stage and had consulted her mother, who claimed him mistaken, but she had, at his urgings, set off for Windsrest to assure both that Emmalie was no longer planning to so risk her reputation by presenting herself on the stage and, further, to learn her reason for doing so.

On Lady Leonie's return, she had fobbed him off by assuring him that Emmalie had no further theatrical ambitions, and as to her reason, who could tell what the girl would do. He himself had imagined several reasons for her actions—from the obvious, that the emotional dramatic instinct she depicted to him while reading and which had further showed itself by wishing to live in such a castle, had run amuck with her, and she could not contain the clear talent that she possessed until she had exhibited herself on the stage. The other explanation, which he preferred and which promised less danger for her future, was that she wished to see the lady that had supplanted her. In either case, the girl was too dramatic and wild and given to crazy starts, and he was delighted not to have anything more to do with her, except, he was planning exactly how to have something more to do with her. For a moment he regretted not having revealed her stage career, for then she would be in disgrace and would have to marry someone, and perhaps then he could forget his blasted nobility and run to her rescue one more time, and her rescue would be his pleasure. Except, except, now that he sincerely cared for the girl, he did not wish her to have to marry him, but to *want* to marry him. Therefore, he kept silent and stayed away and planned to do so until the Season was fully over. Then he intended to visit her at Windsrest, and hope, perhaps with Lady Leonie along as an encouragement, to summer there, during which he could press his case.

Now, the devil take the girl, she had revealed all. And what did that mean about her? Totally confused and then intrigued, the viscount could think of naught but Miss Marlowe and her stratagems. He was further alarmed by Lady Leonie's not responding to any of his notes, which had him conjecturing that Emmalie was now controlling her. He knew that mad-brained child enough to realize the wilder the scheme, the more likely it came from her fertile, dear little head!

Meanwhile, unknowingly carrying out Emmalie's assigned tasks were Lord Lanadale and Mrs. Reynolds, the dress designer. They had spread the word to all— not only about Emma's shocking appearance onstage, but further that Lord Lanadale was somehow connected with the entire prank, a fact he verified by winking broadly, as well as by further announcing he was to be Miss Marlowe's escort at the ball. That latter tidbit was prodigiously delicious, for was not Lord Lanadale the viscount's closest confidant? Ergo, it followed the former fiancée had been stolen right under Reggie's aristocratic nose! All Society could barely wait for the ball, and those who had not received an invitation were in dismay that they would be missing not only the last event of the Season but undoubtedly the most significant!

Further whispers were that His Royal Highness would be appearing and personally giving the award for the most suitable costume to the theme. From his own royal hand! By Jove, no one would care to miss that condescension!

Shockingly overdue, the viscount's invitation arrived with Lady Leonie's regrets scrawled at the bottom, expressing she had meant this to be one of the first sent, but it had naughtily hidden itself under her blotter! Nonetheless, being so close to her family, he had probably assumed he had been invited all along, had he not?

He had not. He had been dashed overset by this lack of an invitation! Rather he had been considering his course of retaliation. Even now, with invitation in hand, Reggie could not quite swallow his choler. It would justly serve both mother and daughter if he simply sent a note claiming to be otherwise engaged on that evening. Except that would not be believed, as everyone else would be *there*. Actually, he could not bear not observing the occasion.

He must swallow his ire and civilly countenance her ladyship's patently sham excuse and claim he had assumed some such mischance. His response was signed with a flourish so deeply embedded, it relieved his peeve, sufficient to unclench his teeth. And then Reggie was free to plan his costume that must express everything he wished to say to Emmalie without having to open his mouth. And, almost directly, he found one that exactly did so. And that reconciled him to the ball and had him joining all Society in the anticipation of it.

CHAPTER FOURTEEN

ON THE NIGHT OF THE COSTUME BALL, THE FIRST FLOOR of Lady Leonie's house was the site of a general unveiling. For there, upon divesting cloaks and daily selves, one after another of the most select of Society emerged in their costumed personas to ascend to the second floor ballroom.

Queuing on the marble stairs were past to present-day literary characters—or Pericleses to Childe Harolds. One glimpsed Romeos and Juliets, Antonys and Cleopatras, Caesars and et tu Brutes, Mirandas and Ferdinands, Fausts and Helens, Two Gentlemen from Verona, and scores of gentlemen and ladies of uncertain literary reference. Steadily mounting: majestic Lears, regal Danes, kingly Henrys and Richards of different numbers. Neither was there a lack of Desdemonas, Cordelias, nor Ladies of the Lake. And of Hamlets there was a prodigious showing. A good many of the characters were right out of the ton's favorite Gothic novels. Of which the viscount came dressed as a monk—hooded and secretive—to recall to a certain Miss Marlowe the tales they had read together, as well as their moments of closeness.

Lady Leonie, at the top of the stairs, greeted all her guests without once missing who they were and always missing whom they were depicting. She, herself, was naturally Venus. Pug, behind her, Adonis. Her ladyship carried a golden apple to complete her personification, but after a while, having made its point, it was eaten by somebody who could not wait for the refreshments.

Lord Lanadale came, as Hamlet, in search of Emma, assuming she would be attired as Ophelia to reveal her secret. But when Edmund Kean and his wife, Mary, appeared as Hamlet and Ophelia, some of the more observant began to assume Miss Marlowe would not be so repetitive.

"Never been such a squeeze," said an outraged King John to the fairy Titiana, and the lady, though agreeing, did not feel that sufficient excuse for his bending her wings. As the crowd on the stairs finally eased into the wider ballroom, one had room to look round at the decor.

There were painted crowns and calliographed sonnets on parchments. The balcony, overlooking the ballroom, held the orchestra and a suspended banner, reading: "Let Every One Reveal His Secret and Rejoice!" Which, it was supposed, referred to the characters all were depicting. Or, some interpreted it as a promise of secrets to be revealed tonight, presumably about Lady Leonie's daughter. Hopefully it would be something beyond her having been onstage, which was already fully digested. Also well chewed: the young lady's dropping one friend, the viscount, and taking on the other, or Lord Lanadale. The beau monde was eager for additional tidbits, for apparently nothing suffices those well-bred on excess.

Miss Marlowe still had not made her appearance. Just as some were recollecting her ability to be somewhere and be unobserved, a timely trumpet sounded. That announced the ball's tableau, directing the guests' attention to the rear of the ballroom, where a curtained stage was at that very moment being circled by candelabra and lamps. Not till the last one was lit and a blaze formed did a footman bring forth an explanatory sign: THE MUSE CALLIOPE OF HEROIC POETRY.

The theme of the tableau had required excessive discussion between Emmalie and her mother before being selected. The principal drawback was the Muse's dress. It was not noticeably different from the ordinary dress of a young English lady. For England overall was swept by a passion for Greek modes. In architecture, culminating in the facade of the prince's Carlton House. In furniture, with reclining Grecian sofas. But predominantly in fashion: for high-waisted, narrow, yet flowing, gowns were direct imitations of the Greek chitons. Some even had a Greek Key design as a hem trim. Actually, Emmalie herself had worn several gowns exactly of this mode during her first Seasons of insignificance. How then could she be outstanding wearing such a common style?

But Lady Leonie was undaunted, concluding, "It is not specifically known what that *particular* Muse wore—no columns from the court news of the time having come down to us describing Calliope's precise attire. All is supposition. Very like, theatrical thing that she was, she had her own individual taste, as does my own daughter. Is not that possible?"

"Very like, indeed," Emmalie cried out with a whoop of laughter and a hug for her mother. And she set upon designing Calliope's dress on her own. But after attempting several changes of design, Emmalie realized fashion had only halfway borrowed from the Greek original, and the most daring depiction would be to make her chiton *totally* authentic, leaving one shoulder shockingly bare and material flowing across the other from the high-waisted bodice. Nor would Miss Marlowe be content with the current soft and airy muslins, gauzes, or silks in pastels or white. Hardly. For Calliope, living so near heaven, could at will scoop up the glow of sunrise and splash it on her gown. And so would she. The gown was to be of a heavy glowing cloth of gold. With that and her hair, which of late, through Mrs. Windsor's advice, had been religiously rinsed with lemon juice and chamomile tea, giving it highlights that emulated the amber glints in her eyes, she would be a symphony of gilt.

Mrs. Reynolds, as eager as Emmalie to make the gown distinctive, went even further than requested, making it particularly conforming to the lady's rounded form. At the final fitting, Emmalie realized this closeness might be considered unseemly and had a moment's pause, but then recollected that, with her background of appearing onstage, she could hardly pose as a representative of the highest propriety. And Lady Leonie, after all, by example, had taught her the success of singularity. The costume would therefore remain without amendment.

On observing it, Mrs. Windsor assured her she would be delectable to all the gentlemen, not to mention that particular gentleman toward whom this performance was directed. The actress further put Emmalie in high leg with her revelation that a canvas of her fellow performers had revealed the viscount was not currently favoring any theatrical lady with his attentions. Nor was he involved with a lady of the ton, her mother assured. Amusingly and somewhat tardily, it appeared the viscount was at last honoring her last test of celibacy, Emmalie thought while planning an appropriate style for her hair. Earlier she had requested the loan of her mother's coronet for the occasion, but Lady Leonie, with great glee, decided better could be done.

Promptly she visited the Prince Regent. There, using her famous Lady Guile indirect approach, which always made other people offer just what she was about to request, her ladyship began with an appeal to the prince's vast knowledge of fashion and jewels. How could anyone forget the prized shoe buckle he himself had designed? And other recollections of His Highness's past fashion successes were lovingly recalled and even more lovingly listened to. At last, judging him sufficiently mellowed, she described Emma's costume and the problem of the headgear. Gold it must be, but the jewels were a problem. Did he think topazes?

"Topazes! Egad!" the prince ejaculated, personally insulted to have such lowly jewels mentioned in his presence. "Yellow diamonds are the thing! Got me a crown with just such. . . . Odd's blood, that's the ticket! I'll give her leave to wear that canary diamond thing for the evening, what say?"

What could Lady Leonie say but that she was all astonishment, not only at his always knowing just the correct thing but at his generosity! Of course, the real apogee of the entire costume ball would be if His Highness himself were to attend. He assured her he had already decided to do so. But Lady Leonie still sighed, and he must then ask the further cause of her distress and be told she had a momentary picture of the Prince Regent *with* Emmalie while she was wearing the crown, which so went to her heart, she could not dismiss it!

"But what's the hubble-bubble! I shall dashed well ask the young minx for a dance!"

"But . . . the image I have is of you as Zeus! For Zeus, or Jupiter, we must have to escort the Muse Calliope in our beginning tableau! And who else combines the majesty of form and face, and yet the glory of epic poetry in one personhood? Anyone less, Your Highness, would make the entire affair second-best!"

Her dejection must not be allowed to continue a moment longer. He instantly proffered himself, an offering he had been making for several years. And in this case, she happily accepted. Before long, he was making a nuisance of himself by enlarging his role and demanding thunderbolts to throw out to the crowd. Some had to be quickly made up and the orchestra notified to provide the effects.

In one short visit to Carlton House, Lady Leonie had achieved not only a crown jewel of England for her daughter but the royal prince himself to introduce her to the ton! What else could Emma wish!

Emma wished her mother had not so arranged matters. For she had planned to be the cynosure and had an actress's misgiving in losing her solo appearance. But before she retorted in this manner, she realized the benefit of being presented by the prince and was properly grateful to her mother, admitting, as Lady Leonie herself exclaimed, no one else could have achieved such a coup!

Not being able to rehearse her hairdo with the crown, Emmalie had arranged her hair in its new style of front ringlets and a waterfall of curls falling from the uplifted back section, assuming the crown would fit nicely over that. Not till the night of the ball did she realize her error. Ceremoniously the prince's own liveried guards delivered the chest to her apartment, whereupon, with as much of a royal air as possible, Emmalie dismissed them. She must be by herself to cherish this moment. After opening the lid, the young lady had to close her eyes at the splendor within. There was a blaze of gold! Not only was the crown itself golden, but there were seven large canary diamonds of at least ten carats each, surrounded with circles and circles of smaller, clear whites. Altogether, it glowed like a berayed sun. Yet it was so much of a weight, two attempts were required to lift and place it on her head.

Stepping back and gazing at herself in her cheval glass, Emmalie groaned. She not only felt weighed down by it, but looked it. The crown covered all her hair and a good part of her forehead. How much more fitting would have been her mother's simple coronet! But Emmalie was not to be defeated on this her night of nights. As she had been taught onstage, when another actor commands all attention, one must do something spectacular to eclipse the competitor. The only way to live up to the sparkling crown would be to loose her own spectacular feature, or her long hair that came down to below her knees. And she did so. Then once more she placed the crown on her head, slightly further back. Now with her long train of hair spilling out from the crown, the lady seemed to belong to it. Several stately walks before that glass assured her of that symbiosis.

Cries of approval came from Miss Spindle, who then began to sob audibly at the sight of her transformed charge. Her mother entered next, and while one could not say she was reduced to tears, her eyes did glisten a mite while expressing her prideful approval and giving her daughter her own yellow diamond earrings as the last touch. No further bolstering was required for Emmalie's entrance. She was ready, indeed.

Accompanied by her guards, the crowned lady slipped through the small door behind the curtained stage and there removed her crown, placing it on the podium ere positioning herself. From the ballroom came the trumpeted announcement: "Behold Calliope: the Muse of Heroic Poetry, our symbol for this evening, and her crowning by Zeus himself." And last minute, almost as the curtain was lifting, the Muse's partner took his place onstage.

The entire ballroom of people emitted one loud gasp. At first all one could observe was a lovely young lady with astonishingly beautiful light brown hair spread out about her, like a mantle, as she knelt before a corpulent elderly man with ruddy complexion. And then, the gasp turned to cries of approval as it became clear it was the Prince Regent himself standing there! He was dressed as Zeus, by Jove, and waved a jagged, pointy stick decorated with spangles. When he was so good as to throw it out among the crowd, accompanied by a booming sound from the obliging orchestra, it was understood to be nothing less than a thunderbolt. Several others followed in rapid succession. The prince then proceeded to laugh and accept with becoming modesty the great applause this simple act had won him.

The lady was still curtsying almost to the ground, in great reverence, so that her face could not be seen, but it was suspected that she was the daughter of the house. The action of the tableau was to be the placing of the crown upon Emmalie's head to signal the Muse's royalty for the evening. And while the young lady waited for that gesture, the prince touched her shoulder thrice with his thunderbolt and then signaled she was to rise. This dubbing was a surprise and another example of the enriching of his part, or mayhap just a royal's reverting to habit when holding a swordlike appurtenance. In time, he recollected the crown (princes never totally forgetting those) and hurriedly placed that on her waiting head. The golden crown with its matchless canary yellow diamonds won even more gasps, as Queen Calliope rose and viewed her subjects. The now royal couple was amply applauded and even cheered! To which both responded with gracious acknowledgment. Another surprise: rather than a closing of the curtain at the conclusion, the duo smilingly stepped down the stage steps directly into the crowd. As if a wind was rippling through the guests, all bowed before them. In the center of the ballroom they stopped, and the prince held out his hand, at which immediate point the orchestra began a waltz. And the regal pair was off into an exuberant exhibition of twirls and whirls that left His Highness winded and red of face.

"Odd's blood, you are a delightful morsel, Emmachild," the prince remarked. "What say, did we have them all agog?"

"You always do, Your Highness. My mother told me there was never a more romantic prince in all the world, even in the storybooks, I daresay. With its romantic theme, no one could more fittingly have begun this ball."

"What ho! As smooth and sweet as your mother, egad! We got their eyes popping with that there crown. Got to take it back to the royal vaults, you know. But no point in leaving things like that to molder. Not while there's a young head like yours to grace it for the night."

" 'Uneasy lies the head that wears a crown,' unless it be borrowed, I expect."

"Rather! That is, what did you say, m'dear?"

"That dubbing was an unlooked for honor. Am I truly made noble by that knighting, or was that also just borrowed finery? Ladies have received the Order of the Garter—was that the Order of the Thunderbolt?"

"Oh, I say. Awake upon every suit. Dubbed you, ain't I? Made you a dame, by Jove. Shall we design a medal and ribbon in the shape of a thunderbolt? Jolly something, that? What say, Dame Emma?"

"Having heard my mother speak of the shoe buckle you designed, I shall be most anxious to see the perfection of that order—and to be the second member of it, after My Gracious Highness, Lord of all Thunderbolts! You are all kindness."

"Princes like to have their kindnesses reciprocated, what? Could have a coach waiting for you tomorrow night, take you right to Jupiter's Mount Olympus!" He stopped dancing to fully laugh at his own sally, which she was obliging enough to join in and which everyone noted. When they had quieted to mere smiles and back to waltzing, the prince whispered, "Odd's blood, got me a poem Dame Emma should hear and approve."

"Delighted, Your Highness."

"The delight, I assure you, shall be all mine. Top ho!" And grinning so broadly, he bowed his gratitude for her promise and for the dance in one.

Lady Leonie was next on his list to honor and proposition. He had an emerald bracelet for her and hoped she would see him tonight, before hearing of his request to her daughter.

Lord Lanadale was given Emmalie's next dance, and she was quick to whisper the prince's making the knighting official and the promise to design a medal for her order.

She deserved several medals for her beauty, he was quick to respond, adding as well that the jewels in her eyes outshone even those in her crown. And when she was claimed by her next partner, Basil rushed off to spread the titled tidbit.

Before several more dances, the entire ballroom was made aware the title was authentic. Immediately Lady Leonie stopped to congratulate Dame Emma and rejoice in her daughter's social success. So oft had she wished for this moment—to have everyone complimenting rather than commiserating on her daughter! Her ladyship must needs touch the glittering girl with the golden crown on her head to assure herself it was her very own Emmalie. But she was not, she was Dame Emma.

Mother and daughter had given the lie to the rumor of Emmalie's being onstage by merely ignoring all who lacked the delicacy to inquire on that subject. The presence of Mrs. Windsor and Mr. Kean, however, did much to propagate it. But neither Lady Leonie nor now Dame Emma were concerned. She was graced by the prince's favor. She was adored by the gentlemen. Lord Lanadale had already proposed by his second dance. And the Duke of Monteford had come close in his first.

Having so many years been on the fringes of Society's approval, looking on from the sidelines at all the frolic, Emmalie was finding this evening as heady an experience as her moment of applause on the stage.

If only it would continue in this manner, Emmalie prayed, and for some time it did. For she was ceaselessly requested for the honor of a dance . . . or a moment's converse. At one point she glanced at the ceiling-high pier glass that reflected back the crowd of titled gentlemen about and she, the golden glowing point of light in the center, and Emmalie knew she would always remember this moment. For truly, it was more joyous and more supreme than ever could have been seen in one's dreams.

Good heavens, even the young ladies and their mothers wished to be in her presence. All expressed interest in viewing her crown in closer proximity or wished to hear the details of the prince's dubbing. Wherever she moved, the crowds were, if not speaking to her, speaking of her. Most universal was the pronouncement of her as "a jewel in herself." Repeating that to Lord Lanadale, on the principle it was too apt to be kept to herself, he instantly seconded it, even improved it, calling her "a jewel among all women!" That, too, was immediately welcomed by the object of all these praises.

For the first time in her life Emmalie was filled with conceit. Appearing as another character and being applauded for it had been heady, but naught next to being praised for herself, and by her mother's own crowd! And the most considerable degree of felicity came from the conviction that she deserved the praise, for she had outshone even her mother, who had been reduced to being just one of the crowd at her own ball! It was a moment of supreme triumph. Actually Emmalie's little heart could hardly bear any more joy. Yet she wished for more. She wished for the ultimate—for the viscount to bow to her and acknowledge she was what he had been searching for all his life. She, a woman he could truly love, in exclusion of all others, for she was the most beautiful and most desirable of all his ladies.

The viscount held back from adding the crowning touch to her evening. Indeed, he had held back so completely, he had not even approached her for the privilege of one dance.

In his dark monk's outfit, Reggie, on the sidelines, watched with a sardonic gleam in his eye and an unsmiling mouth. Lord Lanadale, having made a full circuit of the ballroom with his remark of Emma as "a jewel among all women," proffered it to his friend. Instead of the usual agreement, the viscount coldly replied, "Would it not be more accurate to say, rather, a *gem*? Surely the lady in question is not of a size to be a *jewel*. Indeed, the only thing about the lady that seems to have noticeably enlarged is her self-importance."

By the time supper had been served and concluded, Emmalie's head was weary from the weight of the crown, and she signaled the guards to watch it, while she rested her neck.

" 'Uneasy lies the head that wears the crown,' " a voice whispered. And Emmalie turned to face a monk.

"Have you come to be my confessor, Sir Monk? Or to entice me to sin?" she asked with a slow smile, revealing those dimples he loved to trace in his imagination.

But though the monk smiled, it was a cold one. She, who had found it so easy to capture all the other men, was finding him a challenge. Perhaps it was because she had removed her crown. Its added height had increased her confidence, and now like a magic talisman, without it, she felt herself diminishing. Or was it the scorn in the cold blue eyes that once had had such warmth for her?

Immediately she thought to reach for what her mother would say, and the words came quickly, smoothly, with the same teasing little smile, "Ah my lord, are you a monk in earnest?"

"Is there anything about you of late in earnest? Or are you all one sham performance? An actress on the stage and one in Society."

Her face flushed at the anger he was exhibiting. She attempted to reach him once more.

"But you are my Gothic monk, here to frighten me, are you not—with a stern, forbidding air? When you turn about, shall there be just a skeleton to reduce all the ladies to trembling and swoons?"

"I would I were a skeleton to put the fear of God in your false little self."

"How false?" Emmalie exclaimed, her anger catching fire.

"You are a trumpery piece! For all your genuine jewels, you are less true tonight than you ever were. I wore this monk outfit to remind you of our evenings in Gothic mirth, indeed, but in faint hope of reviving in you another memory. . . . And the Emmalie I knew would have understood.''

''What? That you are the Abelard to my Heloise? Yes, I nearly dressed myself as a nun to speak to you thus. To remind you of the moments when with our books open before us,'' (and she airily quoted his translation) '' 'our hands went from those well-read pages to each other's hands instead.' '' She grinned, having outjockeyed him by not only knowing to what he referred but by being the first to put it into words.

Yet rather than admitting her dextrous pass and smiling with her at its palpability, he gasped in disdain. ''You laugh at words that once meant so much to us!''

''I! It was not I who laughed at what we were. You found it not sufficient and preferred the falsity of Miss Kitty. Well, my performance was superior to hers! And now, as well, I am the most acclaimed of all the ladies of our set. I am the queen of Society.''

And at that she turned and retrieved her crown from the guards and placed it once more on her head. It gave her back the height and confidence he had cut down from her.

''Admit it,'' she said with a pleased smile. ''Am I not desired by every gentleman in attendance here? Am I not what all your life you have admired and wanted?''

''No, Dame Emma, you are not anything I ever could or did admire,'' he responded grimly. And taking out his quizzing glass, he gave her one of his long and nerve-wracking examinations. ''I wonder why I ever thought I saw something special in you, after all.'' And beginning to turn away, he concluded with a bored sigh, ''When others valued you lowly, I saw your uniqueness, yet it was clearly I who was mistaken. For now, as the ultimate lady in Society, it becomes clear that you are, after all, totally insignificant, because you are at long last just like everybody else.''

''As are you,'' Emmalie exclaimed huffily, and signaling one of the hovering swains awaiting anxiously, she danced off.

Neither the viscount nor Dame Emma came close the rest of the evening. Both were shocked by the anger sluicing through their veins. Emmalie could only think of all his searing words and how they burned in her breast. Why had she not seriously come to cuffs with him and put him in his place? Because ladies did not demonstrate even a smidgen of hackle—certainly not when being the cynosure. Otherwise she could have said something more devastating than that simple, inane, "As are you." But she had been caught unprepared by his reaction. So certain was she that he would say, "Now you are everything I ever wanted," how could she accept his saying she was everything he *never* wanted?

Through the rest of the evening, the young lady of the house drew all the gentlemen's interest but one. The viscount danced with Lady Daphne, the current Season's diamond, which had Emmalie nearly stopping him and crying out from her heart, "Cannot you see, *I* am the principal diamond of the Season; why are you settling for less?" And further to ask from her heart, "If you want her, why not me?" But she danced on. And on.

As for the viscount, he merely kept in place his mask of indifference and retired early, making it obvious to all that he was escorting Lady Daphne to her carriage.

And after that, the ball for Emmalie was flat and unendurable.

CHAPTER FIFTEEN

So MANY PEOPLE AFTER THE BALL CALLED TO INQUIRE after both ladies' health that it was nigh onto having an assembly. Lady Leonie left word she was resting, please to leave their cards. But Emmalie was unable to rest. So fired up was she by the viscount's treatment she must be up and doing . . . up and receiving the callers who to a man, if not woman, reassured her of their admiration for herself and the ball.

Dressed in one of her new peach creations with her hair in a whirl of face-framing curls, she looked like an angelic child, everyone declared. Never had a lady taken Society so much by storm, especially after everyone for so long had ignored her. "Blossomed" was the word being passed around to explain it. Not that they had never appreciated her, but rather that the girl herself was a "late bloomer." And now she had become a belle of the magnitude of her own mother, with promise to continue so for some time . . . sharing Lady Leonie's saloon and, with many a smile it was added, perhaps even her admirers!

Lord Lanadale wished to identify himself as her principal admirer by calling several times that day. As for the viscount, he committed the cardinal insult of sending his servant to inquire after the ladies' healths, rather than being gracious enough to call himself. Emmalie could not forgive him for the slight, and even Lady Leonie was astonished at his behavior.

Her ladyship's costume ball had ended the Season

with a flare. Now most of the lords and ladies were preparing to repair to country estates or the continent or to resorts such as Bath or Brighton. Brighton beckoned Lady Leonie in the rotund form of the prince. She owed His Highness, at the very least, her presence at his favorite resort, for not only his appearance at the ball, but her nonappearance at their subsequent assignation. Especially since her note of refusal had included her daughter as well as herself. He was crestfallen but inured; Lady Leonie had made refusal an art.

Meanwhile Dame Emma, in a social whirl if not frenzy, was accepting as many gentlemen's invitations as she could, being taken for rides and picnics and shining at the one or two remaining small parties.

Yet throughout, Lord Lanadale was her constant escort. Of all their jaunts, she favored the visit to the Tower of London, which brought a regret of Caesar upon viewing the other lions at the royal menagerie and a regret of her golden crown at the tallow-lit viewing of the Crown Jewels. She gave a royal wave to her abandoned headgear while Basil dropped compliments to the effect that the crown was crestfallen at no longer being near her, as he would be, and so forth.

Outside, she observed the Yeomen Warders in their Tudor uniforms, which must percourse remind of the viscount's near arrest by them. And that called out her first full smile of the day. If one could go back, mayhap she would play her cards differently. On the other hand, she played the hand she was dealt, and now at least she was free of a gentleman who lacked a heart in spades. A knave whose clubbing had reduced her from a diamond of the first water to a lady of no worth at all!

Brighton was once more being talked of at home, but Emmalie yearned for retirement at Windsrest and thus informed her mother. Lady Leonie had so enjoyed the social Dame Emma that any evidence of the old Emmalie and her reclusive ways sorely disappointed.

"My dearest," she replied. "I hesitate to indicate the obvious, both priding ourselves on being above that, but I must point out that you have garnered marriage proposals from half the eligible lords in London. By next year you shall probably have offerings from the other half. Why do you persist in behaving like a pea-goose over just one? Holding to him buckle and thong? Clearly Reggie is not suited for marriage. He is scarce sincere in his current attentions to Lady Daphne either, I vow."

"He is never sincere. He is a rackety hedge-bird, and if I could shoot him in his heart I would, but he should not feel it, for there is merely a huge empty space there," Emmalie countered, all the while her hands twisting the golden heart the viscount had given her, which she wore once more around her neck.

"Ah, my poor Emmalie," her mother said softly, resorting back to the diminutive, since her daughter seemed once more to be a little girl. "It is my fault for having embroiled you with that heartless knave. I knew he was one, and yet I allowed you to risk your heart over him—but actually because I thought only the very best, the nonpareil of all, would finally reach through your defenses. As indeed he has."

"Yes."

That simple word, with no extenuation, no regrets, no fault-finding or blame, reached Lady Leonie even more, and she sat next to her daughter and took her in her arms; and for the first time, since a child, she rocked Emmalie and hugged her. None of her noble friends would have believed the sight from this unmotherly woman. No one but Pug, who entered and smiled, seeing the woman he loved exactly as he always knew her to be—of the warmest heart, for all her surface brittleness and distance.

Sitting at their feet, Pug finally spoke. "Why not put him to another tetht?"

So surprised were the ladies at his not only knowing

their situation, but having what seemed to be a sensible suggestion, they both looked down, freshly viewing the young lord's childlike face. This slowtop had begun to spin.

Asked to explain himself by Lady Leonie, Pug was quick to do so—or as quick as a gentleman given to the fashionable lisping could contrive. The viscount, if he recollected correctly, during the time when Miss Marlowe was giving him tests, had never enjoyed himself as much. Gone—the jaded look in his eyes. Either he relished being tested and performing as a gallant knight, or he loved Miss Marlowe . . . or both.

"Both," Lady Leonie cried, hugging Pug.

This act had him lisping, "Fellowths not thuch a damned nail, I thay. Loveths Mitth Marlowe, by Jove. Clear ath a looking glaths."

And, therefore, on such a shaky support as Pug's instincts and Lady Leonie's confidence in them, Emmalie allowed herself to engage in staging another test for the viscount. And by the time the entire plan had been worked out in full detail, Emmalie felt bobbish enough to put off her return to Cornwall, concluding doing was better than dying.

In mutual satisfaction, all three, therefore, went off to write notes.

The viscount was occupied with his most enduring passion: giving his last touch to his full-blown cravat, which, it was his delight to note, could never be quite emulated by other gentlemen, either in its height or intricacy. Today he was to display another one of his unequaled talents, driving a high-perch phaeton to the veriest inch. He would be taking up Lady Daphne and was girding himself to have to once more discuss their meeting at Brighton where all the ton would be congregating. Lady Daphne had been repetitively wishing his assurance that her parents had rented in the vicinity of his own Brighton house. The next time she did so, he swore to himself, he would reply that while his home was in the vicinity, it was very likely *he* might not be. For whether he would or not summer in Brighton was becoming so fatiguing a decision, he assumed being there would be equally so. Actually Brighton Society was the same people one left in London. One could begin a conversation at a town assembly and conclude it with the identical person at the Brighton Royal Pavilion. Oft making the same observations!

Another person excessively boring the viscount with talk of Brighton was Basil, while lounging in the viscount's sitting room. He had consistently failed to win Reggie's attention, until he mentioned Dame Emma's refusing to join her mother at the resort, despite his valiant efforts to persuade her to do so during their visit to the London Tower to nostalgically view her famous crown. The mention of Emmalie in conjunction with the Tower could not but arouse a recollection of their time there, which encompassed his kissing the astonished lady down every step. That memory made a sizable dent in his ennui. There was even a small smile beginning, until Basil wiped it away by bemoaning all the gentlemen Dame Emma had refused, including himself. And *himself*, the viscount recollected, responding shortly, "That is her forte—she refuses gentlemen quite neatly," which sunk both lords into philosophic contemplation of that lady. Reggie could not but remind himself, with pique, that one of the reasons he had left Emmalie behind at Cornwall was the fear she would not be up to his weight in Society. Ye gods! he had been solicitous of her being too much in *his* shade, and now she was throwing her shadow over all! So shaken had Emmalie's supremacy left his lordship, it took him a moment to realize Basil was presently shaking him as well—to indicate a footman with a note.

Recognizing Lady Leonie's handwriting, the viscount read it directly and with more than tolerable attention.

My dear Reggie,

I apply for your help in this moment of distress, for you alone are aware of my dear Emmalie's mad-brained starts. I have trusted her to you before and feel only you can rescue her from her wild ways. Her own dear Spinny alerted me that after winning the affections of practically every eligible parti, she is submitting to the Regent's importunities. He has not desisted since the evening of the ball. Gifts a'plenty have invaded my home, as well as letters which he has done her the honor of writing himself, despite the stiffness of his fingers. And most constantly requests a private meeting. Till tonight, she has held out. But now has agreed to meet him at Carlton House. He is sending his yellow chariot with the discrete purple blinds for her, and you know what that indicates. I am distraught. I can think of no one else to turn to, but you who had, at one time, a special relationship with her. Come, at once. A mother's hopes are in your hands. If you cannot succeed in persuading her against this rash step, the girl is lost, and I shall be forever in despair.

In haste, Leonie.

Twice over he read the letter. After a moment, he raised an eyebrow. That last line was surely doing it too brown for Lady Leonie! But then, she had, of late, shown a remarkable interest in her daughter, quite above the usual. Emmalie had a way of rousing such, as he had learned to his regret. Why then should *he* concern himself about that lady? Basil, here, was breaking his heart over her. Best turn the letter over to him. The viscount had almost moved the note under Basil's nose (which was twitching with its usual avaricious curiosity), but then stopped and placed the note in his vest pocket. No, the matter could not be turned over to Basil! He would not only botch it, but make the lady's name a byword. Not that she did not deserve it! Al-

224

though the missive proved her still not up to snuff in Society's ways, he concluded in satisfaction, anticipating saying as much to her.

Hurriedly, the viscount sent Basil away and wrote a note excusing himself from his outing with Lady Daphne. The prodigious amount of relief he felt upon doing so alerted him it was time to shab off from that flirtation. Thereupon, his lordship added some well-honed lines of general dismissal, beginning with his being too seasoned to season in Brighton, after all, much to his regret.

Free at last of all obligations, he set about replying to Lady Leonie and found himself, for the first time in a while, a picture of a gentleman awake upon every suit and in pursuit! His steps had a quickness, his eyes an alertness, his lips an insuppressible smile as he moved about making his preparations and cross maneuvers.

Upon receiving the viscount's response, both Lady Leonie and Emmalie read it almost together:

My dear lady,
Be not alarmed. I shall endeavor to rescue your daughter—since I apparently have experience in that area. Permit her to go to the assignation. Then merely invite the prince to come to you—if necessary send the emerald ring. I do not believe he should refuse that invitation which he has been awaiting for nigh onto a decade.

Your obedient servant, Reginald.

"What is the man planning? To overtake the prince's yellow chariot, I expect. Or since that shall be occupied by His Highness coming to me, more likely send his own thus disguised." Lady Leonie neatly arranged in her mind her friend's maneuvers and then smiled. "And from that carriage spirit *you* away, I daresay. What ho! That should be an adventure!"

"Yes," Emmalie agreed, but she was peeved by the

225

tone of his reply. "Is he doing it for your sake . . . or because he cares for me? His words do not depict a man in love. Nor one in fear for his loved one. Rather it sounds very like a gallant performing a duty for an honored friend."

"Nonsense. Reggie prides himself in always appearing in control. I have rarely seen his feathers ruffled in any situation."

"I have."

"There. That is the most heartening observation we have heard yet."

"But . . . look you, how he still thinks so lowly of me . . . that the prince would drop me in a moment to be with you."

Lady Leonie smiled at that and allowed that the prince had been her most ardent admirer for a good long time. "Whether it is genuine affection or that he had never succeeded with me, both Reggie and I know that if I, at long last, offered him a private meeting, he would abandon any lady, no matter how beautiful."

"Charming, Mama. You put it in just the correct way to restore one's confidence. I intend someday to have some of that elegance of style."

"I am in sore need of all your spare compliments, my child, considering how that blasted lord has arranged things. Not that I intend to send my emerald ring, but I daresay I must actually invite the prince for a private meeting! Good heavens, greater love hath no mother than to give herself to His Royal Highness for her daughter's honor. I shall expect at least a monument."

Emmalie, preparing to rush to plan an outfit for her adventure, stopped at that and bit her lip. "No, you are correct, I cannot accept so great a sacrifice. I shall write a letter to the viscount that I have uncovered the scheme and . . ."

"What a load of gammon. Dear child, you do not really believe after years of experience in holding off that royal lecher, I cannot continue to do so. I shall simply allow him to kiss my hand a few times and then either faint or pretend I have a cold, for he dreads contagion . . . or some such, and then dismiss him. Have no fear. Ah yes, I have it, I shall pretend to possess some information against his traveling wife, Princess Caroline. That always enrages him so much he is incapable of any romantic thoughts!''

Mother and daughter laughed in delight at the brilliance of the one and the hope of the other and prepared for the adventurous evening ahead.

CHAPTER SIXTEEN

DAME EMMA WAS DRESSED IN A LIGHT SILK PELISSE OF aqua over a pale cream crepe gown with such a plunging bodice, it was clearly a style that bespoke an assignation. However, the pelisse modestly covered all, temporarily. In her reticule she carried an implement of protection in the unlikely event that all plans went awry.

Stepping into the yellow chariot, Emmalie noted that Lady Leonie had been correct in her supposition that it would be disguised into an exact replica of the prince's private means of amorous transportation. Not only did it similarly have purple blinds but, she noted in alarm, they were down even though it was dusk. The coachman and outriders were silent and discreet in their actions, merely bowing her in and driving off at a smart pace. Believing that any moment she was to be waylaid by a rescuing viscount, Emmalie was all anticipation. Yet as the horses moved forward and nothing occurred, she felt some anxiety. Continually Emmalie peeked from the corner of the nearest blind. London was not only under wraps of the fading day, but a fog was adding further obfuscation. Yet the ballad singers and street peddlers were resolutely carrying on. Their sounds blended with the clip-clop of the fast-paced horses. With what unheard of alacrity were they transporting her to her destination! Indeed, in only a few more paces they came to a stop. Eagerly Emmalie waited for Reggie to open the door and pull her from her fate worse than disgrace.

The door opened. It was done so however by the coachman, not the viscount. Crestfallen, Emmalie hung back and then resolutely stepped out. Only to note with grave consternation the classical portico of six Corinthian columns, which clearly indicated she was directly before the Prince Regent's Carlton House. That could not but fill her with alarms at the viscount's strategies. Rather than rescuing, was he revenging himself on her by making her assignation with the prince a reality? Lady Leonie, as of Emmalie's departure, had not yet received a response from the prince to her note, but she had not refined too much on that, claiming that the prince never felt the need for common civility. But Emmalie was disturbed then and now doubly so, fearing their well-laid plan was being unlaid by some other hand. Nonetheless, she was here and could do naught but play the game out. The newly dubbed lady stepped through the doorway, as if on cue for her entrance.

Fluidly, that did more to arouse her alarm, Dame Emma was passed through the royal halls. Her only relief was that she was still on the ground floor and not being ushered up to the private apartments. At that point, Emmalie decided, she would draw the line and fall into a swoon. Except the royal servants might be accustomed to such tactics and simply carry her insensate body into the Regent's bed—a dismaying conclusion which had her on guard against the guards as well.

Yet the liveried men were keeping their proper distance. Rather, the same outrider from the yellow chariot was directing her through the first floor toward the crimson drawing room. Somewhat reassured by the locale, Emmalie continued walking on the velvet carpet with its insignia of the Garter. The double doors between the state apartments were open. Turning round Emmalie was relieved to observe she was not being followed either by any attendants or an intended.

Unlit and ahead—the recesses of the throne room. Onward lay the conservatory. Without pause, she was ushered through that stained-glass, plant-filled area—directly into the garden. And left there.

Obviously an alfresco rendezvous.

But with whom? If actually the prince, the viscount had played her false and himself arranged for His Highness to be there. Otherwise, it must be the viscount himself, and he was simply using all these dramatic delays to increase her sense of discomfort, for agreeing (he supposed) to meet the royal seducer. Touching the security of her implement of protection in her reticule, she proceeded through the garden. There, as evening had fallen and none of the strung lamps lit, the sighting continued uncertain.

A nightingale was singing its heart out. What an idiotic, romantic bird, she thought—indicating the young lady was hardly in a prime mood for a clandestine meeting. Swaying in the breeze was a weeping willow, a branch of which, hanging low, disordered her hair, catching in her topknot. She disengaged herself and went further into the recesses of the garden. Spotting a seat by a walk and disgusted by this orchestration, Emmalie decidedly sat down, hands folded in her lap. If any seducer were out there, he should dashed well have to put himself to the effort of finding her himself. She had gone her limit!

After a while the nightingale was joined by another, but Emmalie was left alone. Could it possibly be that the viscount had just arranged for her to have to wait in vain for the prince, and that was to be her punishment? That she was to be given a royal slip by His Highness, who would be with her mother, while the viscount all the time would be in his own sitting room laughing at her plight?

"Top ho, little miss."

Emmalie turned. The voice, unaccountably, was very like the prince's. The shape in the dark, admittedly cloaked, was of a corpulence that bespoke His Highness.

She stood up and faced the garbed figure. The neck

had a full scarf that partially covered the face and a top hat, which while appropriate for evening wear, was not quite the thing, she assumed, for a lovers' jaunt in a garden.

"Your Highness," she began, testing the figure further. "You startled me."

"Always do. Startling is my forte, don't you know? Especially little things like you." And he laughed his high falsetto laugh.

Something had gone amiss, Emmalie feared. Rather than being tipped the double by the Regent, was the viscount placing her in the very devil of a hobble by placing her in the royal roué's hands? And yet . . . yet . . . Emmalie decided to test him—that being *her* forte.

"I arrived with great expectations of your fulfilling your *promise* to me."

"Always fulfill my promises to ladies, egad."

"Please then, begin," she instructed. "I shall be listening with the greatest of all possible attention."

A moment's silence and then the figure temporized, "Too cold."

"Pity. You are, however, rather warmly wrapped. And you were so anxious to demonstrate . . . *it*."

She paused, expectantly. Having a vague promise of a declamation of one of the royal poems, if this were the authentic prince, he should remember. Or if not remembering, imperiously say as much. But an imposter would only continue to sham it, hoping for a clue. Although an amazingly apt imitation of His Highness, by now Emmalie was convinced she was in converse with the viscount. That is, she was almost positive it was he. Heavens, she hoped it was he!

"Are you not going to begin?" Emmalie pressed, feigning surprise at the delay and beginning to enjoy the viscount's position.

The prince moved closer and took her hand and placed a loud kiss on the palm of same.

Pulling back in outrage, Emmalie cried, "Your Highness! I cannot possibly allow any such attentions, especially when you are being so discourteous as to refuse to meet your commitment. . . ."

"Dash it. Ain't likely to remember me promise to every lady! Royal prerogative to forget. Odd's blood!"

"You have wounded me to the quick. Am I *every* lady?"

"Refresh me memory," came the royal order.

He was breathing loudly, and she remembered the royal prince doing so behind the curtain when the two were together. A sudden doubt assailed her that it might be His Highness, after all. And his memory was known to be as faulty as his promises. To verify, she carried on with a total sham. "Did you not promise to sing?"

"Frog."

"Oh, no. I cannot possibly settle for that. You promised most faithfully to imitate a nightingale. I should not much care to hear the sound of a *frog*!"

"Meant frog in throat, what? Not able to perform at me best, egad."

"Egad, indeed. How dreadfully disappointing. Heavens, my mother has never ceased to extol your most exalted voice, and when you promised to give me an exact demonstration of not only the mating song but the mating habits of the nightingale, I could not resist the offer."

"The mating habits!" The viscount's voice came through in his surprise. In a moment he had caught himself. "Quite so. Come here my little bird."

"Perhaps if you rang for tea?"

"Tea? Odd's blood! Why the dashed should you wish tea rather than me?"

"I meant for the frog in your throat. To clear it. I shall be quite devastated not to hear your impersonation. I understand you are quite a mimic!"

A cough was all the reply she received. He was obviously sparring for wind.

"Most disappointing," she concluded, her eyes in

the shadows playfully dancing. At that moment a nightingale trilled uncontrollably. And Emmalie gasped and urged, "Ah, Your Highness, answer it! Hear, it is calling for its mate. *You* must respond!"

"Have to settle for its own mate. I have mates enough! Odd's blood! Not adverse to showing me own mating habits though." Of a sudden the muffled man refused to be further dallied with. In an imperial manner he approached and commanded, "Bird-witted little thing, ain't you? A plucky little pigeon! You coo for me, and I'll trill for you, what?"

Attempting to avoid him, Emmalie cried, "Please, Your Highness! I had hoped for a more subtle approach from you!"

"I say, no need for subtle approaches, egad. Not princely, that! To the devil with these preparations. 'Pon honor, let's bag the brush! Tally-ho!"

Alarmed in actuality, Emmalie attempted to quickly step back, when she was clasped against the burly breast.

"Good God, don't trifle with me!" he exclaimed, having difficulty with both her squirming and keeping his voice properly falsetto. "I have been pushed past all endurance by your charms. I beseech you, ease my royal sufferings!"

And forthwith he pressed several kisses on her protesting mouth. Her eyes and throat were similarly splattered upon. And always he returned to silence any of her interruptions by kisses of such length and depth that she was finally unable to reply, even when given breath to do so.

For a moment Emmalie considered allowing this disgraceful deception to continue. It would be fitting revenge indeed, if she allowed this sham prince to win her. Never would the viscount be confident that she had not succumbed to a crown rather than to himself! He should be totally flummoxed. But Emmalie's own emotions refused pretense. She could not bear allowing the viscount to handle her in this manner if he were not in earnest for himself. And mostly, mostly she needed to do something to gain control of herself. And so reaching into her reticule, she fumbled, found her implement of protection, a scent bottle of rather larger than usual proportions, and during a particularly exuberant exhibition of twisting and turning, managed to open it and thoroughly douse this Banbury prince-viscount with her scent!

"Good God!" the drenched gentleman exclaimed, stepping back.

"You seem, Your Highness, to have been so . . . so athletic as to have unstoppered my scent bottle. I expect it is a timely coolant for us both. I request you bathe yourself and consider it a lesson for attempting to turn me up sweet when I had trusted myself to your honor. Good night, sweet prince, and flights of nightingales sing you to your rest. I leave you to them and . . . the frogs."

And ere the coughing, sputtering lord could speak, Emmalie had run through the garden, through the columned side entrance, past the startled guards, and had signaled for a hack, gone before the viscount could quite collect himself and get a full breath!

CHAPTER SEVENTEEN

ON HER RETURN TO WINDSREST, EMMALIE ORDERED her butler to deny her to all, even if the prince himself were to call. Upon reflection, she amended, "*Especially* if 'tis His Highness!" For a significant second that addition gave the butler pause, and then in perfect butler fashion, he merely nodded. He had his orders.

Heavens, Emmalie had had enough of Society. She had explained to her mother that the viscount had been particularly offensive. Rather than meeting their test of his feelings for her and coming to her defense, he had—coldhearted thatchgallows that he was—merely used her helplessness to offend her honor and make free use of her person, under the blatant disguise of being His Highness. And he had only proved once again how unworthy he was of any true woman's affections, and she had only proved to herself once again that she could only love that rackety, ramshackle knave. So much the worse for her. She would turn her face on Society and all other men and retire to her castle, until she had learned to forget him. And then perhaps she could come back.

Lady Leonie was not above half-pleased that their stratagem had so fallen short, especially since she had had a particularly difficult time with the amorous prince. But she had finally succeeded in ridding herself of him by spilling tea on his favorite waistcoat. Admittedly that was cause for a permanent breech with His Highness, since she could not have done anything he could least forgive. Not for naught was he known as the First Gentleman of Europe. His attire always was of first consequence to him. He would have left offended to the quick, had not Lady Leonie been quicker to compliment him on the fit of the waistcoat but feel the tea stain was all for the best, as the print was of not sufficient boldness to depict his character. With that viewpoint he could not but agree and conclude that perhaps a bolder print might be selected.

"Something with as much dash as your personality and yet with as much subtlety as your understanding. Yet overall, with a delightful wit about it to capture the sparkle of your conversation." Immediately, he felt she alone, knowing him so well, must visit his tailors with him on the following day, and that being decided, he left well satisfied both with the lady and the stain.

As for the viscount, Lady Leonie was prepared to throw up her hands at his deviousness. His intransigence had sunk him beneath reproach, she felt. And while she could not but endorse Lord Lanadale's proposal, she allowed that her daughter did need an appreciable time to recover from Reggie's gross and unforgivable tactics. Impersonating a royal! Heavens, that was nigh onto a criminal offense, and she had a good mind to inform the Prince Regent of the viscount's use of not only his conservatory but his personage.

Happily Lady Leonie had second thoughts of the public exposure for her daughter, and even more fortunately Pug reminded her of their appointment to travel to Brighton, and she became so absorbed in preparing for that departure, she was, at last, brought to allow her daughter's retirement to her castle. They parted this time with a close embrace and exchanging mutual affections and mutual superfluous suggestions on taking care of oneself. Lady Leonie was turning more to Pug for her ease of mind, gradually discovering it was possible to prefer fellow feeling rather than an exciting duel of wits. That meant hers were dulling with lack of use, she told herself, which must be a result of being so often in Pug's company or from age when one preferred peace of mind to anyone's piece of mind.

It was with some relief that Emmalie had left the heat of London. The dust particularly seemed to rise up and wipe out one's horizons. And the air was so stagnant, it had made her spirits heavy. Here, near the sea, she took reviving breaths of air and felt herself healing.

No longer did she feel the need to curl her hair into the mass of ringlets that had so won her acclaim. The brown hair was once more in its straight and natural arrangement. She wore a ribbon to keep it back and a light yellow muslin dress and still, despite her new unconcern, had a well-favored appearance. Especially since her cheeks were oft aglow from her vigorous walks. Returning from such, she spotted in the distance an elegant coach approaching with a coat of arms that could very well be the viscount's. On the run, she entered the castle calling to the finally astonished butler not to in any circumstance permit the lowering of the bridge!

But her instructions arrived after the fact. The gardeners, feeling themselves still the viscount's people, had instinctively given him entrance. Having charged her citadel, she would at least not grant him audience, Emmalie concluded, reminding the butler to deny her. Then in some dudgeon, she waited for the butler to announce the viscount's departure. Instead, totally flummoxed, she saw Reggie himself coming into her sitting room.

"You are not to enter my apartments, nor indeed my castle! Gnasher! Remove his lordship from my presence!"

The mastiff, not up to snuff on the intricacies of the relationship between a gentleman and a lady, mistook the order to mean he give Reggie the usual greeting—which consisted of practically toppling his lordship in his bounding affection. Not till they had had a friendly

237

wrestling match did both dog and erstwhile former master compose themselves sufficiently to turn to the highly vexed new mistress. Gnasher settled himself happily at her feet as if he had acted exactly as ordered. "Toady," she said aloud in contempt, "this castle is filled to its turrets with them!"

"Jolly decent of them all," Reggie merely said, with a self-satisfied smile. "And that calls to mind another rather decent fellow. I had a prodigiously interesting discussion with Pug."

"That must have been quite an effort," she responded.

"Not at all. There is more behind that childlike face than one would assume."

"Do not, I pray, attempt a diversion from the point. You have *not* been invited into my castle, and I request that you depart—especially from my private sitting room. Your entrance here clearly shows you lack even the veriest shred of delicacy. You have, my lord, sunk beneath reproach."

"Speaking of sinking, I am a trifle fatigued. You should invite me to sit down, you know," he said with gentle reproof.

"How dare you! I shall not invite you to be seated. I am inviting you to depart. Which should scarcely be necessary if you were a gentleman as well as a lord!"

"Have I not passed your final test of entering your guarded dungeon?" he replied with mock affront. "In faith, I am prepared to sweep you on my horse and ride with you *ventre à terre*, carrying you, my prize, back to my own castle, except, of course, we are back in my own castle, after all."

"Not much of a gallant," she scoffed. "For you scarcely had a challenge here—with my entire staff rushing to make it all easy for you."

"Would you rather I had swum the moat and climbed the battlements?"

"Yes," she said simply and honestly.

To which he laughed outright. "But think of the pollution in the moat! I should catch my death, doubtless. Rather a shabby sort of honeymoon if you had to perform another role—that of a nursemaid. Although having seen you performing so many diverse roles, I would have to admit you should do it to perfection. Actually one remembers with some dismay ever concluding you could not rule Society. It showed a serious lack of confidence on my part. For after having conquered *me*, everybody else, even en masse, must per course be a lesser challenge."

At that Emmalie suddenly sat down.

"Thank you," he said, and sat down next to her on the settee.

"Why is it necessary for me to ask you to leave?" she asked with a sigh. "One need not rule Society to know its rules, and a principal one is that if a lady so much as hints that a gentleman's presence is offensive to her, he instantly departs."

"Life has its disappointments, does it not? Alas. But you have turned your back on Society, so its rules do not apply here. Nor have they ever, between us. And as for yourself, it is ironic to hide behind the conventions when you have broken every one in your madcap ways! I daresay you change roles so oft one would assume you a strolling player. First, a shy suffix to your mother, then a lady of heart and soul, then an actress onstage, and lastly a ruler of Society. Miss Marlowe, Emmalie, Ophelia Browne, Dame Emma—which are you?" he asked dryly. "Or do you not know who you are and what you want?"

"I want you to leave," she said, unable to countenance his jabs.

"Then why did you follow me to London?" he pressed. "To prove what? And to whom?"

"You do not stand in such position as to question me. You long ago broke our engagement—what I do and who I am is not your concern. Yet here you are,

239

still making a May game of me and my feelings. There is a limit to my accepting such mockery, and I have reached it!''

All amusement left the viscount as he realized she was in earnest. "You are the one who originally made a game of our relationship," he reminded her with some attempt at self-justification. "You, the one who feared the honest feelings between us . . . asking, no, insisting we remain friends only. And I, obeying the rules of Society, playing a gentleman's role, submitted and left you here, untouched. And then you began another game. Coming to London, to prove what? That whatever lady or world I chose, you could best me and my choices? And upon my humbling myself to come here, I find yet another persona, or mayhap it is Miss Ophelia Browne featured in a new comedy entitled: 'The Outraged Chatelaine.' Ah, where is the honest Emmalie who won my heart here in Cornwall by not hiding behind Society's sham manners? Are you not aware you are desecrating the very walls of this site of our awakening to each other by all this playacting?''

The viscount surprised himself with his vehemence. But, in effect, she had asked for a frank discussion, and if that was what she wished, he would act in kind.

On her part, Emmalie was equally desirous of fully airing her griefs. Every feeling was offended at the nonchalant way the viscount had rearranged the facts from his vantage point. Rising and turning to collect herself, she impatiently brushed away several betraying tears. But his lordship, his chivalry always to be relied on, was quick to act first, wiping her eyes with his own handkerchief and with his lips.

The affront of that was not to be borne! In the heat of her ire, she found her voice at last and, pulling away, cried out, "Stop this dalliance! You have already won and discarded me, you should go on to your next challenge! I expect there are several ladies in the kingdom that you might have missed in your philandering and should not allow that there be a gap in your record!''

Belatedly Reggie was sensible of his having jumped his fences before coming to them, and he muttered at the mull he was making of this. He'd hoped all explanations could wait until he had clasped her to his heart, and then perhaps they would not be needed. But she was maintaining such a degree of reserve, he sensed the necessity for his backing up. Apparently there were still hurdles between them that had to be carefully overstepped. Yet he could not restrain himself from taking one last leap by impetuously exclaiming, ''Pug told me you had turned down all other gentlemen . . . because your affections were engaged.''

''That is so,'' Emmalie parried. ''My affections are engaged by a higher source.''

Smiling at that and tightly reining his straining self, the viscount matched her social manner by temporizing, ''Ah, His Highness. I have heard, indeed, that he is pursuing you. What a delightful difference you make to his usual blue-eyed matrons. Lady Hertford, I believe, is a grandmother.''

''Well, apparently, both of us have our feelings engaged. When am I to wish you and Lady Daphne joy?''

''I daresay Lady Daphne shall someday find her joy, but I had mine the moment I parted from the lady.''

''You are heartless. Another young lady dropped by the wayside. How can you live with yourself?''

''It is you I am asking to live with me.'' One more attempt at bringing the matter quickly to the touch.

''Why?''

The viscount's eyes softened. ''That's my darling. You are back to your direct ways. Apparently your newly acquired social veneer is not lasting. A mite more directness on both our parts would have prevented the need for so many other fatiguing relationships. And to prevent further misunderstandings, I shall directly say

Pug also claimed the person who had won your heart was myself."

"The more fool you to believe such a fool as Pug."

"I found him to be quite a sensible young man. His only sign of mental instability is the fidelity he has shown to your mother. Indeed, whether on his own or at your mother's behest, he openly confessed that Lady Leonie's letter about the prince's opportuning you was meant to once more put my affections to the test. One hoped we had all long since graduated beyond this mania for testing with which you seem to have affected all, especially in regard to myself!"

"Certainly not! That is, there was no such test!" Emmalie flushed vividly and then exhaled. "Oh, fiddle! How can you expect me to have the slightest affection for you, considering how cruel you were to me at the ball, telling me I am a *nothing*? Naught to you, in faith!"

"Is that what is sticking in your lovely throat?" the viscount exclaimed in relief at having found his way clear to his love. "Let me retract it. For, in faith, rather than naught, you are everything." And Reggie, wishing to continue this discussion at a closer range, sought to regain his position next to his now seated lady by shoving off the reluctant Gnasher, who was playing dog in the manger alongside her. With an oath and an extra push, he succeeded, and then turning to Emmalie, openly, unreservedly exclaimed, "You are more than everything to me. Note how honest I am being. Indeed, I admit to being wild with jealousy that night . . . and disappointment. You showed me, as you showed all Society, that you could give us all the lead. But I had fallen in love with you here at Windsrest precisely because you were not like any of the ladies I have so long known."

"Yet I was not enough for you then, I collect," she said coldly, not allowing him to evade. "Apparently you wished to continue with ladies you had *so long known.*"

And he sheepishly owned as much. "There is something of that. Upon your offering me all, I wished to have *less* as well. Not till you proved how easily you could conquer the beau monde did I comprehend I had been using its social patterns as a protective covering for my feelings—had been doing so since I came into my majority. And then wondered why my life was so lacking. There I was—endlessly repeating the same social steps, as if lost in the pattern-card figures of a quadrille, until you came along and tripped me out of that elegant dance. So it seems, months ago, Miss Spindle had the correct answer. I *was* searching for my true love and found her and through her, myself."

Remembering that awkward moment of Spinny's taking it upon herself to declare the viscount's love for her charge had Emmalie unconsciously grinning and flushing all at once, and she was unable not to respond softly, "Miss Spindle is . . . always correct."

At which he pulled her into his arms and whispered, "You are a wild, mad-brained girl, and that is why you are the only lady I have and shall ever ask to be my bride—for you are the only lady I have ever truly loved and still do so."

So close were they, almost eye to eye. Emmalie stared at him, weakening. Although her heart was lighter, she shied away last moment. There were still a few more hurdles to be gotten over and one major obstacle of an affront that rankled and must be assuaged, and so she demanded, "If you loved me, why did you purposely *break the last test* and fly to Miss Kitty Jones's well-used arms?"

"To prove how much I loved you."

"Flummery!"

"Nay, 'tis true. No greater act of love was ever shown than for a gentleman to spare his lady by seeking the arms of another woman."

"And a woman known the world over for her *beauty*. What sacrifice! The mind boggles!"

"Yes, Kitty is quite beautiful. But in a boring way. And as you have met her, do you really think her conversation would be of the kind which could keep me interested? Actually, so fatiguing was she, I jolly well consider *that* liaison my greatest trial for your hand. Further, I chose her deliberately because I was certain it would make the most brouhaha, allowing you to cry off without a single stain on your honor. Loving you in earnest, I could no longer play games to force you into a relationship you were so clearly against. Recollect your own attitude of our time here. Did you not request that we remain just friends? I knew then I would not allow either myself or your mother to force you into an arrangement you were not yet prepared to accept. For your sake I had to give you sufficient cause for refusing me. Such that even your mother would not be able to swallow. Therefore, I made my action . . . blatant. And Miss Kitty is about as blatant as one can get."

Emmalie could not help but fully smile at that. And then pausing to digest his comments, she shook her head in wonder at the realization of how unimportant Miss Kitty had been all along. He was eyeing her questioningly, and she explained, "Heavens, it appears I am indebted to Miss Kitty in more ways than I assumed. For if I were not so determined to meet Miss Kitty, I should never have appeared onstage, which freed me of my self-doubts. And later, establishing myself in Society also developed enough of my assurance to conclude I was not wholly without merit—enough to merit a prize of your caliber. Actually, I have learned all our time apart that one has to accept oneself before being able to share oneself with another. I made myself entitled to you. *That* is what I was telling you at the ball and what you were particularly obtuse in understanding!" Her vexation of that evening could not but resurface as she concluded with some asperity, "You were supposed to

244

crown the affair by proposing! And you ruined it instead!''

"If I recollect, you had sufficient crowning," the viscount responded, equally reliving the ignominy of that evening, but then he smiled ruefully and admitted, "Through that entire ball I was so out of frame, so knocked acock by jealousy, that you who were all mine at Cornwall had now become everybody else's—dash it!—I scarce recollect what I said! The fact is you are the loveliest lady of all Society and stage . . . and my heart."

"Do not give me false coin, my lord," Emmalie said calmly. "A simple admission that I have your heart forever is all the compliment I require."

Not only did he instantly acknowledge that, but accompanied that admission by taking the opportunity to obliterate the last bit of distance between them and pulling her into his arms. All hurdles had been cleared, and they could henceforth ride together in concert. But in the midst of their embrace, she broke away and exclaimed in astonishment, "Heavens! You kiss strangely like the Prince of Wales!"

"Good God, you knew all along that was me!"

"Certainly. While telling you all, did not Pug tell you Mama and I expected you to rescue me from the Prince? I did have a moment's fear our plan had miscarried for your impersonation was quite extraordinary. And that was why I tested you with the sham promise from the Regent to sing like a nightingale."

"You little minx!" And Reggie could now fully join her in laughing at that recollection which also brought out the daunting effect of her dousing him with her scent. Her laughter was more extensive than his on that point as Reggie was now focusing most of his attention on holding her hand tightly—so she could not pull away from him and even began to nibble on her fingers.

Delighted to have her digits thus distinguished, she added that her mother had suggested she should have allowed him to win her in the Prince's guise. But she would not gull him thus, fearing he'd be forced into a marriage declaration.

"My darling girl, I scarce need to be forced into doing what I most desired this last year. From our moments here in Cornwall and when I had to fight a lion to rescue you and then a king—it has always been my earnest wish to win your heart."

"Oh," Emmalie said airily. "You have always had that since you rescued Boots. And since we read the love letters of Heloise and Abelard, I longed to abandon myself to your love." And she helpfully undid a button on her long gauze sleeve to allow him to kiss up her arm. "Mother assured me I could have no better teacher."

Abruptly, he stopped his kissing and, looking at her twinkling eyes, responded in as severe a tone as he could henceforth ever use to his love. "If that is the final test of me—or your subtle way of discovering whether I have ever been your mother's lover, the answer is no."

"Yes, Mama says that as well. Of course it is quite reassuring to have your confirmation."

"Odd's blood! I swear . . ."

"And upon your royal oath as well, thank you! But your gentleman's word was sufficient. I told you I should always accept it."

"I was swearing that I have had enough of your mother!" he interrupted—his smile holding on with difficulty. "Kindly do not mention her to me until we have the occasion to present her with her first grandchild!"

"Mother, a grandmother! Isn't that returning evil for good? She brought us together. No, I do not believe I could bring myself to do that to her."

"It is not likely we shall be taking her wishes into consideration on the issue of our issue! Now, once again, may we please not mention Lady Leonie—at least until I have finished my second proposal to you?"

"Oh, but it was Mama who proposed for you the first time!"

"Egad, you have gone your length trifling with a gentleman so violently in love. Your mother should have taught you not to laugh at a gentleman in such a vulnerable position—not to laugh at all during a proposal, it is singularly bad form."

"No, Mama said that . . ."

"Not another maternal word! I shall have the last word on her, for I cannot help but recollect her assurance that you were such a silent girl. Yet since then—although your words have been the most meaningful ever spoken to me—I would appreciate your presently ceasing to speak long enough for me to finish my offer!"

"Ah, is that what you're doing? I say, you are making rather a botch of it, aren't you? You have wasted half our time together on my wrist and witticisms. I advise you to go a more direct route and with more sweeping romance!"

Groaning at that, Reggie promptly picked her up and held her on his lap, putting his hands on either side of her face and staring at the golden imps dancing in the center of her laughing eyes. Then softly he whispered, "It appears the only way I shall finally keep you still is to continually stifle your words between my own lips." And he thoroughly did so. "Is that romantic enough?"

But when Emmalie was allowed to breathe free, she said immediately, "That did not stop my *thinking* about Mama."

"Wretch. You have tried my patience beyond all permission. Are you telling me that at that moment you were thinking of your *mother*?"

"Indeed, I was thinking that Mother has once again been proven to know best. You *are* the perfect gentleman for me."

"Let's kiss to that!" he concluded softly. And they risked being redundant and wildly sentimental by doing so again and again. And again.